CHAOS
AND
KINGDOM

A Financial Thriller

by J.S.B. Morse

Chaos and Kingdom: A Financial Thriller

www.GodsOfRuin.com

Published in the United States by New Classic Books, an imprint of Code Publishing. For distribution opportunities, please contact publishing@code-interactive.com.

ISBN 1-60020-051-6
978-1-60020-051-9

First Edition

*For Ludwig von Mises, Milton Friedman,
Frédéric Bastiat, and the other great
thinkers who have paved the way
for a truly free society.*

The one who saw all I will declare to the world,
The one who knew all I will tell about,
He saw the great Mystery, he knew the Hidden:
He recovered the knowledge of all the times before the Flood.
He journeyed beyond the distant, he journeyed beyond exhaustion,
And then carved his story on stone.

Prologue

The emergency room doors flung open with a crash as a group of medical personnel hurriedly rolled a stretcher through the triage area toward Trauma One. The unconscious young patient's shoulder-length blond hair framed her peaceful but unresponsive face.

As they rushed down the stark white hallway brightly lighted by fluorescent bulbs above, the resident doctor assessed the patient's breathing then looked up and in a levelheaded tone asked, "Did she take any drugs?" His question was aimed at the patient's friend, a worried woman in her mid-twenties trying to keep up with the group of nurses and doctors.

The friend, who wore a ratty black dress and intentionally disheveled hair in a punk clubber style, shook her head. Black eyeliner streaked down her face as she wiped moisture from her eyes but she remained silent, just staring at her friend.

"Miss?" the doctor asked, then repeated, "Miss, did she take any drugs?"

"Um, I don't know," she replied loudly but uncertainly.

"Miss, this is very important," the doctor said focusing his gaze on the woman as the group rolled into an emergency room. "Did she take any narcotics?"

"Uh, I don't know! I can't think!" she blurted out loudly. "We smoked a little weed before the club. She said she wasn't feeling very good, but I didn't know she was going to just collapse like that in the middle of the dance floor!"

"I don't see any track marks," one nurse announced.

"Any chance she ingested Rohypnol?" the doctor asked while raising the patient's eyelids and shining a pocket-sized flashlight into each eye. Her pupils were equal, round, and covered half of the iris, so he counted out opiates. However, her pupils did not dilate normally in reaction to the light, indicating potential damage to the nervous system.

"What?" the patient's friend shrieked.

"Roofies, roach, circles? The date rape drug?" the doctor tried to clarify.

"Uh, I don't know!" the young woman's voice quivered, "We bought our own drinks."

"Blood pressure's normal but her pulse is a little erratic," a nurse added as another placed a tourniquet on the patient's right arm and injected a needle into her vein. Within seconds the nurse had a liter bag of saline bolusing into the patient.

The friend looked at the patient and called out, "Rosie . . . Rosie baby wake up!"

The physician turned to the patient lying unconscious on the bed. "We're going to take care of your friend, okay? Everything's going to be all right." He turned to the head nurse. "Have you seen anything like this?"

The nurse responded in a metered tone, "Well, I've gotten word of a virus spreading—it's extremely volatile. This patient fits the bill."

"What is it? What are they calling it?" the doctor asked.

"Roger at County called it Chinese encephalitis."

* * *

In a small conference hall, Jacob Tanner was giving a presentation to a room full of intrigued investors. He stood six feet tall in his new department store suit and his thick head of hair, which contained only a few gray hairs, was gelled into a tightly cropped wave. Winter clouds had left him fairly pale, but he was an attractive man by most standards. The lighting in the small banquet room was dim to allow better contrast for the projection of slides that accompanied the businessman's presentation.

"As I've explained," Jacob said, "we've tried tirelessly to find the cause of this strange disease and we have yet to isolate the causal abro-virus though we believe it is related to the Japanese encephalitis virus—the most common in the world—which is transmitted by mosquitoes or ticks. We believe Chinese encephalitis is similarly caused."

Jacob Tanner paused to gather his thoughts before continuing. "Despite the fact that we haven't isolated the cause, our treatment, Symbalia has been highly successful at treating the symptoms of Chinese encephalitis, which are much worse than similar viruses. Now, without treatment, three to four days after infection, typical flu-like symptoms will start to present . . . ." Jacob Tanner pressed a small electronic device in his hand to advance the slide show to reveal images of sickly patients stricken with the disease.

"But just days later, the patient will exhibit extreme symptoms such as muscle weakness, seizures, or paralysis."

Jacob clicked to the next slide, which showed a man with dark blue circles around his eyes. "A telltale signature of this condition is the myste-rious discoloration that occurs around nearly all of Chinese encephalitis patients' eyes."

Jacob clicked to advance the slide show again. "Of course, if left untreated past this stage, the patient will likely die."

* * *

In the hospital emergency room, the young patient had begun to convulse. Her body violently shook and slammed against the padded bedding.

The doctor called out his orders, "I need four milligrams Ativan stat! And let's get some labs people. I need a CBC, complete metabolic panel and blood tox screen," He attempted to maneuver the young woman onto her right side to help facilitate her breathing.

"I've already drawn the labs," a nurse reported.

Another nurse drew up a vial of the sedative Ativan and injected it quickly into the IV.

A clear fluid began gargling out of the patient's mouth and, as the sedative took effect, her tremors subsided. Once the convulsions ended, the doctor suctioned out her mouth and rolled the patient onto her back again.

"Her pulse is all over the place, blood pressure's still normal," a nurse reported, then added, "temperature's 101."

Another resident ran into the room and demanded, "What's the situation here? I got a page that we had a patient coding."

The resident responded, "No, she's not coding, but her vitals are erratic, she's post ictal. Gave her Ativan for what looked like a grand mal seizure. We're waiting on the labs." He leaned into his colleague. "I haven't seen anything like this. It looks like she OD'd on something, but her friend doesn't think so. Just marijuana earlier in the evening. Joan says it looks like something they've been seeing over at County—something called Chinese encephalitis."

"Can we treat it?" the doctor asked.

The other doctor pursed his lips and shook his head.

* * *

"And after three to six weeks of therapy with Symbalia, patients are typically back to normal—the myelin sheath around the patient's neurons do regenerate, although we have seen some signs of regression.

"Now, since this disease is still very rare, we have been able to obtain orphan drug status from the FDA," Jacob Tanner informed the room of investors. "That has provided us with vital funds to get to where we are today . . . but we're currently at risk of losing our federal funding. The good news is that we have enough funding to continue producing Symbalia indefinitely. The bad news is that the funding is still out there in all of your pockets," Jacob said with a smile and received a few laughs. "If you invest with us today, not only will you be making a wise financial

decision, but you will also be preventing tragedies like the one I had to endure."

Jacob clicked the slide forward and a picture of him and his sister showed up on the screen. Jacob's sister, who looked substantially younger than he, had wavy, shoulder-length blond hair and wore a smile in the picture as her big brother embraced her.

"Two years ago, my sister was rolled into an emergency room just forty-five minutes away from here. She had what was then the unknown condition, Chinese encephalitis. If Symbalia existed then, my baby sister would have lived. Instead . . . ," Jacob paused and put his left fist to his mouth, choking back a surge of uncontrollable emotion, "Rosie passed away that night—one of the first victims of this horrific epidemic that is now raging across the country."

Jacob looked out to the crowd of investors. "Since the cause is as of yet unknown, we don't know when or where CE will strike next. Please, I beg of you, don't let the tragedy of CE strike a loved one of yours. You can make sure that no one else has to suffer the pain of a sudden and tragic death like the one in my family. Invest with us today and ensure the production of Symbalia for generations to come. Thank you very much."

Jacob gathered his papers and backed away from the podium.

CHAOS

AND

KINGDOM

PART 1:

KAIZEN

One

Better. The thought came to Jacob Tanner as he observed the haggard Axelaris Pharmaceuticals factory floor below him through his office's panoramic window. He watched intently as one of his employees went about his normal routine below, moving back and forth between a gangly combination of machinery and a laptop stand just feet away. The diminutive worker wore a tattered T-shirt and trudged through his repetitive procedure but that wasn't what concerned Jacob.

"One, two, three, four," Jacob hurriedly whispered to himself as he followed the worker's behavior.

So engrossed was Jacob that he all but ignored his director of scientific research, Marc Johnson, who was droning on about something right behind him. The words were more of a nuisance than anything, Jacob thought as he focused back on the employee twenty feet below. ". . . twelve, thirteen, fourteen . . . ."

Jacob's austere office walls were bare except for an old framed picture of him and his sister, a diploma from Harvard Business School, and a banner, which hung above the panoramic window, reminding the CEO and his visitors to, "Teach a man to fish."

Marc Johnson continued talking but his words fell on deaf ears as Jacob finished counting, "Twenty-four." He paused for a moment, bouncing an idea around in his head, then turned toward Marc.

"Jacob?" Marc asked expectantly.

"Excuse me for a moment," Jacob said, then walked around Marc and out of the office.

A minute later, Jacob Tanner threw open the doors to the factory floor below his office and was hit with the cacophony of breathing

hydraulic pumps beneath paint-chipped steel arms, an intestine of greased chain tracks, and heavily worn piston joints. Jacob waved at the factory foreman and called out, "Hey Smitty, shut her down. Shut her down."

Smitty, an overweight, scruffy-looking man in his middle thirties, was seated on a raised stool five feet above the floor, looked quizzically at his boss and once he received confirmation of Jacob's intention, depressed a red rubber button enclosed by a metal ring on the station in front of him. A loud buzzer echoed through the facility and the noises from the machinery whimpered to silence. The bustling factory seemed to deflate as everything came to a standstill.

"What the hell?" One worker yelled, then noticed the CEO of the company walking through the factory floor and covered his mouth.

"Everyone gather 'round." Jacob Tanner instructed with a firm but friendly tone as he waved his employees toward him. A group of a dozen workers congregated around one particular machine. Jacob walked toward the worker he had observed from his office window and asked, "How's it going, Jim?"

Jim nodded. He was a thin five-foot-nine with a worn and disheveled appearance. His shirt read, "You look like I need another drink," and his face projected a similar sentiment.

"Jim," the CEO said as he put his arm around his employee and raised his voice so that everyone could hear, "you operate the filler machine correct?"

Jim's wide eyes gave Jacob an apprehensive look, slowly nodding.

"It's okay, Jim," Jacob reassured the man, "you haven't done anything wrong." The two stepped over toward Jim's station. "Now, can you show us the general procedure you follow here at the filling station?"

Jim nodded slowly and started with a thick drawl, "Well, the bottles come in from the arranging machine and I have to make sure they're all lined up right, but they's never messed up much." Jim nodded at Jacob with a smile. "Then the filler does its thing and before the bottles can get moved down the line, I walk over here," Jim said taking four steps down

the line to get a good view of the next stage in the line. "Now, I decide which of the three downstream saniti—santini—"

"Sanitization," Jacob helped out his employee who seemed to be getting nervous.

"Yeah, them stations. And I walk over here," Jim said as he moved through the small crowd of onlookers to a laptop station and imitated typing on the keyboard. "I direct the line to whichever station looks most empty, then I go back and start it all over again."

Jacob nodded. "Good Jim. I'm sure you're doing exactly what you were taught. But there's a problem." The CEO looked around to his employees to see if any of them could guess what it was. "The problem is that it takes you 24 steps to complete a procedure that could take just three or four or maybe even none. Those 24 steps take time and time is money and, in our industry, money costs lives. Notice how all the empties are building up here upstream of your station?" Jacob raised his arm and directed the crowd's attention to the empty pill bottles grouped in front of the filler machine.

Jim bulged his eyes and stared at his boss.

"It's okay, Jim, it's not your fault. We just don't have the most efficient process in place." After a brief thought, Jacob waved a burly employee over to the laptop stand. "Chris, help me with this." He unplugged the laptop and secured one side of the metal stand that was holding the laptop. Chris gripped the opposite side and the two lifted the stand then brought it over toward Jim's filling station. Jacob looked for an outlet to plug the laptop in and found one under the filling station, which he kneeled down to utilize. He stood up and looked at the filling machinery and thought for a second.

"Anybody have a Phillips-head screwdriver?" Jacob asked and he held out his hand.

Chris looked down to his tool belt and pulled out the requested tool then handed it to Jacob, who was looking at the ventilation hood over the filling machine. Jacob used the screwdriver to unfasten the hood and Chris stepped closer to support the hood until it was completely unfastened.

"There," Jacob said as Chris walked the ventilation hood away from the station. "I don't even know why there's a hood here. Jim do you know why there's a ventilation hood here?" Jacob turned to look at Jim.

Jim shook his head with a confused look. "That ventilation duct is never on. I don't know why we have a hood there."

Jacob viewed the renovated workstation. "There. Now, you can stand right here and see the counter for the downstream station and you can easily direct the traffic on the laptop all without moving one step."

Some of the employees cracked a smile and others nodded.

"Twenty-four steps down to zero," Jacob said with a grin and a pat on Jim's shoulder. He turned to address his employees, "Now, remember what we talked about at the all-hands yesterday? It's called Kaizen. It's Japanese and it means 'change'—*kai*—and 'better'—*zen*—change for the better. I want this factory to be in a constant state of flux toward a better, more efficient state. That's the goal and it's the only way we can improve and become more efficient.

"Now, don't worry. Kaizen isn't about making you all expendable and sending your jobs overseas; it's about making you as effective of a team as possible. The more efficient each and every one of you is, the more people we can help with our product. And believe me, we *are* helping. By doing what you all do here at our factory, you are actually improving and saving the lives of thousands of patients out there."

A middle-aged woman in the group of employees smiled at her boss's sentiment.

"Jim . . . you are a lifesaver. Marge, you are a lifesaver. Smitty, you too."

Smitty allowed a wide grin to creep across his weathered face.

Jacob continued, "And we can save even more lives by being more efficient. If any of you see any sort of waste in your job or if you see some way to improve your daily routine, I want you to tell me and we will make the change, okay? For the better." Jacob nodded and clapped his hands. "All right, let's get this puppy back up and running and save some lives!"

The workers slowly dispersed and walked back to their respective stations. As Jacob walked back toward the office doors, another employee, Marge Sorenson, walked up to him.

"Mr. Tanner. Mr. Tanner," she said with urgency. "I think you're forgetting something."

"Hi Marge. What am I forgetting?" Jacob said, not slowing his stride.

"This factory was designed strictly to the Good Manufacturing Practices guidelines. You were here when that FDA man told us exactly how the laptop stand was to be positioned. And I don't think he's going to like you just up and taking off that ventilation hood, Mr. Tanner. That laptop station and that ventilation hood were put there for a specific reason in accordance with state and federal law and that FDA man is coming here this afternoon, I don't think you should be altering the location of those things."

Jacob nodded in understanding and smiled at Marge. "Marge, have I ever told you that you're excellent at what you do?"

Marge stared wide-eyed at her boss but did not respond.

"Thank you for your attention to details like that, but I know that the FDA agents are going to see the improvements we've made and I understand that they're probably not going to like it."

"Well, why would you want them to see that then?" Marge asked.

Jacob smiled at Marge. "Let's just say that I want to open up a dialogue."

Marge did not know how to respond. "Oh," she said, then turned and slowly retreated toward her office.

Back in his office, Jacob resumed his stance in front of the large window overlooking the factory and smiled after seeing Jim smoothly operating his station without the unnecessary steps.

"Now," Jacob said turning to Marc Johnson with a grin, "you were saying?"

* * *

Marc Johnson was incredulous. Not only was the CEO of his company ignorant of the nuances of pharmaceutical regulatory policy, he was unwilling to listen to an expert on the subject, namely, him. As the chief researcher for the company, Marc was tired of pleading. He had been dealing with the FDA and other government agencies his entire life and understood the ins and outs of the industry. But his boss clearly did

not. Jacob Tanner was strictly a businessman and didn't grasp the importance of the checks and balances offered by the protective federal agencies. Still Jacob was the CEO and held the reigns of the company.

"I hate to sound like a broken record on this but we simply need the government." Marc Johnson implored the CEO. He used his left hand to pull his chin-length, greased hair away from his face and behind his ears as he poked a toothpick between two molars with his right hand. The crisp white lab coat that he casually adorned belied his slovenly attire underneath.

"You do realize what this company would be without it, right?" Marc persisted. "I know that you've been out there trying to bag private donors and all that good stuff, but where has that gotten us? None of our funding throughout phase one and two was from your private investors, it was all from the FDA grant. And, don't forget, they lowered the mandatory requirements in phase three—the only reason we could pass muster with just 23 test subjects was because of ODA."

Jacob sorted through some papers on his desk and repeated, "ODA," as an ambiguous confirmation or question to Marc Johnson and did not look at his director of pharmaceutical research.

"The ODA, the Orphan Drug Act? Does this sound at all familiar?" Marc Johnson asked, slightly miffed.

Jacob nodded unconvincingly.

"Jacob, you know better than I do about the profitability of my drug, but I don't think we're making any money. If it weren't for our grant and decreased testing requirements, we would never have made it out of trials, not to mention all the grant money we got through ODA. I know you don't want to believe it, but we need to play ball with the feds. They own us."

Jacob pressed his lips together and exhaled through his nose in audible dislike of Marc's words.

Marc cleared his throat, then asked, "Jacob, did you hear me?" Marc shook his head in disbelief, then spoke intently, "Three years of sleepless nights during development, eighteen months of clinical trials in which I

nearly had a nervous breakdown every week. That's not to mention my entire post-doc spent on this theory. Jacob, this is my baby. I'm not going to throw it away because of a ridiculous rift between you and some FDA inspector."

"Look, Marc, you are the best. You were further along on this treatment than anyone else. That's why I hired you."

"We need to play ball with the FDA, Jacob," Marc said, glad that he finally got the CEO's attention. "It's that simple."

Jacob Tanner took a deep breath and stood up from his desk chair. "Marc, if it weren't for the FDA and its contrived approval process, Symbalia would have been available to the public two years ago. Can you imagine how many lives we could have saved in that time? The FDA cares about making sure we don't hurt people with our drug; they don't care about the disease out there that could hurt more people if it weren't for our drug. Now, they're pulling the plug on us at the end of March but people are still counting on us to produce, Marc—people like my sister when she got sick. It's my job to make sure that we can continue producing Symbalia so that more people don't end up like her." He pointed to the factory floor through his office window.

Naïve fool, Marc thought. "What do you mean, 'if it weren't for the FDA'? There's no such thing. They run the show."

Jacob raised his right index finger then said softly, "Not everywhere, Marc. The FDA doesn't run the show everywhere."

Marc contorted his lips, then said, "You're thinking only like a businessman . . . people's lives are at stake for Christ's sake."

Jacob looked intently and sternly at Marc. "I'm quite aware that people's lives are at stake here, Marc." He tapped a picture frame hanging on the wall that contained a portrait of his sister. "I'm quite aware of that." The two stared at each other in a tense standoff until Marc nodded and quietly left the office.

Two

"I told you so!" Marge Sorenson screeched as she ambled into Jacob Tanner's office. "I told you so Mr. Tanner!"

Jacob dropped the collection of bills in his hand and peered up to the factory manager with a skeptical grin. "Yes, Marge?"

"That man from the FDA is here and he went straight for the filling station where you made those changes earlier." Marge lifted her arm toward the panoramic window to indicate where the FDA agent was. "It's like he knew you were going to change something."

"Okay, okay. Calm down, Marge." Jacob said and patted the air in front of him to facilitate calmness. "Now, tell me what happened."

"He's going to cite us! He says the factory ain't in accordance with GMP. I said he was going to say that exact same thing earlier today!"

"Yes you did," Jacob agreed.

"Jim is talking with him now," Marge added.

Jacob nodded, then looked behind him to the factory floor and pursed his lips at the scene below. "Jim probably isn't the best spokesman for us, huh, Marge?"

Marge did not answer but stared impatiently at her boss.

Moments later, Marge was following Mr. Tanner onto the factory floor toward the FDA agent who was conversing animatedly with Jim Reynolds. As Jacob approached, he could hear the discussion between the FDA inspector and Jim above the machinery noise.

"I don't like the sounds I hear when you open your face, sir!" the FDA inspector yelled. Graying hair swooped over the perspiring forehead of the FDA inspector as he thundered. He was just under five feet eight inches tall but his wide girth made him more imposing than he would

have been otherwise. When the inspector opened his mouth a noticeable sliver of his canine tooth emerged. It looked fake and painfully sharp.

"You, you big dummy!" Jim retorted. "You ain't the boss of me! Jacob's my boss. I don't have to take orders from no FDA patsy."

The FDA inspector fumed and burned a look into Jim. "Patsy, huh? You best watch your tongue, sir. I could have you arrested. I could have you all arrested."

"Bullshit, Colombo! You can kiss my white ass." Jim turned around and spanked himself.

Jacob reached out his hand as he burst between the men, "Whoa! What's going on here?" Jim immediately returned to work at the sign of Jacob.

The FDA agent turned to Jacob. "Well, well, well. If it isn't Mr. Tanner," the agent said with a fake smile. "So nice of you to finally join us."

"Gary," Jacob said with a nod to the FDA agent and held out his hand for a shake.

"That's Inspector Javert, Mr. Tanner," Gary Javert said, ignoring Jacob's attempt at civility and instead pointing behind him at the filling station where Jim had been working. "This station is not in accordance with the Good Manufacturing Practices."

Jacob nodded. "Yes, inspector, I understand. We made improvements to the process just this morning, in fact, to reduce waste—"

"I don't care if you changed it to save your grandmother from a burning building. This station is not in accordance with the GMP. Under Section 501(B) of the 1938 Food, Drug, and Cosmetic Act, 21 US Code 351, I am authorized to enforce the GMP—"

"Yes, yes, I understand," Jacob said to move past the formal presentation of authority.

Javert looked at Jacob and continued, "You need a ventilation duct and hood and this electronic equipment cannot be within 15 feet of the filling station," the agent declared as he pointed to the laptop stand. "I explained this to you last time I was here, Mr. Tanner. If I wasn't so chari-

table, I would say that you changed this equipment to *deliberately* antagonize me."

Jacob bowed his head slightly and raised his hands, "Gary—Inspector Javert—you know that's not the case. Look, I understand your concern. But if you'll notice, there is no harm being done here. The ventilation hood is intended to collect dust particles from the filler, but, as you can see, we are producing gel-caps, not tablets. There is no dust to be collected by the ventilation system."

"Well there might be," the agent shot back.

"No, we've had air quality tests by qualified professionals. I can show you the report. The air in this factory is as clean as it can get."

Gary Javert shook his head as he bit leftover particles of lunch behind his closed lips. He said, "Mr. Tanner, in my 20 years of service with the FDA, I've seen just about everything. I've seen companies try to sell surgical knives that were rusted through and through. I've seen dangerous levels of DDT in grain intended for breakfast cereal. I've seen a company trying to sell prophylactics with holes in them. I've even seen a human corpse packaged in a bag of coffee beans. I have seen it all," the FDA inspector continued, "but I've never encountered someone as insolent as yourself, sir. You're like a modern day Gilgamesh."

"Gilga—?" Jacob repeated, confused.

"You have an adulterated pharmaceutical here and you are endangering your employees and your customers."

Jacob shook his head, "I'm not endangering—Gary, there is no harm being done here to the product and certainly not my employees. I would know if it was causing harm. I am in this business to *help* people not harm them. This factory is perfectly safe."

"I don't care if this is the safest factory on the planet Earth," the agent said slowly as if disciplining a child. "It does not meet the GMP industry standard."

"Wait, wait, wait, Gary," Jacob said. "You agree that there's no harm being done here with these alterations?" Jacob asked intensely.

"That is inconsequential, Mr. Tanner. You *must* maintain your factory at or above the industry standards."

"Well, if I may, what good are the industry standards if they don't protect from harm?"

"The standards *do* protect from harm—"

"Evidently, not in this case—in fact, it appears that the standards are actually *harming* us by restricting us from being as efficient as possible."

"Look," the agent said snapping his head back in disgust, "I'm not going to sit here and argue with you, Mr. Tanner. Fix this or I will shut you down."

"You do realize what we make here, right?" Jacob nodded rapidly.

Javert was silent for a dramatic moment and looked into Jacob Tanner's eyes. "Oh, I know all about what you make Mr. Tanner—your snake oil with which you ripped off thousands of innocent people with lies. Keep building your wall, Gilgamesh."

Jacob shook his head, "What are you talking about? Gary, we no longer manufacture that product. We have one product here, Symbalia." The CEO raised his hand and pointed to the bottles in the assembly line. "And it just so happens to be the only drug on the market that effectively treats Chinese encephalitis. If you shut us down, you put thousands of sufferers at risk."

The FDA agent was silent and let a wispy grin creep over his face. "My dear man, I wouldn't think of abandoning those poor people. I would simply nationalize your company and make your drug available for *free*. The drug would still be available, but you simply wouldn't be able to profit from it."

Jacob Tanner stared at the FDA agent, incredulous. "You don't have the authority."

Javert maintained his smile, revealing his razor-like canine teeth. "Oh, surely, you've heard of the HEAL America Act, Mr. Tanner? It authorizes my office to seize certain pharmaceutical companies that would be better suited under the auspices of the federal government. Yours would be an open and shut case considering you've repeatedly failed inspec-

tions, not to mention the fact that the FDA has already invested millions of dollars in your company through your grant."

"Now, sir, I'm sure we can come to an agreement here," Jacob said with a conciliatory tone.

"Typical," the agent said as he straightened up his posture. "When you're faced with losing your precious little company, you want to acquiesce. You make me sick, Mr. Tanner."

"I'm sure if you understood the situation better . . . ," Jacob said but did not finish his thought.

"You have two days to fix this." The agent flicked a finger toward the filling station. "Or you will find yourself shut down."

Inspector Javert walked past Jacob and Jim and toward the factory exit.

"Gilgamesh?" Jacob whispered to himself as he watched the inspector leave.

He felt his phone vibrate in his pants pocket and mechanically reached down, pulled it out and answered, "Tanner here."

"Jake the snake!" the cheery voice on the other end of the line said.

Jacob smiled. "Berto! How the hell are you?"

"Man, life is good, I tell you what!"

"That's good to hear," Jacob responded.

"Hey, I'm in town tomorrow and wanted to get together—you still looking for funding?"

Jacob raised his eyebrows at the coincidental question. "Of course," he confirmed.

"Well, I think I may have the answer to your prayers."

"I like the sound of that." Jacob smiled and headed back to work.

Three

"Man look at us," Roberto Rodriguez said warmly. He wore a button-down shirt with sleeves rolled up and had an even, Latin complexion with straight black hair, neatly combed to the side of his head. Roberto Rodriguez seemed to have a permanent, genuine grin and this moment was no different. "We were going to change the world, remember?"

Jacob's smile was subdued as he nodded. "Yeah, I remember, Berto." They were sitting at a rustic wooden table with a pair of plastic cups filled with water and three dishes filled with a various brown sauces in front of them. Jacob bounced his knee and looked around impatiently.

"We were going to be industrial giants and change the world," Roberto reminisced.

"Improve the lives of everyone on Earth," Jacob added.

"And make a killing along the way," Roberto said with a chuckle and a wink. "But the man's got you down now?"

Jacob shook his head. "No, it's nothing. It's just . . . it's crunch time, Roberto. People are relying on me. If I don't get some major funding within the month, I might lose the company when the grant runs out."

"What you mean you might lose the company?"

"It's this new law that allows the FDA to seize pharmaceutical companies for," Jacob sarcastically said, "the public welfare."

"You're shitting me."

"No." Jacob shook his head. "Some genius thought it up as a way to keep down for skyrocketing health care costs or something."

Roberto shook his head. "Of course the endless spigot of federal funds has nothing to do with skyrocketing health care costs, huh?"

"I mean, at one end, people are needlessly dying from diseases since the FDA is so backed up in the approval process, good drugs aren't released, and on the other end you have them restricting businesses to the point that it's impossible to produce drugs that *have* been approved."

"What'd they say?" Roberto asked with a smile, "If a thug kills you, it's murder; if the FDA kills you it's just being cautious."

"It's impossible," Jacob said dismayed.

Roberto brushed it off. "Ah, you don't really need to be concerning yourself with all that now, Jakey. What you should be concerning your-self with now . . . ," he said, changing the subject, "is the barbecue they're going to bring out in a little bit." Roberto clapped and rubbed his hands together. "Woo-boy, I love coming back to this place! Now, they're going to bring out some potatoes and a corn dish, but you need to ignore all that noise—don't let any of that sidetrack you," Roberto instructed with an anticipatory grin. "And don't even think about looking at the bread. You want to keep your eyes on the prize. You need to keep focused on the world-class ribs and brisket they're going to be bringing out. I mean you only have a limited amount of stomach space and you don't want to be filling up with any of that other veggie garbage."

Jacob nodded, amused.

"Shoot, man! But, of course, the whole point of this here exercise is the sauce. The meat is good, but it ain't nothing without this sauce. And they got some killer sauce here—probably the best outside of Texas."

Jacob smiled at his giddy friend.

"I tell you, sometimes I just want to drink the sauce straight out of the bowl." Roberto chuckled.

"Man, you'd trade your wife for a plate of ribs," Jacob joked.

"Don't tempt me Jakey." Roberto laughed. "So, speaking about the wife, how 'bout you? You find you a ball and chain yet?"

Jacob shook his head. "No way José. I cherish my freedom too much."

"Aww, that's just an excuse. You'd give up anything for the right girl I bet," Roberto asked.

Jacob shook his head. "She'd have to be perfect."

"Perfect, huh?"

Jacob nodded.

"Really, though, what does that mean?" Roberto inquired. "Perfect?"

"We've talked about this, Berto," Jacob said angling his head backward, thinking for a moment. "Okay, I'll tell you," he said flipping his hand in the air. "One of my professors at Harvard—a great man—once said that everyone on Earth was a slave to money, marketing, whatever you shoved in their face. He said that they all would notice a billboard instead of the moon next to it even though the moon is a much more spectacular object. He said that some people choose to look at the moon but they only notice the bright part. Only a few are really free and see the entire thing—even the part of the moon that isn't fully illuminated." Jacob moved his hand in a round motion in the air to reflect the moon. "I'm waiting for a girl who sees the whole of the moon."

Roberto looked at his friend with his usual grin. "What the hell was that, Jakey boy?" he mocked and let out a chuckle. "You been listening to your hippie-ass parents too much!"

Jacob smiled and shook his head. "Man, you can't handle anything deep can you?"

"No, that was real pretty—it was like one of them inspirational posters." Roberto chuckled.

"Man, it's beyond your IQ, I guess."

"No, I understand. You like werewolves."

"I want someone who isn't a slave to what they shove into our faces—someone who is really free! That is beauty."

"You know what's beautiful?" Roberto said hitting his friend on the arm. "A big ole plate full of barbecued ribs with the sauce dripping off the edge. Now *that's* beauty."

Jacob laughed, "You're hilarious."

"No, this is serious stuff, amigo."

Jacob smiled and took a swig of water. "Thanks, by the way," Jacob said, looking at his friend. "Thanks for setting this meeting up—really."

Roberto nodded. "No problem man! I probably can't help you with your moon women, so this is the least I can do for an old friend."

Jacob shook his head and laughed.

At that moment, a hostess directed a businessman wearing a crisp Armani suit to the table at which Roberto and Jacob sat. The two men stood up and shook the businessman's hand.

"Peter Driesel," Roberto said, "this is Jacob Tanner, president and CEO of Axelaris Pharmaceuticals. Jacob, this is Peter, president of Nexus Capital Group."

"Director of acquisitions, *not* president," Peter Driesel corrected Roberto dryly.

"Whoops, almost gave you a promotion there didn't I?" Roberto asked through a chuckle.

Peter was not fazed by Roberto's comment. He looked at the weathered table and sat down, placing his briefcase on the table. He then lifted his briefcase moved his hand over the wood surface and rubbed his fingers together to remove any residue. Peter moved his briefcase to the bench to his left and opened it.

"Have you had the ribs here, Peter?" Roberto asked with a friendly tone.

After a terse shake of his head, "I don't eat meat," Peter said.

Roberto frowned but nodded his head. "Oh," he hummed.

"If you don't mind, I'd like to get directly to business," Peter said.

Jacob nodded. "Great. Have you had a chance to look over my proposal?"

Peter answered, "Yes. You have an untenable business model, Mr. Tanner. You produce an orphan drug, but look to manufacture it and distribute it without your current FDA grant. Further, this disease your drug treats—Chinese encephalitis—the cause is unknown, correct? And we don't know if it's going to be around in six months much less five years. It could be another bird flu—a lot of hype with no real threat. You do have patent protection though, correct?"

Jacob breathed in deeply, soaking up all the negative assessment. "Yes, but I've had trouble with the FDA recently and I don't know if that will be honored or if they will want to revoke our patent or what."

"What do you mean trouble?" Peter asked, squinting at Jacob.

"Well, the FDA inspector assigned to us is bucking for a promotion or something and he's trying to use that new HEAL America Act to seize my company." Jacob noticed a weary face across the table from him.

Peter shook his head in confusion. "Mr. Tanner, forgive me, but what do you expect me to do here? You want me to fund a company that is losing money and has no guaranteed prospects of a solid return on investment?"

"Mr. Driesel, with all due respect, Chinese encephalitis is a real danger and it's affecting more and more people every month—it's growing to epidemic proportions. Mr. Driesel, I'm sure you or someone you know has a loved one that will be affected by Chinese encephalitis. I myself have suffered a loss in the family from this horrible disease. We need to keep producing Symbalia so that no one else out there has to deal with the pain and suffering that my family went through."

"Sir, you're giving me warm and fuzzy. I have sweaters in my closet and a golden retriever in my back yard to give me warm and fuzzy. What I need from you is a cold hard case for making money. I don't care that your 90-year-old granny is suffering from this disease; if you're not making any money treating it, it's of no interest to me. You're going to get the same response from everyone you talk to in my position."

Jacob nodded. "I see."

Peter Driesel pulled out an executive report of Axelaris Pharmaceuticals from his brief case and surveyed it. He hummed, then looked at Jacob. "Your salaries and benefits package are way above the national average. Have you thought about terminating your employees and hiring some migrants? I'm sure they could sufficiently handle the workload and you could save hundreds of thousands of dollars."

Jacob smiled but shook his head. "I can't do that, Mr. Driesel. These are my employees. They are what drives my company and I can't let them down."

Driesel put the paper down. "Have you considered relocating the company to Ur?"

"That's what I've been trying to get him to do!" Roberto agreed.

Jacob looked at his friend, then questioned Driesel, "Ur, you mean the special administrative charter city in Texas?"

"Yes, that's where Roberto and I are based. It's completely tax-free and will save you a considerable sum."

Jacob nodded. "I have considered that, yes. But again it would be painful to relocate my employees from their homes and families."

"If you'll excuse me, you seem far too beholden to your employees, sir. If you start thinking like a businessman and not a charity worker, it may help you become profitable." He paused, then added, "However, until you develop a stronger business model, I cannot endorse your company."

Peter pursed his lips. "That orphan drug program you were in is a great way to fund unprofitable drugs like yours. Government is great at losing money. I am not. It sounds like you've had your issues with the FDA, but I believe at this point that is your best bet."

Jacob looked down and acquiesced, "Right."

Peter closed up his briefcase, stood up, and extended his hand toward Jacob. "If you'll excuse me."

A startled Jacob stood up and shook Peter's hand, as did Roberto.

Peter said, "If you can come up with a profitable business model, please, by all means, come down to Ur and talk to me. I'd be glad to look it over." He half-smiled and stepped over the table bench, paused for a moment then turned back to Jacob. "On second thought, I doubt he will have any more interest than I, but I can put you into touch with an associate of mine. He deals in high-risk ventures. I can't promise you anything, but this gentleman can make a profit selling sand in the Kalahari. If anyone can make something of your company it's him."

Jacob nodded eagerly. "That'd be great, Mr. Driesel. Any lead will be greatly appreciated."

Peter Driesel took out his phone. "Do you have Bluetooth? I can forward you the information." Peter eyed Jacob's phone, which was sitting on the table.

"Sure," Jacob confirmed. He picked up his phone and tapped the screen, which remained black. Jacob let out a moan of discontent. "I'm sorry," he said looking at his phone. "I need to get another phone, this one's always dying on me."

Without missing a beat, Peter took out a business card and a pen and wrote a name and phone number on the back. He handed it to Jacob. "The guy I want you to contact is Martin Gall, he's—"

"Wait, Martin Gall? *The* Martin Gall?" Jacob said jutting his head toward Peter.

Peter nodded. "Yes, do you know him?"

Jacob rolled his head and looked down at the table. "I don't *know* him, but I know *of* him, of course. The guy's a genius, a legend."

"Yes. He's a very capable businessman," Peter agreed.

Jacob smiled. "That would be unbelievable, Mr. Driesel. I'd love just to meet the guy."

Peter nodded. "Well, there's his assistant's contact information. Get a hold of her and she'll set up a meeting. He'll want you to come to Ur as well, but it would be worth it. I wish you the best of luck, Mr. Tanner."

Peter then secured his briefcase, walked away from the table, and exited around the corner of the restaurant.

Roberto hit Jacob on the back and laughed, "Shit man, notch one more failure to your list."

Jacob maintained his stare in the direction of Peter Driesel's exit.

"You know . . . Harland Sanders had a really good idea at the age of 65 but he was rejected over 300 times before someone wanted to buy his pressure cooker and *secret recipe*. Now there are 10,000 Kentucky Fried Chicken restaurants with his mug on the sign."

Jacob turned to his friend and smiled but said nothing.

Roberto added, "You can't give up, man. You'll make it work."

"Thanks man. You're always good for a pep talk." After a moment's thought, Jacob said, "If nothing else, it will be great to get a meeting with Martin Gall out of this—he's an absolute legend."

"Yeah, I've heard of the guy. He's a big name down in Ur—got one of the tallest buildings there."

"Martin Gall is the most incredible business mind to come out of Harvard ever—he was five years ahead of me. He led a revolution in minimization and elimination in the workplace. He's just very inspirational—his book was what inspired me to create Amelior. And," Jacob said, surprising himself, "he's also actually a dedicated philanthropist. Each year his charity gala raises millions of dollars for a great cause. I think last year he raised enough money to build an entire orphanage for the lost children in Uganda. All private funds."

"Well maybe you can get me some tickets to his gala this year—I've been trying to get my hands on some. At least something good would have come out of this meeting."

With an open mouth, Jacob looked at the business card Peter had given him. "Martin Gall."

"Well, it sounds like you'll be following me down to Ur, o-boy!"

Jacob nodded and agreed, "Sounds like it."

Roberto spotted their waitress bringing a plate of sizzling meat toward their table and clapped his hands and rubbed them together. "Here we go, Jakey! I'm glad Peter took off, you can never trust a man who won't eat barbecue." Roberto laughed at his joke and reached for a chunk of meat before the waitress had placed it on the table.

Four

The glass, concrete, and steel towered above Jacob Tanner's head in the warm Texas air. He was trying to estimate the height. Seven? Eight hundred? He wondered.

"This one is going to be around 1,300 feet tall. Gall's building down the street is 1,200 feet," Roberto Rodriguez informed Jacob looking up at the structures.

The clamor of construction filled the atmosphere of the Ur city center and Jacob tried to soak in the ambiance of the frenzied, productive activity. Nearby, dump trucks kicked up dust and the smell of fresh-cut lumber and aluminum wafted in the air as a hive of construction workers swarmed the site.

"Crews are working 24 hours a day, seven days a week. This structure is going up at the rate of two floors a day. It should be completed within four weeks. Faster than anything else of its kind."

"Unbelievable. And what's that building over there?"

"Oh, the thick zigzag lookin' building?" Roberto pointed to a metallic structure about a mile away that carved through the sky like a large angled bracket teetering impossibly on one end. "Believe it or not, that's going to be a ski resort."

"A what?"

"Yeah—they're building a ski resort in hot-as-hell South Texas of all places. Can you believe it?"

Jacob shook his head. "No, it's amazing."

Roberto continued his tour. "Tell me about it Jakey. Just look around. Three years ago, this whole area was brush and swamp. There was absolutely nothing here. And ever since they secured charter city

status, the place has just exploded in growth. I don't think anyone has seen anything like it. London in the nineteenth century, New York at the turn of the twentieth, Las Vegas, Dubai—no place has seen growth like this."

"You would know," Jacob agreed.

"Right, you know my firm handles some of the biggest construction projects in the world. We were on a number of projects in Dubai during their boom and I can tell you that was nothing like this. I think they had about twenty percent of the world's cranes in 2007. Well, over half of the world's cranes are right here in Ur right today. *Half.*"

"Amazing."

"I tell you what," Roberto confirmed. "And these buildings aren't all there is. They already got a gorgeous river walk down in Hayek Town and they're putting up a real nice museum up in Jefferson Heights."

"Wow. And all this construction is to code?" Jacob asked, pointing around the area toward several new buildings.

"Well, you see, that's what's amazing about all this. There is no code."

"Excuse me?" Jacob asked.

"You know, there is no code. At least there isn't an overarching code that mandatorily applies to every project or district. And even if there was a code, there's no government agency or bureaucracy here to enforce it."

"How's that?"

"This is what I've been trying to tell you Jake, there's *no* government here. None. It's a completely free society."

A smile began to creep over Jacob's face. "And it's working?"

"That's what everyone was wondering when they started building this place. It seems crazy—you take fifty thousand people, stick them in a place with no government and just one law and see if they behave."

"And are they?"

"Look around, man. Not only is it working, but it's working better than any other system in the world ever has."

"Well, with these buildings, how do they ensure safety and structural soundness?" Jacob inquired.

Roberto put his hands out to facilitate his explanation. "Okay, so, it's really remarkable what they're doing here. Any company or entity who wants to construct their building hires their crew or multiple crews and they also hire an auditor. Now hundreds of these auditors have cropped up here in Ur in order to do exactly what the government was ostensibly doing on the outside. Only these companies are doing it at a fraction of the cost of their mirror government agencies because no one would voluntarily pay those fees charged by government." Roberto elbowed his friend. "Like, it doesn't take two million dollars to inspect a skyscraper, right?"

"I don't know. Does it?"

"Not by dang sight. Anyway, these auditing companies have gained a lot of prominence. The buyers are going with the most critical auditors because the future tenants of the buildings want to see that it's being built right. For instance, Google is planning on moving its headquarters into this building. They hired their own auditors on top of the one the building manager has hired to make sure everything's in line. So instead of one measly government bureaucrat looking into the construction of the building, you have whole teams of people making sure the thing is built right. There are even auditors of auditors to make sure the audits are being done correctly."

"That's a lot of auditing. How does that affect things on your end?"

"Well, I'll tell you what, all the redundancy can be kind of a pain, but I think it's worth it in the long run. We want to be known as the best construction outfit in the industry, so we bring on the most scrutiny for our projects."

"And I'm sure they have auditors for pharmaceutical companies too?" Jacob asked.

"Yep. I know of two companies right off the bat that approve quality of pharmaceuticals and nutraceuticals. Burnett & Jones is the biggest and most reputable—you'd probably want to work with them. And I

know several retail chains that won't purchase drugs unless they've been approved by these auditors. I know Whole Foods and Costco both require the top approval from at least Burnett & Jones."

"Makes sense. So how is Burnett & Jones different than the FDA?"

"Well for one, they ain't going to stop you from producing your drug—I know of a couple who have come here to escape the FDA and release their drugs immediately. No one has the authority to shut your company down. And they won't hold your drug up while it makes its way through some bureaucratic bottleneck. All Burnett & Jones does is their best to ensure your product is safe and does what you claim it does. Then they slap their seal of approval on it and the retailers feel comfortable selling it."

"So, what? Do the retailers pay for the auditors, then?" Jacob asked.

"For the most part," Roberto confirmed with a nod. "If big pharma was paying for the audits, there would be a conflict of interest, so the burden is placed on the retailer."

"Ah," Jacob said in reply.

"That way, there's no Enron going to happen here."

"Right, but doesn't that drive up costs for the consumer?"

"It does, but the lower overall costs of doing business here in Ur offset the higher effort dramatically. Labor's extremely cheap and materials are less without all them taxes."

"I love it. It's exactly what I've envisioned. You probably save millions doing business here."

"Woo boy! That's why every company and their brother want to be here. No forced regulation and no taxes. Look around man. This is growth!"

Roberto led Jacob along a sidewalk that was crowded with a tarp-covered fence designating the boundary of a construction zone. Dust billowed up over the fence as rugged workers on nearby three-story scaffolding communicated to each other in Spanish.

"So, if there's no regulation—"

"No *government* regulation," Roberto corrected his friend. "There's all sorts of self-regulation."

"Right, if there's no government regulation, there's probably no police force either?" Jacob asked.

"You got it. No *official* police force run by the city or anything."

Jacob shrugged his bottom lip and hummed, "Interesting."

"Yeah, does that sound scary to you?"

"No, no, I could see it working."

Roberto acquiesced, "Well, it is safer here than outside Ur. They take security very seriously here. I mean, you remember your drive down here? The checkpoint at the border with the hand and retina scanners? The district up there, Washington Heights, pays for that—completely supported through private funding, by the way. And that checkpoint on the highway you drove in on is sponsored by my company, of course."

"Oh man, now you're speaking my language. This gets into the question of positive externalities and whether the benefits from a police force and a safe society outweigh the costs of supporting the police. I guess here, they say that the positive externalities don't outweigh the costs."

Roberto shook his head but maintained a grin. "Man, I don't know what the hell you just said."

Jacob smiled. "Right, a positive externality is the benefit that the whole group gets from a part doing something good. For instance, the government provides a police force but everyone benefits from the safer society. Theoretically, that should mean that everyone should have to pay for the police force."

"Right. But here, everything is individualized and privatized. If you want to protect your warehouse, you can pay for your own damn security."

"And so everyone has their own security force?"

"Not really. There are a couple big firms that specialize and provide security for everyone else. My company goes with Triple 'S'—Shield Security Systems. They're pricey, but top notch. The other big one is Keynes Aegis."

"It sounds great, but then again, why should your company have to worry about security? Doesn't it make more sense to just leave all that to one single police force?"

"Well, that would be nice if we could rely on a police force to protect us, but even outside where there's one ubiquitous police force, crime still happens and companies are required to hire security forces. This way, if Triple 'S' fails us continually or becomes corrupted, we can go to Keynes or some other firm."

Roberto looked around the construction site as Jacob thought about what he was saying.

"Really, though," Roberto continued, "the only way to really protect everyone is for *everyone* to be in charge of protection. Each building downtown will have their own security because that protects them best and we let Triple 'S' run our checkpoint to protect our own interests. For example, we're promoting our highway as the only traffic-free highway on Earth. So, of course, it's in our best interest to insure that the cars that are driven on the road aren't going to break down or cause a ten-car pile-up. We want to make sure drivers can get to our clients as soon as possible."

"Clients?"

"Yeah, clients."

"You mean the drivers?"

"Not really. We want to make our roads free to travel on for the drivers, so we require the companies that we connect with the road to pay for that service. If you own a shopping mall and you want customers, we can get them to you safely and efficiently, but it's going to cost you."

Jacob squinted. "Of course, roads cost money."

"Right. And there ain't no taxes here to pay for the roads, so somebody's got to foot the bill. Our business model determined that the companies benefiting from the roads should be the ones who pay up. And it seems to be working out just fine. Without heavy property taxes, people are willing to chip in for state of the art roads."

Jacob nodded, letting the idea sink in. "No taxes . . . ."

"That's right, Jakey! Every transaction here is 100 percent voluntary. You're going to love it here man!"

Jacob nodded. "I know you're right, Berto."

"Woo boy! And you haven't even had the Barbecue down here yet! When do you meet with Gall?"

"This afternoon."

"You nervous?"

Jacob shrugged his lips and nodded. "A little."

"You'll be fine, o-boy." Roberto patted Jacob on his back and the two left the construction site.

Five

Jacob sat quietly in the front office in the executive suite of the Gall Enterprises building. His briefcase rested on his knees and he surveyed the stark, angular design of the room, which stretched upwards to twenty feet. The only other person present in the office, a middle-aged secretary, was situated across the room from Jacob and operated a desktop computer. Both Jacob and the secretary tried to ignore the shouting that was emanating from behind Martin Gall's office doors.

"I want his ass on a platter!" was heard through the thick mahogany doors. "You got that?"

Jacob's eyes widened and he looked at the secretary for some guidance.

The secretary presented a fake smile. "Mr. Gall will be with you shortly."

Jacob nodded silently.

The muffled shouting continued and a moment later a burly man in a navy blazer opened the main office door from the inside. The security guard stood at the door and looked up as someone else, a 50-year-old, downtrodden man wearing an old beige suit walked through the doorway with his head down. Behind him was a man in a sophisticated black suit with a pink- and red-striped tie. His thick hair was gelled back and gave an additional two inches to his six-foot-four frame.

"Leslie," the man in the black suit barked at the other as they left his office. "If this deal falls through . . . if you fuck me on this . . . ." He tapped his index finger in the air at the other man but did not finish his thought.

"Mr. Gall, I promise," the man in the beige suit said as he turned around to face his tormentor.

"A promise is a bunch of words, Leslie. I want the fucking goods."
Mr. Gall pointed at the man in the beige suit again. "If you fuck this up, I
will personally string your balls up and feed them to Allie."

Who's Allie? Jacob wondered.

After a short pause and an uncomfortable smile from Leslie, Mr.
Gall continued, "I'm not joking."

The man in beige looked around to seek some support but received
none from the aloof assistant and the stunned Jacob.

"All right, now get the hell out of here," Gall said to Leslie in a
suddenly friendly tone. He patted the shocked man on the shoulder and
turned back to his office ignoring the patient Jacob.

The assistant called into the main office, "Mr. Gall, a Mr. Jacob
Tanner is here to see you."

"Send him in," Mr. Gall called back without slowing his stride.

"Mr. Gall will see you now," the secretary said after turning toward
Jacob.

Jacob raised his eyebrows and stood up. He walked through the door
at which the security guard was posted and stepped into Martin Gall's
office. The room was a combination of simple, geometric furniture and
gaudy marble appointments. The warm ambiance of recessed lighting on
the walls contrasted the cold, hard edges of the angular chocolate brown
furniture scattered throughout the office.

Jacob watched Gall as he walked toward a young man sitting at a
workstation in the corner of his office. He yelled out, "Bobby, whataya got
for me?"

"I found one, Mr. Gall," the bespectacled man said turning toward
the executive. "P/E is under 20 and the alpha is 1.15."

Martin Gall chuckled, "One point one five? The crap I took this
morning has more alpha than that. Are you trying to waste my time with
that bullshit?"

Bobby turned away reticently. "Right. Sorry, sir."

"Keep at it," Mr. Gall tried to give the young man support. He walked
around his desk near the center of the office and slapped the keyboard,

moved his index finger down his computer monitor, then nodded to himself as Jacob observed silently.

"Okay," Martin Gall said looking up at his guest. "You are Jacob Tanner from Arkansas. You want some money for your company? Pharmaceuticals is it? All right, you have exactly five minutes to knock my socks off."

Jacob swallowed and looked down to gather his thoughts. "First off, I want to say you're my biggest fan—"

"Oh?" Gall responded curiously. "I am?"

"I've read all your books. *Greed Is Grand* was absolutely brilliant. You really show how self-interest leads to better conditions for the entire world. You're a real—"

"Okay, okay, I get the picture," Gall said and glanced back at his computer monitor. "You worship me. Fine. Join the club. Let's move along."

Jacob nodded. "All right, Mr. Gall. So, I founded a pharmaceutical company seven years ago to help people—"

Gall shook his head subtly. "Again, skip the bullshit, Tanner. It sounds like you're trying to sell me on you as a person. I just want the facts. A great man once said that a friendship founded on business is better than a business founded on friendship. Now, I don't want to be your friend, I just want you to tell me what *you* need in order to make *me* a shitload of money."

Jacob looked down to reset his mind. "Right, okay. I need cash to lease my factory, pay employees, and pay down my equipment."

"All right, all right, Tanner. You're asking me to help you out, but you haven't used the magic word."

Jacob paused and smiled. "What *is* the magic word?"

Gall grinned, "'Money.' The magic word is 'money,' Tanner."

"Well our grant was for $5.2 million per annum," Jacob said unhesitatingly.

Gall looked calmly at Jacob. "I understand but how much do you *need*?"

"I can get the job done with four," Jacob confirmed. "That on top of current sales will get us to where we need to be."

Martin Gall's eyes darted around for a second before he spoke, "Now, Driesel said you were a charity case. Let me get this straight, you are not profitable currently, correct?"

Jacob lifted his chin, "Not right now, no. Our sales numbers are still very low but I know that if I can streamline our processes and cut on waste I can get very close. And I estimate that, with the current rate of increase of diagnosis for the condition, we will be profitable within a year or two."

Mr. Gall shook his head. "Whoa, whoa, whoa, Tanner! You and I could be taking a dirt nap in a year or two. That's not what I want to hear. So, what's the disease this drug treats?"

"It's a neurological condition. No one is sure about the cause but we think it may be a flavivirus antigenically related to the Japanese encephalitis virus. Most likely it's being spread by mosquitoes, but that has not been confirmed. There's a new theory that says CE comes from bed bugs."

Mr. Gall shook off the scientific description. "Upside?"

"Symbalia is the only drug available that treats the specific symptoms of this disease. Upside is potentially very high."

"What are we talking about here, Tanner? I want figures."

"Our break even point is 100,000 prescriptions monthly. With economies of scale we could be seeing a profit of one million every month if we double that."

"That's a big *if*." Gall repeated skeptically. "Tanner, I'm going to be honest with you. This sounds like a crapshoot. You don't even know what the hell causes this disease, right? You don't know if it will fade away by next year or will be the next Black Plague turning everyone into zombies. You're in debt and not making any money."

Jacob sensed his opportunity slipping away, "Sir, you're really my last hope. I've talked to every venture capital group in this country and I've gotten absolutely nowhere."

Mr. Gall scrunched his face, "What the hell, Tanner? You giving me a guilt trip? I'm not the Salvation Army. That shit may work out there in Arkansas, but it won't work here in Ur."

Jacob looked at Gall. "How do you mean?"

Gall let out a chuckle. "I mean your guilt trip may work in Arkansas where you have some government tit to feed off of. It's difficult to actually make money if you don't have the FDA keeping you fat year after year, huh? I know exactly where you are, Tanner. An example, I just sold a million units out of my New York manufacturer on a government contract. A million units of what?" Gall paused to let Jacob answer, but he did not. "Fuck if I know and I don't care to. I don't even care if these units do what they're supposed to do. What I care about is making the sale. And I *can* make the sale because the people who make decisions owe me favors."

Jacob listened silently.

"My competition in that contract, Bob Numbnut over at Motorola, spends all of his time trying to make his superconductors a thousandth of a percent more efficient or his processors a billionth of a percent faster, but with just one phone call to a friend of mine I can get a regulation passed into law limiting the use of devices to a type that only *I* can provide. Connections, Tanner. That's the name of the game."

Martin Gall turned to the wall to his right. On it hung a dark brown leather whip situated on a wooden peg. A bronze plaque was situated below the whip but the inscription was unreadable to Jacob as far away from it as he was.

"You see that whip?" Gall asked and waited for confirmation from Jacob, which he got. "That was a gift from one of the most successful businessmen in the modern age, Bernie McAlvie. And he said that *I* cracked the code. How do you get people to buy your product when it's inferior to the competition's? You break out the whip and get the animals working for you. You target the jackals at the capitol—you get them to write the law that favors your product—and you get the masses of sheep to follow along."

"That technique wasn't in your book," Jacob said under his breath.

"Could I do that here in Ur? Hell no, I couldn't. Who's going to write that law? That doesn't happen here. There are a lot of great things about this place—it's the Wild West—but to make it here you have to produce. Take your situation, for instance. You were doing quite well, I take it, back in Podunk or wherever making your little orphan drug under the auspices of the federal government. But once you take away your FDA grant, you're up the creek without a paddle, aren't you?" Mr. Gall pointed in the air. "Out there, making money is simple depending on who you know. It's a bit more difficult in here without friends in high places. You actually have to make something worthwhile that people will buy. A difficult concept to grasp, I know."

Jacob shook his head. "But Symbalia *is* worthwhile, sir. It helps the lives of thousands of people. It really works."

"Save it for your church group, Tanner. If you're not making money, you're not helping Jack W. Fuck."

Jacob pursed his lips and looked around the office. "Well, I see your mind was already set, Mr. Gall. I won't waste any more of your time." He took a step back. "But I'm wondering, if your mind was already made up about this, why did you agree to see me?"

Martin Gall thought for a split second then explained, "I agreed to meet you, Tanner, because I know about you. A few years ago, you introduced a drug that was going to revolutionize the world. It could heal depression, joint pain, any number of fictitious conditions that the pathetic masses complained about. What was it called?" Gall raised his hand and snapped for assistance from Jacob.

"Amelior," Jacob said.

Martin continued, "Right, Amelior. And you made an absolute killing. That is, until the story broke that Amelior was no more than an inert compound—that it was a fucking placebo. Now, you got crucified for that. People said you were a snake oil salesman that you were evil incarnate—"

"But Mr. Gall, Amelior really worked. The studies were conclusive. If someone *believed* they were getting better from a placebo they *actually* got better!"

Gall assumed Jacob was joking and laughed at him. "Funny, Tanner."

"I'm serious."

Gall shook his head, "Look, you can cut the crap with me. You don't have to sugar coat it. You saw an opportunity to make money and you took it. A sucker is born every minute, right?"

Jacob let out a proud smile. "Well, it was a business opportunity—"

"Tanner, I'm not *condemning* you. It was a brilliant move! I think it was fucking genius that you were able to slap a label on some bullshit chalk pill and call it a wonder drug. Absolute genius."

"Okay, it was a pretty clever business move, I guess," Jacob said, allowing some pride to show.

"I mean, shit, if you can sell a million chalk pills at a 2,000 percent markup, you can sell anything. Unfortunately, your new drug, what's the name . . . Symbalia isn't chalk and it doesn't have a 2,000 percent markup. I don't want Symbalia, Tanner, I want Amelior. Bring me Amelior."

Jacob breathed deeply and nodded. "I see."

Martin scanned Jacob's face with a flat, distant look. He then turned to his computer before explaining, "Now, if you'll excuse me, I have some business to attend to."

Jacob nodded with a disappointed air and looked around the office. "Of course," he said, dejected. Jacob slowly paced toward the office door. His mind was reeling in rejection and a loss of what to do next. Where was he to turn? Who could save his company now?

"Oh, Tanner?" Martin Gall called toward his guest. Jacob braced for more verbal abuse. "Talk to Jean out front. She'll write up a contract and get you set up with a warehouse in the Rand sector."

A smile crept across Jacob's face at Gall's words.

"You have one month to start making me money and I don't care how you do it—fire every employee and replace them with fuckin' slaves, start charging an arm and a leg for the drug, switch out the ingredients

with horseshit—I don't care, just show me the fucking money. If that doesn't happen, you're out on your ass."

Jacob rushed back over to Martin and vigorously shook his hand. "Mr. Gall, you won't be disappointed. I'm going to make you a killing, sir, you just wait!"

Martin Gall looked away from Jacob, "Well, you better. Now get the hell to work."

Jacob couldn't contain a wide, child-like grin as he turned around and briskly walked out of the office.

Six

Nasty, brutish, and short. Isn't that what Hobbes had said natural life was like? Gary Javert contemplated as he looked at himself in his car's rear view mirror. Hobbes had been right of course—the natural state of man was a tribal state of constant warfare and it made for an awful existence. In the natural state, a man could do whatever he wanted in order to preserve his own life or property. He could kill another man to improve his life or wealth or he could band together with a group of people to destroy another tribe and plunder their wealth. Bellum omnium contra omnes— war of all against all. That's what true human nature was like.

But mankind was smarter than that, Javert thought. It had invented the concept of government—a guiding force, based on a social contract in which the people agreed to give up some of their tribal, antiquated freedoms in order to live in the peace of a civilized society. And society had entrusted public servants like him in order to maintain civility.

Javert recognized that some people didn't want to abide by the social contract, however. Those people were typically the naturally strongest of the population and sought a return to the nasty, brutish, and short barbaric state of nature, mainly because they could thrive in such an environment, he reasoned. People like that would have no problem stealing from the weak, pushing around the defenseless, or toppling the legitimate sovereign authority under which they had gained their power—the government itself.

Jacob Tanner was such a person, Javert thought. Not only had Tanner previously stolen from people with the promise of a panacea in the nutraceutical Amelior, he had somehow finagled his way into an FDA

grant, which had supported his new pharmaceutical Symbalia, and he was planning on capitalizing off of that drug at a stunning rate.

Tanner was part of the unprecedented gouging of the American public by pharmaceutical companies that had driven up health care costs and forced millions into a situation in which they could not afford health insurance. The entire health care system, Javert thought, was out of control. It had reverted to Hobbes's state of nature—a corrupted system in which the strong took advantage of the weak and profited only when people were sick. It wasn't a *health* care system, after all, it was a *sick* care system and would not be remedied on its own. The system needed a cure. Of course, that's why Congress had passed the HEAL America Act—the Health Enterprises And Liabilities of America Act—granting the FDA new authority to seize certain key pharmaceutical companies in order to provide their vital drugs to the public for a fraction of the cost. Only when companies stopped profiting on sick people were people going to truly heal.

Gary Javert opened his car door and stood erect in the late morning air, straightening his suit jacket, before closing his car door. His late-twenties assistant, Nicholas Debbs, trudged through the dew-covered grass on the parking lot median toward Javert. The assistant was tall and gangly in his inexpensive suit, which did not quite fit.

Nicholas Debbs carried a melancholic air with him and moaned more than he spoke. When he got to Javert, he asked, "Sir, don't you think this is a little overdramatic? I mean were the paramilitary soldiers really necessary?" There was no conviction in his question, just a sound of futile sarcasm.

Javert was slightly taken aback by the question but he did not let Nicholas's melancholy dampen his evident giddiness. "This is what we live for, Mr. Debbs. This is a modern day O.K. Coral; this is Pat Garrett going after Billy the Kid and Eliot Ness taking down Al Capone. We are the hippest law enforcement officers alive."

Nicholas Debbs did not roll his eyes, but looked away from his superior with distaste. "But the guns, sir? This is a pharmaceutical company."

Javert slowly turned to Nicholas with closed thin lips and squinted eyes. "Mr. Debbs, behind those doors is a collection of hardened miscreants who have persistently defied authority and broken the law and the GMP. They are the barbarian horde, the brutes, the vandals," he said pointing to a nearby office building. "They could have guns trained on us right now. We don't know what to expect."

Nicholas pursed his lips and shrugged. "Great we all get to go home early today because we'll all be dead."

Javert ignored Nicholas's sarcasm and turned toward the imposing building in front of them.

Four men with all-black military fatigues and badges, which read, "Office of Criminal Investigations," approached Gary Javert. Each officer held an assault rifle at a 45-degree angle toward the ground away from Javert.

"Men," Gary Javert shouted, "follow my lead." He stepped off a grassy median in the parking lot and walked toward the front doors of Axelaris Pharmaceuticals.

"We going to see any hostiles today sir?" one of the OCI officers mumbled at his superior.

"Quiet, officer!" his superior retorted.

The four hunched-over OCI officers walked behind a confident Gary Javert and a lagging Nicholas Debbs. Each officer took turns scanning the surroundings for suspicious behavior but found none in the peaceful office park.

As Javert approached the tinted window doors in front of the building, he turned to his team and squinted. "Let's take one back for the American people. Let's do some good!" Gary Javert turned back to the doors and pulled them open with a dramatic rush.

A stark empty room stared back at agents as the OCI officers poured through the doors and directed their weapons at each corner of the front office, securing the perimeter.

Javert's eyes bulged as he took in the scene. He slowly followed the OCI agents into the building and turned toward the swinging doors that

led to the factory floor. He exploded through the doors and stopped in his tracks, stunned. The factory was empty.

Two at-ease OCI officers walked into the factory behind Gary Javert and shrugged. "Uh," one officer said, "take what back?"

Gary Javert looked around the stark rooms and fumed. "This isn't the end Jacob Tanner," he whispered under his breath. "You can run, but you can't hide."

Seven

"What have you done Jake?" the elderly baritone asked on the other end of the line. It was Eli Tanner, Jacob's father. "You're giving up the grant?"

Jacob was sitting at a round table in the posh lounge of the Grand Ur Hotel waiting for a meeting with Marc Johnson when his father had called. After a familial summary, Jacob found himself on the defensive. "Dad, we were going to lose the grant anyway," Jacob explained, "and the FDA was threatening to shut down my plant. It was the only way to keep producing our drug."

"Well why were they going to shut your plant down, son? Maybe it was for a good reason?"

"Dad, you're siding with them and you don't even know why they did what they did!" Jacob blurted.

"Well . . . why *did* they do it?"

"It's this guy at the FDA. We've been butting heads for years now. I'm just trying to produce something worthwhile, dad, like I've always said. I want to help people and I know I can do it but this FDA inspector seems to have it out for me—he just wants to micromanage every little detail and he even threatened to take over my company under a new bill they passed in Congress."

Jacob's father chuckled. "Well, you know how I feel about that, son."

"What? You would have the FDA take over my company? Dad, the FDA can't even handle their current case load as it is, why do you think they will be able to handle running several drug companies on top of that?"

"Son, you know my position on those pharmaceutical companies and those mega-corporate debacles. Some things are just better off under

government care—you know, for benefit of the people." His voice was earnest and pleading.

"Dad, are you kidding? They're talking about taking over the entire pharmaceutical industry. Government can't even deliver mail or issue drivers' licenses efficiently—I mean if you needed to get a package to someone across the country tomorrow, would you use FedEx or the post office? If you need to get your driver's license, would you rather go to the DMV or AAA?"

"We're not talking about the DMV, son."

"You think some government bureaucracy can effectively produce Symbalia let alone every drug needed for every disease?"

"Yes, son. When we're talking about things as important saving lives, we need someone who knows what they're doing to be in charge—a central authority who's responsible to the people not dominated by *yetzer hara.*"

"*Yetzer hara* dad?" Jacob shook his head. "Dad, how many times have we gone over this? The best way to allocate resources for the people is the price system and the profit motive, *not* some central authority."

Jacob's father hummed, "I don't know . . . ."

"Look, what are you using to talk to me with?"

"Uh, I'm not sure—"

"The phone you're using to communicate to me with?"

"Well, I'm using my phone."

"Cell phone?"

"Yes. I got one of those new Viper phones." After a hesitation he admitted, "It's pretty cool."

"Right. Did some central authority think that up and produce it for you or did a corporation do it to best serve your needs? I mean, you probably remember when a central authority was in charge of the national telephone system, they offered one standard black rotary phone and they said, 'Here, it doesn't matter if this is the best we can offer because you can't get any better so this is what you're going to get.' It's only later, when they broke up the monopoly that you get all sorts of variety and techno-

logical advancement in the phone industry. You open the system up to competition and your *yetzer hara*—your profit motive—drives companies to produce the iPhone, the Droid, and the Viper. One person can't do that; a government bureaucracy can't do all that but in the right structure, the profit motive can. We need creativity and innovation in every industry."

"But son, you act like there wouldn't be any creativity under a well-run government program."

"Just think of it, dad. What if you put the production of pop music under the control of the federal government? Do you think you'd get more or less creative music if that happened?"

After a momentary pause he admitted, "Probably less."

"Right. And I want that creativity in my industry too. I want to be a part of an exciting, innovative, and productive culture in the pharmaceutical industry that helps people get what they want and efficiently and effectively. That's why I moved the company here to Ur where there's no government and no FDA licking its chops to take us over."

Jacob's father grumbled then asked, "What do you mean no FDA down there, Jake? Do you think that's a good idea?"

"Yes!" Jacob replied emphatically. "The FDA is just a regulatory bottleneck that holds back production. It's great that there's no FDA."

"But we need regulation, son, especially in the drug industry. Do you want to take drugs that haven't been thoroughly examined by a reputable government agency?"

"Dad, you act like the FDA is perfect. Even after all the extensive testing, the FDA still approves drugs that hurt people. I mean, Vioxx passed the rigorous standards of the FDA and people still died from it. The only way to ensure that people are protected 100 percent is to prevent any drugs from reaching market at all. That way no drugs will harm anyone. Of course, hundreds of thousands of people will die without the drugs, but that's not your concern is it?"

Jacob was silent for a moment, then continued, "I read somewhere the other day that American companies spend over $2 trillion in order to

comply with the 82,000 pages of federal regulation. Yeah, sure, dad, some regulation is needed in my industry, but don't you think the amount we have is a little excessive?"

"No. I think we need *more* regulation!"

Jacob shook his head. "It's just that there will be a point when the mountains of regulations absolutely crush industry and no one will be able to produce anything anymore. There will be no pharmaceuticals—at least no new ones. Don't get me wrong—they *do* have auditors down here making sure the product is up to snuff, but there's no federal bureaucracy threatening to take over the company on a bureaucrat's whim."

"I don't know son, it's just that I'm worried about you. You can't keep doing this."

"Doing what dad?"

"These crazy, get-rich-quick business enterprises."

Jacob rolled his eyes. "Dad, what are you talking about? I'm producing an extremely helpful drug right now—one that would have saved Rosie, remember? It's not a get rich quick scheme. And, as a matter of fact, I'm *not* getting rich quick, I'm actually losing money—a state of affairs that I intend to rectify as soon as possible, but nonetheless, that's the case."

"I just don't know son," Mr. Tanner repeated.

After a moment's silence, Jacob posed, "I take it mom is still mad at me too?"

"Well, son, she *never* wanted you to go into business, you know that. All the stories you hear about corporate malfeasance and the Enrons and the Worldcoms. Corporate America just breeds an immoral, corrupt people."

"You know those are bad apples. That's not me, dad. Does she realize that I'm helping to save thousands of lives?"

"Oh yes," Jacob's father confirmed. "She just can't understand why you couldn't have started your drug earlier—before Rosie got sick. Maybe instead of fooling around with that damned placebo."

"Thanks Dad," Jacob sighed.

"It just doesn't seem right. If you weren't just trying to rip those people off—"

"Dad, I was trying to help people. Placebo actually helps people when they think it's working."

"That's what you keep saying."

"Because it's true," Jacob said, deflated.

"Well maybe if it wasn't for that, you would have developed a drug that actually helps people. And you might have saved your sister's life."

"Dad, it's something I think about constantly. I'm doing everything I can to fight this thing now. You just can't change what has already happened."

"I don't know Jake. I just don't know."

"Look, I have to go."

"Okay, son."

"Hey, dad, have you ever heard of Gilgamesh?"

"Gilgamesh? The ancient myth?"

"I guess. What was it about?"

"Oh, Gilgamesh was an ancient king—a tyrant—who wanted to build a wall around his city. He was ruthless and forced his people into manual servitude. I believe the myth was about his struggle with the gods. It's one of the oldest stories known to man."

Jacob smiled at the thought. "Sure, I get it. Thanks dad."

"No problem, son."

"Will you tell mom I love her?"

"I will."

"Thanks. Love you too dad."

"Love you too, Jake."

Jacob ended the call, closed his eyes, and put his right fist up to his forehead and shook his head.

The young men of Uruk he harries without warrant,
Gilgamesh lets no son go free to his father,
Gilgamesh lets no girl go free to her bridegroom.
The warrior's daughter, the young man's bride.

Eight

"It's impossible," Marc Johnson said walking up behind Jacob Tanner. He sat down in the chair opposite Jacob at the hotel lounge table. With a shake of his head, he said, "One month? Forget about it."

"Oh come on Marc," Jacob Tanner pleaded with his director of scientific research.

Marc sat back in his chair across from Jacob, shaking his head. "No, you're asking me to develop a completely new drug. In one month. It's just not possible."

"Marc, I'm not asking you to develop a completely new drug. I'm asking you to figure out what we can eliminate from Symbalia without reducing its effectiveness."

"It would take trials, testing. It just can't be done in the time you're suggesting."

"Look, you said it yourself—we used the shotgun approach for active ingredients—that we included some of them just to cover our bases?" Jacob peered into Marc's dodging eyes. "Can't we isolate those ingredients and just replace them with filler?"

Marc looked at Jacob. "You want to produce another placebo, is that it?"

"No!" Jacob exclaimed. He patted his hand in the air and calmly explained, "I want to keep the active ingredients. I just want to get rid of the wasted *inactive* ingredients. We just can't afford them any more."

"Look we know this formula works, it would be extremely risky to alter that without the necessary trials."

"We're not starting from scratch here Marc. I just want to improve on what we have."

Marc muttered, "Five fucking years of testing," under his breath and shook his head in dismay.

"Look, Marc, can you just look at it from my point of view? We need to cut costs. Either I fire people like you and replace the rest of the staff with migrant workers . . . or we simplify the product and get rid of the waste. Either we eliminate the unnecessary ingredients or there will be *no* ingredients. There will be no Symbalia. And you and I will be out on the street begging for loose change."

Marc shook his head and sunk into a thoughtful pose. He hummed then mumbled, "On a chip?"

"What's that?" Jacob asked.

Marc shook his head and looked at Jacob as if he was doing him a favor. "No, I just remember a colleague who developed a technique to test therapies without involving animal testing. He put human cell tissue on a glass slide in order to test lung disease. He called it the lung-on-a-chip. I'm wondering if I could use this technique to test the cause of CE. That way, we could be sure which ingredients are absolutely necessary and which ones can be removed."

A smile crept across Jacob's face. "See, I knew you were up for this."

"Yes, Jacob, I'm up for it. But give me two years or twelve months at least not one month for Christ's sake! What you're talking about is completely unorthodox. You're thinking like a businessman again. But this isn't economics, Jacob, this is science!"

"Everything is economics," Jacob said under his breath.

Marc stood up from the lounge table and looked down at Jacob holding his right index finger up at the CEO of the company. "It was your ego that got us in trouble with the FDA. This is *your* fault." He flinched as if to add more, then shook the notion off and walked away from the table muttering, "Your fucking fault . . . ."

Jacob yelled back to his exiting colleague without turning toward him, "We'll talk about this tomorrow, okay?" and he returned to a stack of papers in front of him on the table. Marc did not respond before stomping

out of the lounge. After a moment of pretending to review a report, Jacob brought his left hand up to his eyes and rubbed.

"Scientists," a feminine voice caught Jacob's attention. "You can't live *with* them, and you can't drive them off a cliff in their stupid little hybrid cars."

Jacob produced a confused smile as he brought his hand down from his eyes and looked at the bar to his right. A slender figure was perched on a stool with crossed, naked legs and an elegant hand dangling a martini glass. She had a sophisticated air—something out of early twentieth century high society, Jacob thought—but she wore a friendly smile, which was disarming. The youthful woman's auburn hair was held up but some locks found their way down her cheek and bare neck. Her complexion had a warm tone to it—not the freckled, fair skin that you would expect with auburn hair like hers—and her soft, supple pink lips completed a perfectly composed visage.

Jacob wondered to himself why he hadn't noticed her before. Had she been sitting there long? She was certainly noticeable, Jacob thought. He smiled at her. "Well, Marc's very pigheaded, but he's absolutely brilliant."

The woman thought about it and squinted, trying to size up Jacob. "And you're the pig farmer trying to harness the wild pig?"

Jacob tilted his head downward and grinned. "Well, yes, I guess you could say that. I'm the president and CEO of our company. Marc is my lead scientist."

The young woman eased off of her stool and sauntered toward Jacob with her right hand extended. "I'm Regan, Regan Matson."

Jacob stood up and shook her soft, smooth hand, then asked, "Reagan, huh? You must be a big fan of the former president," he said almost as a question.

Regan's eyes bulged and she shook her head. "My parents were huge fans. Me? Not so much. Luckily, it's spelled differently. R-E-G-A-N," she explained.

"Ah, so you were the radical hippie in the conservative family? You don't look like the typical radical hippie type." Jacob quickly scanned the length of Regan's feminine figure. "It looks like you take showers regularly."

Regan smiled. "Looks can be deceiving."

"It's funny. I'm the opposite. My parents *were* communal hippies and I ended up at the top of the class at Harvard Business."

Regan maintained a seductive half-smile and said unconvincingly, "That is funny, mister . . . ?"

Jacob looked down abruptly and cleared his throat, "Uh, Tanner. I'm Jacob Tanner."

The two shook hands again and, with a smile, Regan said, "It's a pleasure to meet you Jacob Tanner."

"Likewise." Jacob extended his left hand toward the empty lounge seat across from his. "Can I get you a drink?"

Regan sat down and put her martini glass on the table. "Oh, I don't drink."

Jacob scrunched his face and gave a questioning look to the young woman's martini glass, then back at her.

"It's a Shirley Temple. Alcohol dims the wits and I wouldn't be *anything* without my wits."

Jacob smiled at what he figured was a joke. "Oh, I wouldn't say that . . . ."

"Neither would I," Regan said with a sultry smile. "So, Mr. CEO, I overheard you when you were talking on your phone about the FDA . . . ."

Jacob raised his eyebrows. "You heard me talking about the FDA? You'd make a good spy Ms. Matson."

Regan smiled. "So what's your beef with the FDA?"

Jacob breathed in and thought about how to phrase it. "They wanted to take over my company."

Regan nodded.

"Why do you ask?" Jacob wondered aloud.

"Well, I kinda have a beef with them myself."

"Oh really?"

"Yeah—they're trying to basically criminalize small organic farmers—you know the people that produce those healthy, all-natural foods that have nothing to do with big agriculture and don't profit Monsanto?"

Jacob smiled. "It sounds like you're passionate about this."

"Have you heard of the Food Safety and Modernization Act? It puts all food grown within our borders under the jurisdiction of Homeland Security. Can you believe that? A little old granny could be arrested for smuggling if she brought her homegrown tomatoes to the farmers' market. It's like the Patriot Act for food."

"Wow—sounds pretty ridiculous."

Regan nodded. She felt herself getting a little carried away so she changed the subject. "So, what about you? What sort of devious little scenario are you plotting with your pigheaded scientist?" Regan leaned in toward Jacob and rested her elbow on her crossed legs. The angle of her torso allowed Jacob a glimpse of her well-designed figure, which Jacob observed momentarily before returning his gaze to Regan's eyes.

Jacob noticed his hands beginning to perspire and cleared his throat. "Well, it's not devious really."

"Is it a secret?" Regan said with widening eyes. "Tell me! I just love secrets."

Jacob shook his head. "No, no. We're actually just developing a drug—"

"Ah, so you're a drug dealer. I knew there was something dangerous about you."

Jacob smiled. "Funny. No, we produce a pharmaceutical that treats a rare disease called Chinese encephalitis—it's a terrifying condition that's sweeping across the country. I don't know if you've heard of it." Jacob realized that he might have started boring his company.

"Yes, the neurological condition, caused by mosquitoes or something," Regan said.

Jacob raised his eyebrows and moved his head back, stunned. "Yes, you've heard of it?"

"Of course."

"I'm impressed."

"You should get used to that."

"What?"

"Being impressed."

"With you?" Jacob asked with a smile.

Regan nodded in a matter of fact manner. "So, what's the hullabaloo with your scientist?"

"Well, we need to cut costs in order to become profitable and I'm asking him to change the magic potion, so to speak, and focus on the effective ingredients by cutting out the ones that aren't doing anything, so we can bring down costs."

"Oh, that's not very sexy at all. Is it always about profit with you people?" Regan asked, disappointed.

"Not at all," Jacob replied. "I actually just want to get the drug out there and help all these people, but we lost our federal grant and our new investor is requiring us to be in the black within a month or he's dropping our funding."

"It's a dog-eat-dog world," Regan said and nodded. "It's a bit different here, huh?"

"In Ur?"

Regan nodded.

"Yes, it is," Jacob slowly confirmed.

"It reminds me of Vegas. So much fun, but so much sin."

Jacob frowned. "Sin?"

Regan sat upright, "Oh, this is by far the greediest place I've ever been to. And don't tell me you haven't heard of the drug traffic and prostitution rings. There's enough debauchery here to turn any saint into the lowest of the carnal beasts. That's what happens when you get rid of law and regulation and let human nature take over."

Jacob widened his eyes. "I had no idea . . . ."

"Oh, yeah. It's pretty bad. And some very important people are involved in this seedy underground, it's not just the thugs." Regan paused for a moment, then smiled. "But you can carry a beer on the streets here, so they've got that going for them!"

Jacob smiled. "You seem very opinionated. What line of work did you say you were in?"

"I didn't."

"You didn't?"

"I didn't say. I'm . . . ." Regan pursed her lips and looked around the bar. "Let's just say I'm in interpersonal communication."

Jacob repeated her slowly, "Interpersonal communication. How wonderfully mysterious of you Regan Matson. You got anything else for me?"

Regan narrowed her lips into an amused smile. "Nope." She looked at her slim, silver watch adorning her slender wrist and then back to Jacob. "Well, I should be off. Off like a prom dress, as they say." She stood up.

Jacob mirrored her ascent. "Yes, of course. Are you staying here? At the hotel?"

"No, I have an apartment in Hayek Town on the water."

"Well, let me walk you out then." Jacob placed his hand on Regan's back and extended his other hand to allow her to go before him. The two strolled through the lounge into the hotel lobby and toward the hotel's main entrance. "It was a pleasure meeting you Regan," Jacob said as a doorman opened the door to the hotel. "I'd love to see you sometime—"

Regan flung her left arm at Jacob's gut, causing him to flinch, but she maintained her forward stance. "Oh . . . my . . . God!" She yelled.

"What? I was just thinking—"

"Look!" Regan glanced at Jacob then returned her stare toward the night's sky, which showcased a giant orange orb hanging just above the horizon.

Jacob smiled. "Wow," he said in matched amazement.

"I've never seen something so beautiful," Regan breathed and soaked in the scene.

Jacob looked at the feminine figure next to him. "Neither have I."

Regan turned to Jacob and smiled. "It was good meeting you too, Mr. CEO." She placed a piece of paper in his hand and leaned in to kiss him on the cheek. She briskly walked toward a cab, which was thirty feet away in the hotel drive. "Call me!" She yelled out.

Jacob stood motionless and smiled. "Absolutely."

The cab pulled away and Jacob watched Regan speed away without a look back.

Nine

It was just a pencil, Jacob Tanner thought to himself as his sat silently at his desk, but it was a miracle. It was so simple, yet no one person knew how to make it. He didn't spend too much time ruminating on such thoughts, but he was entranced by this idea for some reason. The pencil he held was just a typical yellow #2 pencil, but Jacob had realized that no one could make it and no one even knew how to attempt the act.

He first considered the wood. It had probably been taken from a tree in the Pacific Northwest—Washington or Oregon. You have to obtain some saws to cut down the tree, he thought, and if you wanted to cut down the tree, you would need to somehow create a saw. You would need steel to create the saw and iron ore to create the steel. So in order to get the wood for the pencil, some one would need to know how to extract iron from the ground and create steel. But that was just the beginning, he thought. The graphite in the middle of the pencil probably came from a mine in South America, so in order to make a pencil, you would have to know how to extract graphite from those mines and, of course, how to make little strips of the stuff to put inside the wood so that the pencil user could rub some of it on their paper. And how they got the graphite *into* the wood was a mystery in itself, Jacob thought.

The pink eraser at the back tip was made of rubber, which probably came from some South Asian rubber plant if it wasn't synthetic, perhaps from Malaysia. One would also have to know how to procure rubber if one wanted to create a pencil. That rubber eraser was secured by a small metal ring—Jacob was unsure what metal—that had ridges and holes punched into it to serve its purpose as connector between the wood and the eraser. Jacob searched along the side of the metal ring and found

no obvious seam. How do you create a metal ring with no seams? Jacob wondered.

No one knows how to make a pencil, he confirmed. There's way too much that goes into it.

But that's not the point, Jacob thought. The miracle isn't that no one knows how to create something as simple as a pencil, the miracle is that despite the fact that no one knows how to make them, pencils *are* made. They are made every day and reside in every office and house. Something that no one knows how to create is everywhere. How? No one person dug up the iron ore and graphite, made the steel, chopped down the rubber plant, stamped out the metal ring, and put it all together, and yet the pencil Jacob held had been created. And it was created without an overarching mastermind—without a central authority planning and dictating action. Pencils are created by voluntary cooperation of thousands of disparate individuals speaking different languages with vastly different skill sets and working on different clocks yet all contributing to one cause, that minor miracle in Jacob's hand.

Of course, Jacob thought, not all of the participants in the long production chain knew the product of their labor would result in a pencil and certainly none were interested in what Jacob wanted to write with the pencil—these things didn't concern them in their effort to produce the writing utensil. Each and every one of them played their part because they thought they would be better off in the transaction. Their effort was worth what they got in return, namely their individual wages. The pencil, Jacob thought, was not just a pencil. It represented voluntary effort. It represented international trade and multicultural commerce. It represented the essence of the free market itself.

Jacob stood up, holding on to his pencil, and walked out of his office into his bustling new factory. He looked around in awe as he applied the pencil philosophy to his product, Symbalia. No one person—not even him—knew how to make Symbalia, yet the people that produced the steel to make the machines, the people who created the plastic for the bottles, the people who created the ingredients for the pills, all worked

together with his employees to create that one product. And after the drug was produced, Axelaris worked with FedEx and the airports to ship the product, then the hospital administrators and the doctors and nurses and adjusters at the insurance companies. All of these people cooperated for a cause that would save thousands of lives. No one person knew how to make Symbalia, much less produce, sell, and distribute it as well, yet that miracle happened every day and saved lives.

Marge Sorenson appeared from within her office and forced a smile at her boss who was beaming with joy. "Good morning Mr. Tanner," she said in a low tone. "Everything's up and running. Smitty says we'll be at peak output by the end of the day."

Jacob nodded. "That's excellent news Marge."

"A representative from Burnett & Jones was here earlier also."

"Oh good," Jacob said surprised.

"The auditor surveyed the plant and said everything looked fine. He's going to spot check the product over the next week to test for quality."

"Yes, he explained that to me over the phone."

Marge looked around without anything to add.

"Marge, I wanted to thank you personally for making this move. I understand you have a family back in Bentonville and it's not easy to be away from them."

Marge shook her head subtly. "I need money Mr. Tanner. You don't think I'm gonna let my family starve while I'm looking for work do you?"

Jacob inhaled heavily and pursed his lips. "I know it's tough, Marge—"

"I just miss my boys, Mr. Tanner. . . ." She shook her head in dismay.

"Believe me Marge, I would have stayed in Arkansas if I could. You've been with me, what, five years? Haven't I treated you with the utmost respect and paid you as best I could throughout?"

Marge nodded. "It's just that Tina said that you might be doing this so that we wouldn't like it here any more so we'd quit and you wouldn't have to fire us."

Jacob looked disappointed and tilted his head down toward his employee. "Now, Marge, you know better than to listen to gossip like that. This is the only solution I could think of to save this company. Those patients out there are depending on us."

Marge mustered a closed-lips smile. "I know Mr. Tanner. You're a good man."

Jacob extended the pencil that he was holding and gave it to Marge. "Here," he said. "I want you to have this miracle."

A quizzical Marge scrunched her face and slowly accepted the pencil from Jacob. "Thanks?"

He put his arm around Marge. "Keep up the good work!"

Marge slowly turned and walked back to her office and Jacob headed toward the factory's laboratory.

* * *

Jacob pensively moved past the factory offices biting his thumbnail and scanning to the ground.

He arrived at the laboratory situated at the corner of the factory, noticing the closed door and peering into the windows that revealed the laboratory through opened horizontal blinds. Jacob could see Marc Johnson in a lab coat hunched over a table cluttered with beakers, gas burners, and Petri dishes. Marc was adjusting the gauge on a burner, which was shooting a blue and orange flame into the air when Jacob knocked on the window with a knuckle from outside.

Marc looked up reluctantly and acknowledged Jacob who motioned for the door with a questioning look. Marc waved Jacob in and returned his focus to the gas burner in front of him. He picked up a wire ring and attached it to a stand above the gas burner.

Jacob opened the door and walked toward Marc's workstation. "Any good news, yet Marc?"

Marc did not seem to pay attention to Jacob's question and instead assessed the laboratory construction he had created in front of him. He mumbled, "I've been able to synthesize the myelin sheath and I made—"

"I'm sorry, Marc. Can you pretend that I don't know anything about science for a second and talk in dumb people terms?"

Marc pursed his lips but continued. "The myelin sheath is the layer of material that surrounds the axon in the nervous cells throughout your brain and brainstem, right? So whatever is causing CE is causing this material to deteriorate. In order to determine what the cause is, I created an artificial myelin sheath that we can test on any number of virus strains. Instead of having to test on actual myelin sheath in mice or other animals, we can use the artificial composition." Marc looked at a slightly impressed Jacob and decided to translate into business terms, "It will save us months and hundreds of thousands of dollars."

Marc took a piece of white bread that was positioned to the right of the burner and placed it on the wire ring above the Bunsen burner flame.

"That's excellent news, Marc," Jacob blurted out but lowered his brow and looked at Marc's contraption on the lab table. "And so, this myelin compound is found on bread or something?" Jacob squinted at the bread in confusion.

Marc looked at Jacob and pointed at his experiment. "This? This is toast." He lifted the bread from the burner and took a bite. Through chews, he continued, "The myelin synthesis is over there." Marc pointed to the opposite side of the laboratory table.

Jacob smiled and shook his head, then followed Marc around the table.

Marc spoke up as they walked, "I've given the synthetic myelin sheath a marker and when it degrades as it does in CE patients, we will be able to see it visually."

Marc stopped at the other end of the table and picked up a small glass slide. The glass reflected a neon blue tint at the edges. "These slides are coated with the myelin synth resin—call it a brain-on-a-chip. When the resin degrades it will produce a darkish tint—" Marc picked up

another slide that was a similar size but was covered with a dark gray coat.

Jacob looked intently at the darkened slide. He noticed that it too reflected blue at the edges, but the tint was difficult to make out due to the dark shade covering it.

"Is it like a photograph exposure or something?" Jacob inquired.

Marc pursed his lips in reflection. "More or less, but instead of light causing the slide to blacken, the CE virus will turn it black." Marc raised an untarnished, clear slide up. "Clear, good." Then he raised a blackened slide up. "Dark, bad. The synthetic resin knows."

"So the only thing that will turn this slide black is the pathogen that causes CE?"

"Right. Everyday substances—air, water, germs from your hands—will have no effect on the resin. Only the virus that causes CE will degrade the resin."

"Marc, you're an absolute genius. Have I told you that recently?"

"I know. And no, I don't hear it enough." Marc looked around for a stack of the slides. "We're going to run these through all the likely causes of CE—mosquito-borne pathogens, flu viruses, you name it."

"And just test it until you find something?"

"Basically, yes."

"It's so simple. Why didn't we do this during development?"

Marc looked at Jacob for a moment with a hint of irritation. "Because we were looking for a treatment of symptoms then. We're looking for the *cause* now."

Jacob squinted at the scientist. "I'm not sure I catch the difference."

"It's okay, 99.9 percent of the population would be at a loss if I tried to explain anything to them. You should feel lucky to understand it at all."

Jacob nodded. "And once we find the cause of CE, we'll be able to reduce the ingredients in Symbalia?"

"That's right," Marc confirmed. "Once we isolate the cause of CE, we'll know what ingredients are truly active and which are just along for

the ride, so to speak. We'll be able to eliminate the extraneous ingredients in the treatment and just use the active ones."

Jacob smiled. "And how long do you think it will take to isolate the cause of CE?"

Marc hummed, "Oh, I don't know, a week—week and a half?"

Jacob lifted the slide and nodded. "You're a genius, buddy."

"That's what I keep telling people," Marc agreed in self-praise. He tapped the slide in the Jacob's hand. "You can keep that one as a souvenir."

"It's beautiful. I'll hang it on my wall." He admired Marc's creation. "There's no stopping us now, Marc."

Ten

"Jacob Tanner must be stopped." Gary Javert grumbled and he peered down to his assistant, Nicholas Debbs, who was sitting in one of the office's guest chairs. Javert's office had large panoramic windows facing a green, wooded area just outside of the FDA headquarters in Silver Spring, Maryland, but Javert opposed the harsh sunlight, so the windows were covered with adjustable metal blinds, which effectively dimmed the room. Picture frames were scattered on the office walls, some containing diplomas and others containing photographs of Javert with notable public figures. The most prominent frame on the largest wall contained a picture of Javert with former president Bill Clinton that had been taken at a fundraiser. A less prominent frame contained a picture of Javert with former president George W. Bush, taken at an FDA event.

One frame contained a weathered-looking paper with an FDA mission statement of sorts in script font. It read, "We are responsible for protecting the public health by assuring the safety, efficacy, and security of drugs, devices, and consumer products throughout the country and the world. We are the FDA." The statement had always inspired Javert to help people who counted on him. It was a constant reminder to do the right thing.

Javert eyed the framed statement then continued, "He is a menace to society and must be stopped. How much public funding did he steal?"

Nicholas Debbs shook his head. "Well, I'm not sure it can be technically considered stealing—"

"It is theft, pure and simple," Javert corrected, abruptly.

Nicholas did not argue but instead looked down to the report in his hands. "Total FDA funding of Axelaris Pharmaceuticals was $12.6 million."

Javert shook his head. "Absolutely iniquitous. And he runs off to that charter city to reap the rewards of *our* funding." Javert's face became contorted as his words pierced the air.

"He's not the only one," Nicholas added. "Xavier Pharma and PT & G both moved there as well."

"And we have no jurisdiction down there? We can't seize his assets?"

Nicholas Debbs shrugged. "Right. According to title nine-thirty-four 'A', federal agencies have no authority in that region—"

"How in the world does legislation like that pass? Can you tell me that?"

"Sir, it was part of the compromise Congress made to clean up the disaster in that area."

Javert appeared to ignore his assistant's explanation. "It's an utter travesty, an injustice."

Nicholas Debbs continued, "Well, until they come to their senses, it is law."

"The law . . . ," Javert repeated with reverence. He stood up and scanned his office, thinking.

"Can we even allow a drug on the market from a factory outside of our jurisdiction? Even the drugs made in China and India fall under our jurisdiction," Nicholas added.

"No, in times of shortages in the past, we have approved imported pharmaceuticals from foreign countries abiding their own standards, but this is different. There is no precedent for this. Ur has no FDA representation and thus *no* regulation."

Gary Javert thought he was preaching to the choir, but Nicholas contradicted him. "Well, actually sir, they do have auditors in Ur that supposedly enforce FDA standards in manufacturing and marketing, et cetera."

"They cannot be effective."

"Of course not," Nicholas said sarcastically.

Javert looked at his assistant and squinted trying to read his mind. He hummed, pursed his lips, and then looked down at his desk before pontificating, "Mr. Debbs, how well acquainted with your FDA history are you? Are you aware of the story of Dr. Kelsey?"

Nicholas shook his head subtly.

"In 1959, a new sedative was introduced in the market to help mothers during pregnancy. That sedative contained the drug thalidomide and it caused severe birth defects in children whose mothers took the drug. Thousands of babies throughout the world were born with grievous deformities due to this treatment but none of those tragedies were in the United States, do you know why?" Javert asked rhetorically.

"Because the agent in charge of approval was too busy lecturing his assistant on the history of the FDA?" Nicholas asked dryly.

"No, Mr. Debbs. It was because the FDA did its job. Dr. Kelsey held up the drug. I'm sure those private auditors do a fine job but they are not the Food and Drug Administration. They cannot have the same standards of excellence that we have," Javert shot back. "No, the situation is dire. We need to stop that man before people get hurt."

"Well, we could pull approval of the drug," Nicholas offered.

"No good," Javert said, looking at his desk in thought. "That would reflect poorly on us."

"We pull drugs all the time. What about Vioxx and Zelnorm?"

"But those actually had adverse effects. Not the case for Symbalia . . . at least not yet."

"Well," Nicholas tried again, "we could bring charges of misappropriation of Tanner's FDA grant . . . ."

"No. Time is of the essence and litigation could take forever. And the courts are never reliable."

Nicholas didn't answer. He was tired of proposing ideas to have them shot down.

"No, we're going to need to go deeper if we want to really address the problem. We're going to need to impose our authority in that charter city."

"What does that mean?" Nicholas asked.

"We're going to need to change the law so that we again have jurisdiction in that corrupted chaos."

"Okay. How do you plan on doing that?"

"I have some friends in the Senate. I can pull some strings."

Nicholas pressed his lips together and nodded.

"In the meantime, we could draw up criminal charges on Mr. Tanner."

Nicholas widened his eyes. "Oh, great idea."

"Can you handle that, Nicholas?"

"It is what I live for," Nicholas said as he stood up from his chair lethargically.

Javert smiled and stared into space. "Justice will be served yet."

Eleven

"Marc, I can't hear that right now. I need results," Jacob Tanner declared as he walked his research director through the bustling factory. "We need to know what causes this disease so we can determine which of Symbalia's ingredients treat it. And we need to know soon or else we will be bankrupt and homeless."

Marc looked down and shook his head as he followed the CEO. "Yes, yes, you've used that threat a dozen times, Jacob, but that doesn't really translate into scientific discovery, now does it? It's going to take time to synthesize the mosquito pathogens. We're talking about a thousand million genetic variants and that's just for starters."

Jacob shook his head then stopped walking to turn to Marc. "That's fine Marc, just tell me how I can help. Can we put more man hours on it?"

"We already have the entire lab devoted to it. I haven't slept in a week and I've showered even less."

"And I appreciate your effort, I really do. But we need this, Marc. I can't implore you enough."

"It's not like I can wave my magic wand here, Jacob. Science just takes time."

Jacob held his tongue and thought for a moment before raising his index finger and looking into Marc's eyes. "You can do it. I have faith in you." He patted Marc on his shoulder and turned to continue walking toward his office.

Marc breathed in deeply and put his hands over his tired eyes then slowly turned the other way and walked toward the laboratory.

A moment later, Jacob opened the door to his dimly lit office and pulled out his cell phone. He had entered Regan Matson's phone number

into his contacts but had yet to call her. He paused a moment before selecting her number and pressing the call button.

While the phone rang, Jacob noticed the small glass slide with neon blue tint at the edges, which had been resting on his desk for the last week. He pushed air through his nose and curled his lips in a sarcastic huff, then shook his head. The brain-on-a-chip, he remembered. Some good it did if it didn't work. He picked up the slide, attempted to view the reflected light off of the synthetic myelin resin on the slide, and then tossed it on his desk when the phone connected.

"Hi . . . you've reached Regan's voicemail. I'm either busy doing something fabulous or I saw your number and simply don't want to talk to you. If this is the second time you've heard this message without me returning your call, you really should take a hint. I don't want to speak with you. Please leave a message and I'll get back to you, unless of course I don't want to. Good bye."

Jacob smiled at the irreverent message and cleared his throat as his phone produced a beep. "Hi, Regan, this is Jacob Tanner. I met you last week at the Grand Ur lounge. I'm sorry I haven't called you yet but I've been . . . well, kind of busy. Anyway, I've been invited to a gala next week at the aquarium and I'd love for you to accompany me. Please give me a call when you can. Thanks. Hope you're well. Bye."

Jacob brought the phone around from his ear to look at the screen and pushed the "End Call" button. He tossed his phone to his desk and looked at his monitor in front of him, which displayed a web browser set to a news website. Jacob halfheartedly scanned the screen then typed "causes of Chinese encephalitis" in the page's search box and clicked the search button.

The results showed nothing new to Jacob. There was a report listed in the results involving a Dr. Lipton, but Jacob had already read the inconclusive paper and was not impressed. There was nothing new from the web or from the medical journal search.

Jacob arched his neck and tilted his head up in frustration, then returned his gaze to the screen. Jacob cracked a smile at a thought, then

selected the search box on his browser window and typed "Regan Matson" and clicked the search icon. Jacob scanned the results as they showed up but was disappointed again. There was a video of a band called Matson, a thesis paper from April Regan and Matson Cline, and a number of results involving *Reagan* Matson, but none with the exact name he was looking for. She must be very private, Jacob thought.

Just then, a chill came over Jacob and he shivered involuntarily. He looked around his empty office and scrunched his face. He had an ominous feeling there was another presence in the room. He surveyed the desk in front of him and got an uncomfortable feeling as he looked at the resin slide resting under his phone.

Suddenly, a harangue from Jacob's cell startled the executive. He looked at his phone, which was resting on his desk. The name on the screen was "Regan Matson." Jacob tapped the "Speaker Phone" button on his phone's screen and answered, "This is Jake."

"Well hello, Mr. CEO!" It was Regan's friendly voice. "Sorry I missed your call."

Jacob's smile slowly disappeared as he witnessed a shocking event. An eerie black cloud crept over the myelin resin slide resting underneath his phone. Like spilled rotten blood, the blackness engulfed the glass and stopped Jacob's breath cold.

CHAOS
AND
KINGDOM

PART 2:
SAINTS AND
SCAVENGERS

When the gods created mankind,
They established death for mankind,
And withheld eternal life for themselves.
As for you, Gilgamesh, let your stomach be full,
Make every day a delight,
This, then, is the work of mankind.

Twelve

The pit of Jacob Tanner's stomach fell to the ground and his head began to swim as he stared at the card stock that was covered with the blackening synthetic myelin resin. Jacob slowly pulled off the phone that had been resting on the slide and his eyes darted between the two.

"Jake, it's Regan . . . are you there?" she said through the phone's speaker. With each word that came through the device, the myelin resin on the slide next to it grew darker, slowly but incessantly.

Jacob swallowed and licked his parched lips. A contorted, worried look overcame the man.

"Hello? Earth to head cheese . . . ."

"Uh, right, Regan. Look, can I call you back? Something just came up," Jacob stammered.

"Um, okay. Is everything all right?"

"Uh, I'm not sure—let me call you back . . . ." Jacob quickly tapped his phone to end the call. He was concentrating on the suddenly blackened glass that Marc Johnson had given him and he finished his thought to Regan, ". . . on a land line."

Jacob picked up the slide and walked out of his office and across the factory floor to Marc Johnson's laboratory. Through the laboratory window, Jacob spotted his lead researcher who was bent over a work station pouring a beaker of orange liquid into a Petri dish when Jacob threw open the door to the lab.

"This better be good," Marc said dryly without looking at the laboratory intruder.

"Is there anything that could darken the synthetic myelin on the slide but wouldn't also cause the CE?" Jacob asked with a stern voice.

Marc slowly placed the beaker on the counter with two hands and placed a rubber stopper in the opening. He turned to Jacob with a pensive look. "The marker is designed to react only to degraded myelin sheath—"

"Any sort of electronic interference—could that trigger the marker but wouldn't trigger CE?" Jacob interrupted Marc and himself.

"Electronic?" Marc looked at Jacob pensively. "I'm not sure I'm getting your drift—"

"Is there anything else that could make the slide go black but not actually cause Chinese encephalitis?"

Marc shook his head and looked down. "Well, I suppose it's possible, theoretically. It's not likely. I developed the synthetic sheath in under two days. So, it's possible I could have made a mistake. Why?"

Jacob raised his right hand, which held the blackened slide. "Because I think I just discovered the cause of Chinese encephalitis."

Marc's jaw dropped as he eyed the blackened myelin slide and he rushed over to the CEO. "Shit, Jacob. What did you do?"

Jacob lifted his left hand, which contained his phone. "I made a call."

"Oh my God." Marc understood. He took the cell phone and the blackened slide from Jacob's hands and placed them together. "I'll need to examine your phone."

"Sure, whatever you need," Jacob agreed.

"Something in the phone . . . ?" Marc asked pensively looking at the phone and the blackened slide.

"Marc, the glass was completely clear when I put my phone down on it and once Regan started talking on the other end—I had it on speakerphone—I saw this cloud of black overtake the slide."

Marc looked at Jacob. "I'll get my entire staff on it."

Jacob slowly turned to leave, contemplating his discovery.

"Oh, and Jacob . . . ," Marc added. "Better not tell anyone about this until we know for sure."

Jacob nodded. "Right."

* * *

Jacob Tanner sat down at his desk and stared at it in deep thought. His hands gripped the edge of the espresso-brown wood as if bracing himself from his own discovery. This was big, he thought. He had quite possibly just answered the riddle of the mysterious disease plaguing thousands of people. He was going to save thousands of lives.

He remembered Regan, searched for her number on his electronic contact list on his computer, then dialed her number into his landline phone.

"Hello?"

"Regan, hi, this is Jake."

"Hi there. Long time no speak."

"Yeah, sorry about that. Something came up."

"I completely understand. Life of the CEO must be really crazy! So many underlings to boss around."

"Right." Jacob thought for a moment about telling Regan what had just happened, but his thought was interrupted.

"So, good news for you, huh?" Regan said with a cheery voice.

"What? Huh?" Jacob stammered.

"Good news. The report just came over the wire. There were 37,000 new diagnoses for Chinese encephalitis last week. Your drug treats that disease right?"

"Oh my God," Jacob said, stunned. "Where did you hear that?"

Regan hesitated for a brief moment, then stated bluntly, "There's this thing called *the news*. I'm not sure if you've heard of it. If you turn on your television and push the buttons on your remote a couple times, I'm sure you can find it."

"That's awful."

"Awful? I thought you would have been happy. Yours is the only drug on the market to combat the disease, right? And you hold the patent?"

Jacob arched his neck back and he looked to the dim ceiling. "Yeah, we have the patent. But I don't want to treat people if I can prevent the disease in the first place."

"Well, of course," Regan agreed.

Jacob thought again about telling Regan about his discovery. He shouldn't tell her anything without proof, he thought—shouldn't yell 'fire' in a crowded theater on a hunch. Instead, he asked, "Regan, what kind of phone do you have?"

"Um, I have a Droid."

Jacob was relieved. His phone—the one that presumably caused the myelin sheath to degrade—was a Viper smart phone. It was possible that those were the only defective devices, he thought.

"Why do you ask?"

"Look, you might want to use land lines for the next few weeks as much as possible instead of your cell phone."

"Um . . . okay. That's a little weird. Why?"

"I can't say. Just, can you do that for me?"

Regan was hesitant, "Um, okay. Should I put some tin foil over my head too?"

Jacob failed to catch Regan's quip. "Can you just try? For me?"

"Anything for you, Mr. CEO," Regan patronized Jacob.

"Thanks."

"Is that why you called earlier? You don't want me talking to anyone else on my phone?"

Jacob searched the room with his eyes. "Um, no, actually . . . ," he said with amusement at more trifling matters, "I wanted to invite you to a gala next week that my business partner is hosting. Have you heard of the Gall Gala at the aquarium next Thursday?"

Regan let out a giggle, then said, "Uh, yeah," Regan answered, implying the obviousness of the fact. "It's a good cause this year, save the manatees."

"Well, I'm working with the guy that puts it on and I have a couple tickets."

"And it's a pretty hot ticket, Jacob. You should be honored to be going."

"Oh?"

"Sure, anyone who's anyone will be there. It will be like the Oscars for people who are actually important."

Jacob chuckled. "I had no idea it was that big of a deal."

"Oh yeah," Regan confirmed.

"Well, you'll be my guest then?"

"Um . . . I'm actually busy that night. Sorry."

Jacob nodded. "Right, of course. How about this weekend? You want to catch a show or something?"

"Well, if you really want to impress me with something more than the gala . . . I've really been dying to see the Cirque de la Lumière show that's getting all the phenomenal reviews. I heard Madeleine Pichette is absolutely fabulous."

"Madeleine Pichette?" Jacob admitted his ignorance.

"The French actress and singer—she's so hot. But I heard tickets are impossible to get," Regan said, allowing Jacob a way out.

"No, let me see what I can do. Let's plan on Saturday night, though."

"Great!" Regan said enthusiastically.

"And we can grab a bite on Las Rambla after? I've heard that's fun."

"Sounds super, Mr. CEO. I'll text you my address. Or is that off limits too? I'll email it to you instead."

Jacob smiled. "Yeah, you better email it to me."

"Okay. See you Saturday!"

"See you then," Jacob said and hung up the phone.

He reflected for a moment on Regan then realized there were other people he needed to warn about the disease. He picked up his phone and dialed the number for his father.

Thirteen

"It's completely sold out, Mr. Tanner," Marge Sorenson reported to her boss through the phone. "It's already a hot ticket and more people are coming into town for the big gala. They're scalping tickets for over a thousand bucks! Each! Do you want me to buy 'em at that price?"

"No," Jacob Tanner said through a frown. "I can't spend $2,000 on tickets to a circus. Thanks anyway, Marge."

"Okay," Marge said before Jacob ended their call.

Jacob was seated in Martin Gall's front office waiting to see him. He hadn't heard the usual yelling emanating from Gall's office this time, but the secretary had assured him he was there.

"Mr. Gall will see you now," the secretary said, faking a smile. She continued, "Mr. Gall is on the roof presently. If you would take the private elevator to your right, you will find access."

Jacob nodded and stood up from his chair. He walked to the private elevator, opened the door and selected the only button available, which was labeled "ROOF."

A brief moment later, the elevator doors opened to the bright open air of the Gall Enterprises Building roof. Jacob stumbled out of the elevator door and grasped a nearby railing. He couldn't breathe at the sight—he was standing at the top of a grassy hill, 60 stories above the Earth overlooking the entire city of Ur. To his left he could see numerous office buildings topped with cranes and a vast expanse of farmland beyond the city center. To his right, just a few miles away, Jacob could see the deep blue of Laguna Madre dissolve into the atmospheric haze.

Gathering his bearings, he carefully inched down the hill toward Gall who was standing in a dirt pit surrounded by a three-foot fence at

the bottom of the grassy hill. The familiar rotund security guard stood ten feet behind Gall and observed the executive. As Jacob approached, he made out a shape at Gall's feet. It was a menacing, 12-foot-long, green and brown prehistoric beast with a wide-open jaw. Jacob flinched when he realized what it was and stopped in his place as he surveyed the animal's rough, reptilian casing and horrifying teeth projecting from his fleshy open mouth. The alligator was crouched still with its head arched up toward Gall waiting for lunch, but Gall just eyed the animal as he yelled into his phone.

Jacob looked around and shook his head. Martin Gall was supporting a pet alligator on the roof of his office building. I wonder how many unemployed people I could get to work with the money he spends on this pet, Jacob thought to himself.

"I don't give a shit, Tom," Gall declared. "Either he wants to sell or he doesn't. If he does, great; if he doesn't, it's time to bring in the artillery." Gall noticed Jacob walk toward him cautiously and winked at him while maintaining focus on his call. "Do I have to spell it out for you, Tom? We'll pull the rug out from under him . . . Yes, I know a guy on the Hill who can lean on him a little. You know Hank, right? Okay, I'll talk to you later, Tom. I want this sale . . . okay." Gall slapped his phone to end the call then stuffed it in his pocket. He grabbed the tail of an ambiguous white rodent from the bucket and threw it into the alligator's mouth, causing the jaws to collapse in a violent snap and the alligator to slowly ease away from Gall.

Gall chuckled to himself and eyed the alligator down.

"Fuckin' snappers, huh, Jermaine?" Gall called out to his security guard who nodded in response.

Gall then turned to Jacob and asked, "Tanner! So, did you come here to gloat?"

Jacob smiled and shook his head. "Gloat? Why?"

"Thirty-seven thousand new diagnoses of CE. With that rate of increase, we're going to be billionaires by next week—well, I'm already a billionaire, but maybe you can join me," Gall said with a cackle.

"Yeah, a lot of orders coming in," Jacob said.

"It's going to be bigger than Prozac, I have a feeling. And bigger than that limp dick drug, Viagra."

"Right . . . ."

"The best part about it is that they don't even know what causes this . . ." Gall waved his hand in the air trying to facilitate his thought pattern, ". . . Chinese bird flu or whatever the fuck it is. It's like depression. You have everything you could ever ask for in your life, but you're still sad? Are you kidding me? Here, take my fucking drug, asshole. Oh, and by the way, give me $200. Everything will be peaches and cream if you just take my drug, suckers. Now that's one investment I missed out on. Like Amelior." Gall gave Jacob an exaggerated grin.

Jacob looked down. "Yeah, about that, Mr. Gall. We wanted to cut costs on Symbalia so we put our best scientists to work trying to find the cause—"

"That's my boy, cutting costs even when sales are up," Gall said through a grin.

"Well, regardless, we—"

"Spit it out, Tanner," Gall ordered.

"I think we may have found the cause of Chinese encephalitis."

Martin Gall turned his head slightly away but kept his eyes fixed on Jacob. "How do you mean, *cause*?"

"That's just the thing. People have had it all wrong until now. They thought it was some virus spread by mosquitoes or something. But it's not. Well, we're not sure yet, but I think it may be caused by an extreme form of radiation from cell phones."

Martin Gall burst out laughing. "Oh that's a good one, Jake Tanner."

"No, I'm serious," Jacob said nodding. "I don't know what it is, but it appears something in the cell phone is degrading the myelin sheath around the cells in the nervous system."

Gall put down the bucket and walked around the fence gate to stand immediately in front of Jacob. "What are you saying here, Tanner?"

"I'm saying that in a few days, we may actually know what causes Chinese encephalitis. And that instead of *treating* the disease with our drug, we can just *prevent* the disease from happening altogether."

"Shit, Tanner. You know what that means?"

Jacob nodded. "Yeah, thousands of lives saved."

"Fucking boy scout," Gall said shaking his head. "No, Tanner. This means no more Symbalia."

Jacob nodded in hesitant agreement. "True."

"Right. So what are you going to do with this information?"

"Well, sir, I think it's obvious that we need to get the information out there to the public, hold press conferences, shout it from the mountaintops."

"Whoa! Slow down there greenhorn." Martin Gall patted the air in front of him. "You want my advice? I'll give you the advice of a real fucking businessman. You keep your mouth shut is what you do—at least for a little while. This encephalitis thing could turn into an epidemic. It could be huge—hundreds of thousands of people could be affected and you—*we* are making the only drug that treats the symptoms. Are you kidding? This could be a fucking gold mine! If it turns out to be a flop or when the generics are released, then we can . . . shout it from the mountaintops."

Jacob shook his head. "But, what about—"

"Fuck that. Look, no one has to know. No one gets hurt because Symbalia is effective at treating the disease, right? If the patients are treated, no harm done?" Gall looked for affirmation from Jacob, which he got. "Chinese encephalitis keeps infecting people, and we keep treating them. We're talking potentially hundreds of millions of dollars a week with this thing. Better than any real estate deal I've ever made, that's for damn sure."

"And if some people slip through the cracks? What if some people get sick and aren't treated?"

Gall turned around and stepped toward his desk. "That would be unfortunate, but, to be quite frank, you gotta crack a few eggs to make

an omelet, if you know what I'm sayin'. You have to expect a little sacrifice on the path to progress. I mean do you want to take all cars off the road because some poor asshole gets in an accident? Do you want to stop using coal because some miners get stuck in their fucking dirty-ass caves for three days? No. We keep moving, we keep *progressing*."

Jacob nodded. "I just don't see why, if we can just prevent the disease in the first place—"

"But don't you see? It's brilliant. We're creating a whole industry with the disease, all this business. Without the disease, there'd be no reason for Symbalia. There'd be no reason to employ all of your staff. No reason to rent my factory. No reason to pay the shippers to ship the drug, the hospitals, the insurance companies. The disease is bad, sure, but look at all the production and economy and jobs it creates."

Jacob tilted his head back and let a smile creep over his face. "Ah, I never thought of it like that," he breathed.

"And if it ever comes out that we knew about it, we'll just say we didn't want to be irresponsible printing the results and causing public hysteria before we knew for sure. By the time the dust settles, no one will know what happened and we'll be sipping Dom on the beach earning twenty percent."

Jacob smiled but didn't look convinced.

"Look, this is probably a little too theoretical for you." After a moment's pause, Gall added, "All men can see these tactics whereby I conquer, but what none can see is the strategy out of which victory is evolved."

Jacob scrunched his face. "Excuse me?"

"Sun Tzu." He shook off an explanation. "Look, give you my 100 percent money back guarantee that this is the best scenario. It's best for the economy as a whole and it's sure as hell the best thing for your bank account."

"I think I get it," Jacob agreed hesitatingly.

Gall grasped Jacob's arm with his free hand and left slimy rodent residue on his jacket. He looked intently into Jacob's eyes. "Tanner, in this world there are the gators and there are the fuckin' rats. You either eat or you get eaten. Are you a fuckin' rat?" Gall clenched Jacob's arm to the point where it became painful.

Jacob pensively shook his head. "No, I'm with you Mr. Gall."

"Hell yeah, you're with me. You and I are the same animal, Tanner," Gall said releasing his grip. We're the same beast. We love money too much. I know you." Gall smiled causing the wrinkles on his face to accentuate then he turned back to his alligator. "You know this motherfucker can digest a small human in just a couple days?" Gall turned back to Jacob. "Someone your size might take a week."

Jacob nodded hesitatingly, not sure how to respond to Gall's joke. "Well, I'll let you get back to it."

Gall looked back at Jacob and remembered something. "Hey!" He reached into his left pocket and pulled out an envelope. "I almost forgot," he announced. He held out the envelope and motioned Jacob toward him with his other hand.

"What is it?" Jacob eyed the envelope, then eyed the manacing gator crouched just feet behind it. He reached for the envelope and Gall retracted.

Suddenly the alligator lunged forward and snapped its jaws shut.

"Jesus Christ!" Jacob shrieked.

He retracted his hand with the envelope and jumped back, his heart pounding. Gall laughed as he watched Jacob cower.

"Whoa there tiger, it's all right," Gall said. "Look inside." He nodded toward the envelope.

Composing himself, Jacob opened the envelope and saw two shimmering, reflective gold cards. On each card were the embossed words, "Cirque de la Lumière." Jacob dropped his jaw. "How did you—?"

"I thought you might enjoy an evening at one of the premiere shows in North America."

Jacob nodded. "Wow, this . . . I've been trying to get a couple of these. Thank you!"

"Bury the science on this, Tanner," Gall said with a solemn face. "There's too much at stake here."

Jacob slowly nodded and held a stare with Gall for a tense moment. Gall turned around again and Jacob headed back to the elevator door at the top of the slope.

Fourteen

Jacob Tanner pushed through the revolving door on the ground floor of the Gall Enterprises Building into the warm spring air of Ur, Texas. He slowly walked toward the concrete stairs in front of the towering structure but stumbled before catching himself on the railing. He paused in a crouched state on the stairs and turned around to view the edifice reaching into the sky. It looked like a towering bird of prey waiting to strike. Jacob's eyes followed the perfect lines of the building down to the first floor and the doors from which he had just exited. Above the front doors of the Gall building was the address, "666 Enterprise Blvd" carved out in gold letters.

Jacob looked back to the ground and slowly eased himself down the stairs with the help of the railing. He searched the concrete as he slowly walked down the sidewalk that encased the city block. When Jacob stepped into the street a bicycle flew past him. The wind from the biker kicked up Jacob's tie and he jumped backward.

"Watch where you're going, asshole!" the biker yelled without slowing down.

Jacob looked each way on the path in front of him, which appeared restricted to bicycles and foot traffic. After another biker zoomed past Jacob, he quickly walked across the path and found protection from the sun under a large mesquite tree, the branches of which were sprawling out over a cast iron gate. The gate and tree seemed to belong to a vast nature park, a Central Park of the charter city.

Jacob grasped one of the iron bars and subconsciously attempted to shake the bar, testing its integrity. The fence must have been only a couple years old, he thought, but it reminded him of a solid, well-made

construction from the nineteenth century when large, powerful industrial giants built things to last. Jacob examined the fence and admired the tree that arched above it.

A shutting car door a hundred feet behind Jacob pulled the executive away from his daydream. He turned back toward the Gall building and saw a striking young woman walking from a black Lincoln Town car toward the building, accompanied by what looked like her driver. She was hard to ignore for the fact that a bright red dress clung on to her as she strode to a side door of the Gall building. The woman's hair was unmistakable too—a warm auburn. It was Regan Matson.

Jacob was involuntarily pulled toward the woman though she had not seen him across the pedestrian thoroughfare. She walked up to a sturdy security guard protecting the side door and produced an identification card from her purse. The security guard nodded and scanned the general vicinity while reaching behind him with his left hand to open the door. Jacob watched as the two exchanged words before Regan disappeared behind the door, which the security guard closed behind her. The driver strolled back to his car and opened the driver's seat door.

Tanner let a clump of bikers pass before him then darted across the path and continued a light jog approaching the security guard.

"Hi there," Jacob said with a friendly tone to the beefy man guarding the door.

The security guard looked at Jacob but did not say anything.

"Can I get past?" Jacob asked.

The guard tilted his head as if to say, "You've got to be kidding me," but remained silent.

Jacob lifted his arm and pointed at the door. "That woman, that was Regan Matson. I know her." Still nothing from the security guard. "I just came out of a meeting with Mr. Gall. I am currently working on a project—he's funding one of my projects. It's called Symbalia, I don't know if you've heard of it."

The security guard did not look impressed. "Sir, if you would like to set up a meeting with Mr. Gall, reception in the main lobby will be glad

to facilitate that with you." The guard looked to his right and half-pointed to the front of the building, which was around the corner from the side door.

Jacob didn't look at the front of the building. He kept his eyes on the guard. "You're not going to let me in?"

"Can't do that, sir."

Jacob turned around and spotted the driver inside the Lincoln Town Car looking straight ahead.

"Fine," Jacob said, defeated and dejected. He turned and slowly walked away toward the tram station to return to his factory.

Fifteen

The film technician dropped his jaw as Michelle Torres walked by in a commanding stride. She wore a tight-fitting blouse under a light tweed jacket and skirt. She turned the corner and stood in front of the executive producer's office door. She took in a deep breath as she focused on her argument, cracked her neck by tilting her head to the left, letting her perfectly-styled mahogany hair fall below her shoulders, then straightened her posture again. She reached for the door handle and, after a second's pause, pressed down and opened the door.

The graying Sam Barnes was reading transcripts at his desk when Michelle stomped into the cluttered office. Sam's loose-fitting suit hid an extra 40 pounds of heft but could not hide his tired eyes. Sam Barnes looked up at his employee and smiled.

"Ah, Michelle," he said with a cracked voice. "To what do I owe this lovely visit so early in the morning?"

Michelle looked at the executive without a smile. Instead, she squinted accusatorially. "I want on."

"On air?" Sam tried to act ignorant to what Michelle was referring.

Michelle did not reply but stared at Sam with a burning gaze.

Sam Barnes enlarged his smile and looked down at his desk. "Now, Michelle, you and I both know you will get your chance, eventually. It just—"

"Bullshit Sam! I want on and I want on today. Stone is out and Whitney is in DC. I'm the most well-prepared anchor on staff and I am ready."

"Oh, I know you're ready, dear."

"Don't bullshit me Sam. I've been waiting in the wings for this for almost a year. You know that this job belongs to me. Shit, Sam, I am the future of this network." Michelle raised her right hand and index finger. "The words of the network president, not mine, I might add."

Sam Barnes nodded. "I know, I know." He pushed back his rolling chair from his desk and stood up to walk around to where Michelle was standing. "But you know about the network politics. It's really just over my head." Sam slowly stepped toward Michelle, then reached over and closed the door to his office behind her.

"It is not over your head, Sam. Don't give me that crap."

Sam swallowed deliberately only to stall then wrapped his arm around Michelle. "It's just that Cindy has had more on-air experience and quite frankly she's more appealing to the viewers."

Michelle threw out her hands and fingers in protest to what Barnes was saying. "Thirty-five percent of viewership is Latino, Sam. Don't give me that bullshit. They want to see my fucking brown hair and brown eyes. And they want to hear someone who knows how to pronounce *Ejécito del Pueblo*." She spoke the last words in a perfect Colombian accent. "I want on," she repeated slowly and sternly.

The smile left Sam's face and he looked at his employee intently. "Michelle, look, you've made your case and I will take it into account. But this is how it is. Cindy will anchor today and we'll see about next time Stone is out." Sam gently flicked Michelle's dark brown hair back from her face and smiled at her.

Michelle analyzed Sam Barnes. He was pathetic, she thought. Old, tired, and stale. She was young, vibrant, and talented. He disgusted her.

"All right. You leave me no choice," she said slowly. "If you deny me this, I'll blow the whistle. I'll tell them what happened."

Sam dropped his hand from Michelle's face. "You wouldn't dare."

"Oh yes I would. 'Network Executive Rapes News Anchor' would make a fine headline don't you think?"

"Now, dear, you can't say that, Michelle," Sam said looking away from her. "It wasn't *rape*."

"It was if I say it was. Either way it was sexual harassment and I could have you hung out to dry or arrested." Michelle Torres placed her right hand on her hip and looked at Barnes demanding. Sam Barnes held his tongue in growing anger and simply looked at Michelle.

* * *

The television faded in and colorful abstract graphics flew around the screen accompanied by the pomp of brass instruments. The graphics retreated from the screen and revealed an image of Michelle Torres sitting at the anchor desk in front of an active newsroom.

"This is *Headlines Now*. I'm Michelle Torres. Stone Andrews is off today," Michelle said confidently, beaming into the camera.

"What's being called an *epidemic* by authorities is spreading across the country today as officials are scrambling to uncover the cause." Michelle continued reading off the teleprompter as a three-dimensional image of a human being rotated on the screen above Michelle's shoulder. The model contained a flashing red light emanating from the area of its brain.

"The Center for Disease Control is reporting that 37,000 new cases of Chinese encephalitis have been diagnosed in the last seven days and at least 113 deaths have been attributed to the disease. This puts the mysterious condition in the ranks of seasonal influenza with the number of affected in such a short time. The lone drug approved by the FDA to treat the Chinese encephalitis, Symbalia, is behind in manufacturing and major supply shortages are expected.

"This would compound an already dangerous situation across the country concerning pharmaceutical supplies. A growing shortage of drugs for a host of illnesses—from cancer to cystic fibrosis—has hospitals reeling and scrambling to avoid harm to patients. The number of medications in short supply, as tracked by the University of Utah's Drug Information Service, skyrocketed to a record 260 last year. Symbalia could be added to that list shortly.

"Chinese encephalitis is an extremely dangerous viral infection affecting brain functioning. Some believe the condition to be caused by a virus transmitted by mosquitoes, so it is recommended that you wear insect repellent while out of doors. If you or a loved one experiences any suspicious flu-like symptoms, headaches, or chronic loss in concentration, authorities ask that you contact your local CDC office and seek medical care immediately."

Sixteen

The lights dimmed and the crowd of spectators mumbled a last word or two before the stage lights came up and group of performers, disguised as organic shapes, made their way onto the stage.

Jacob Tanner, who sat in a small balcony section, dropped his eyes to the empty seat next to him, breathed a deep, regretful breath and turned his eyes to the performance. The colorful bodies moved around the stage and around each other in a fluid dance accompanied by symphonic music.

Slowly, the organic figures began contorting and moving in impossible ways and their dance took on new unity. The figures then calmed down and angled themselves as if they were looking up. Just as they did, a beautiful actress floated down from above the stage.

Jacob Tanner had heard rumors about the provocative performance of pop musician Madeleine Pichette, but didn't know what that would entail. She was completely bare, sitting perched on her swing high above the stage, but her nudity resembled more an ancient Greek goddess statue than a distasteful modern music video. She was elegant and beautiful, not, as the tabloids had promoted her with the word "sexy." She did not rock back and forth on her swing but dangled her feet in a playful manner.

Madeleine Pichette began to sing in an operatic voice—not Italian, not French, but some other Romantic language. Her sweet and powerful voice lifted the entire audience out of their seats with euphoric pleasure.

After an awestruck moment, the colorful shapes on stage erected a pole in center stage that reached just below the beautiful young woman. The mass of colorful beings contorted and fell over themselves and some began to climb the statue of shapes. One moved slowly up the pole with

its arms and head first and another was able to extend upwards feet first. Others leapfrogged the first ones and danced up the pole in extreme acrobatic contortions, nearly reaching the top. The nude chanteuse arched backwards in apparent delight when the highest shapes reached up for her.

Suddenly, the lights dimmed, the music turned into a wretched dissonance, and shadowy shapes poured onto the stage from all directions. The dark actors flipped aggressively around the stage and attacked the statue of colorful ones. Eventually, they brought the tower down in a thunderous collapse.

To the audience's horror—the Madeleine Pichette character flipped off of her perch and fell to the clump of dancers below in what seemed as if it could have been an accident.

Jacob raised his eyebrows and watched as the colorful shapes mingled with the shadowy newcomers in a violent dance covering Pichette until they all dispersed and removed from the stage leaving no trace of Madeleine Pichette. Jacob stiffened his neck and shrugged his lips as the lights went down, bringing the Cirque de Lumière's first sequence to a close.

At that point, the door to the balcony opened and an usher directed Regan Matson to her seat. Jacob released a breath of air in relief as he watched Regan tiptoe down the stairs to their row. She was wearing an elegant and shapely dress that consisted of a bust with hanging white squares of satin and shimmering dark gray pattern down the length of the black dress. She held a small white purse and wore a guilty smile as she ambled down two stairs to her seat.

"I'm sorry I'm late," Regan whispered as she sat down and leaned into Jacob.

Jacob shook off her apology. "Glad you could make it."

"Are you kidding? I wouldn't miss this for the world." She grabbed Jacob's hand and squeezed as the lights came up for a second scene.

* * *

"Oh, I love stepping out into the warm air!" Regan sang as she danced into the cobblestone courtyard in front of the theater following Cirque de Lumière. "It's so liberating!" Regan held her arms in the air as she twirled around despite the crowd of exiting theatergoers.

The theater courtyard led into an area called *Las Rambla*, patterned off of a similar pedestrian walkway in Barcelona, Spain. The promenade was alive with street vendors, musicians, and human statues vying for the attention of passers-by, strolling in between palm trees and Texas live oak trees. Warm tropical music and sweet smells of freshly made cinnamon and sugar churros filled the air and enticed the dozens of visitors.

Jacob smiled and followed Regan while allowing her space to flutter about.

"Don't you?" She asked.

"Yes, when I'm not wearing a suit," Jacob answered.

"There's just something mystical about a warm evening breeze. Something invigorating!" Regan smiled at Jacob, then turned and breathed in the night air. "Let's get a crêpe! Let's go swimming! Let's dance in the rain . . . naked!"

Jacob laughed. "But it's not raining."

Regan turned back to her date and leaned into his face. She tapped her index finger on his head and softly said, "Now, let's not let *that* stop us."

Jacob smiled again and shook his head. "So, what did you think of the show?"

"It was marvelous!" Regan said as she skipped along the pathway. Jacob soaked in the atmosphere and eyed the massive trees and cheerful pedestrians visiting the shops and eateries throughout. Strings of white light bulbs hung from tree to tree, giving the promenade a warm glow.

"What did you make of the dragon creature in the end? What do you think that represented?" Jacob inquired.

"That obviously represented greed," she said without hesitation.

"So, the village killed greed?"

"Yes."

"So what did you think of Madeleine Pichette?"

Regan widened her eyes and dropped her jaw. "So gorgeous. I'd do her!"

Jacob closed his eyes and shook his head. "What?"

"I mean, I only mess around with girls every once in a while, but she is so hot. If she was standing right here, I'd totally make out with her."

"How very . . . libertarian of you," Jacob said, eyebrows arched not knowing if Regan was joking.

She looked at him with a sly smile. "Don't worry, Jake. I like men."

Jacob shook off her alluring eyes and returned to a safer conversation, "So, what about Pichette's character? What did she represent in the show?"

"She was Aphrodite . . . love."

"Ah, so the reward for killing greed is love? Interesting."

Regan nodded, then spotted a vendor selling frozen cocktails. She pulled Jacob toward the vendor. "Okay, what did you think they were?"

"Well, I thought the demon was a slaver. You know how he was always hovering over the village, changing their behavior for the worse?"

"Two mango mojitos please," Regan ordered from the vendor. "Yes," she said returning her attention to Jacob.

"Yeah, and Pichette was freedom. When the village was finally able to kill the slaver, the reward was freedom." After a confused moment, Jacob said, "Hey, I thought you didn't drink."

Regan turned to him and shrugged. "You only live once, right?" Jacob tilted his head, then nodded at her response.

"That'll be twenty bucks," the vendor said.

Regan pulled out a twenty from her purse and paid the man.

"You're getting these?" Jacob asked.

"It's only fair. You got the tickets to the show. You probably paid a fortune."

He smiled. "Yeah, it almost cost an arm and a leg." He reflected on Gall's alligator then added, "Well, an arm at least. But, no, it was my pleasure."

"Well, this is my pleasure." She raised her eyebrows repeatedly and smiled.

Jacob took the two drinks, handed one to Regan and held his up for a toast. "What shall we toast to?"

"To love," Regan answered.

Jacob nodded. "And to freedom."

The two tapped their plastic cups and sampled their beverages.

"It's funny how we got such different analyses out of the same show," Regan said. "It's almost like a Rorschach test."

"Oh right. The ink blot test?"

"Yeah, where they present an ambiguous shape and your interpretation of it tells what type of crazy person you are."

"Right." Jacob smiled. "So . . . what type of crazy person are you?"

"Funny," she replied.

"No really, are you a psychologist or something? Is that how you know about all that?"

"Maybe I just go to psychiatrists often."

"Seriously, what *do* you do?"

"For work?"

"Yes, for work. I still don't know what it is that you do."

Regan tilted her head away from Jacob. "Aww, I don't want to talk shop now. It's such a lovely night. Can't we just enjoy the evening?" Before Jacob could answer, Regan asked, "And why is it that people are always defined by what they do any way? Are you defined by the sales you make, Mr. CEO?"

Jacob smiled and looked at her as if she'd caught him in a misdemeanor. "Well, I'd like to think that what I do is valuable to humanity . . . ," He said eyeing Regan but it was clear she didn't want to talk about that. "Okay, let's just enjoy the evening." Jacob looked into the night's sky past

the glowing light bulbs strung from tree to tree to the smattering of stars. "And what an evening it is."

When Jacob returned his view to Regan, he saw that she was running off toward a twenty-foot-wide concrete fountain graced with colorful tiles situated the middle of the pedestrian walkway.

"Let's get in!" She yelled back to Jacob.

Jacob laughed. "Ah, no thanks."

"Aww, come on." Regan sat on the concrete wall to the fountain and unstrapped her heels, then flung them off, swung around and dipped her left foot in the fountain. "Ooh, it feels wonderful!"

A number of bystanders glanced at her then turned away, embarrassed.

"You're crazy," Jacob protested.

"Come on. Join me." Regan put her other foot in and stood up in the fountain. She began dancing around the fountain and singing. "Jacob," she said flicking water from the fountain spout in Jacob's direction. "It's raining!"

Jacob smiled and shook his head. He put his drink down next to the fountain and slipped off his shoes, pulled off his socks and rolled up his suit pants. Regan hummed as she danced over to Jacob and held out her hands to help him into the fountain.

"Here, do you know the Charleston?" She asked.

Jacob shook his head.

"I'll show you." Regan took Jacob's hands and kicked her feet sporadically, splashing water in every direction. "It's really fun in the water!"

Jacob tried to imitate her dance steps but ended up mocking an Irish folk dance instead and couldn't contain a burst of laughter. He concentrated on her steps but couldn't see clearly with all the splashing water.

"You could be the best fountain dancer I've ever met!" Jacob said over the noise.

"And you could be the worst!" Regan teased.

Regan stopped dancing and, looking slightly up, smiled at her damp partner. He looked into her eyes and inched closer to her lips. As if pulled

by an uncontrollable force, the two moved into each other and their lips merged in an exhilarating union. Shock waves rippled through Jacob's frame as he embraced Regan's soft but firm body and held her tightly.

The two were completely entranced with one another and didn't hear the security guard when he approached the two standing in the fountain. "Uh, yeah, I think y'all need to come on down out of the fountain now."

Jacob and Regan continued their passionate embrace, disregarding the interruption.

The security guard cleared his throat obnoxiously and coughed. "Excuse me, folks."

Regan opened her eyes and focused on Jacob but he slowly turned toward the source of the plea. Not only was a security guard staring at the two, but a small crowd of onlookers had gathered to watch the spectacle also. Several people in the crowd applauded the couple and one whistled in entertained enjoyment.

"Oh, right," Jacob said through an embarrassed smile. "Sorry." He slowly led Regan out of the fountain and apologized to the security guard. The couple gathered their belongings and the crowd dispersed in quiet amusement.

Seventeen

Regan Matson dangled her feet over the edge of the wooden pier that stretched along the uneven shore bordering the Hayek Town sector of Ur. The waning moon had risen and was reflecting its light off of the gentle waves of Laguna Madre, but Regan wasn't paying attention to the slivers of light. She stared into the deep blue beyond the reflections.

"I'm warning you, it's not pleasant," Regan said.

"It's fine. I want to know what happened," Jacob Tanner replied.

Regan nodded, swallowed, and began, "I never had a good relationship with my father. He was always too important for us and when he was around, he would do things . . . inappropriate things." She hesitated, the altered course, "I loved my mother, but daddy was an arrogant, conservative drunk. That's what he was." After a contemplative pause, she continued, "One night, my parents were going out to a party and I told my father he was too drunk to drive and what do I get for looking out for my parents? A slap across the face." Jacob was stunned by the story, but Regan shook her head as if relaying the weather. "Nothing new there. He said he was sorry but tore off anyway with my mom in the car. They didn't come back that night . . . . The next day we got a call from the hospital. Daddy had checked in after he crashed the car into a ravine by our house. My mom was killed instantly."

"Oh my God," Jacob whispered.

"My worthless father lived but took my mother from me and my brother."

"That's horrible. How old were you?"

"I was fourteen. Nixie was sixteen."

Jacob looked at her with a scrunched brow. "Regan, I'm so sorry."

Regan shrugged. "Why are you sorry? *You* didn't do anything. It was daddy's fault. Everything is his fault." She shook her head, reflecting, "But his friends in high places cleared his name—they said it was a hit and run—someone else's fault but that was all bullshit."

"What happened with him?"

"Oh, daddy went on to become . . . ," she said and paused looking at him. "Let's just say he's a pretty big deal now."

Jacob let the thought register. What is a pretty big deal? he wondered. "Would I know him? Matson? I don't think I've ever heard of a Matson. What's his first name?"

"Henry," she replied.

"No, it doesn't ring a bell."

Regan glanced back at Jacob and returned her gaze to the water. She ignored Jacob's inquiry. "No, it certainly wasn't all Disneyland and Strawberry Shortcake growing up, for sure. But I learned what not to be."

"Like an alcoholic Republican?" Jacob asked with a smile.

"Right," Regan returned the smile. "Especially the Republican thing. I can't stand what he and his cronies do. I hate them all."

Jacob pursed his lips in empathy. "I'm really sorry to hear that Regan. I take it you don't talk to him much."

Regan raised her eyebrow in amusement and shook her head. "I haven't spoken to him since I moved out at eighteen."

Jacob thought for a moment. "You know it's never too late to change. He may have been an awful person but there's always hope."

"Thanks for the optimism, Jake but my father is beyond hope. He's a disturbed, corrupt man. There are just some things in this world that are hopeless."

Jacob nodded in agreement. "I know what you must feel, but it's never too late. Like, for instance, I took a hardened criminal off the street and turned him into one of my best employees right now."

Regan let Jacob's words sink in then turned to him. "What? How?"

"You want to hear the story?"

"Yeah, I'm intrigued!"

"So, it was a cold night a couple years ago. Marc—my lead scientist—and I were walking to a local restaurant one night and it was a dark and shady road between two warehouses covered in graffiti. Marc says, 'Look out for this guy.' And I'm like, 'What guy?' All of the sudden, he's on top of me yelling, 'Give me your fucking money!'"

Regan's eyes bulged at the intensity of the story and Jacob continued, "So, I'm shitting my pants, right? This guy has me up against the warehouse wall with his massive forearm and he's got a switchblade in the air ready to come down on me. I try to calm him down and I take out my wallet and held out the cash. But he had to release me to grab the cash, so he did and he stepped away and counted it. He was like, 'Nice doing business with you sucka!' and I told him to wait."

"What?"

"Yeah. It was cold out and he only had a T-shirt on. I took off my jacket and threw it to him. The guy was stunned. He was like, 'What the fuck?' So, I told him—this is what I said. I said, 'It's cold out and you're going to need that if you're going to be out here stealing all night.'"

"No," Regan said in disbelief.

"Honest to God truth. I told him that we were going to be getting dinner down at Joe's Diner and that he should stop in for a hot meal and that I was buying. He walked off without a word, but later that night he showed up."

"No!"

"Yeah. He showed up wearing my jacket and ate with us. He said that he never had anyone treat him like that. I told him to think of it as an advance on a job offer. I told him he could be making what he stole every day no problem and he wouldn't have to threaten people's lives."

"You offered him a job?"

"I did. And guess what? He accepted. He took the job and is now managing my shipping department."

"Wow, that's a great story, Mr. CEO. It turns out you do have a heart after all."

"Don't sound *too* surprised," Jacob said through a smile.

"Oh no. I think I'm actually starting to like you."

"You don't look happy when you say that," Jacob said amused.

Regan shook off the comment. "So tell me about your drug. How's it going?"

Jacob looked around. "Uh, it's going well. But I kind of have a dilemma."

"Oh? Tell me about it."

"So, drug sales are way up—better than expected, right? That's great. That's what I want to do—to help people. So, I'm happy, my lead scientist is happy, my business partner is happy. Everyone's happy. But then a couple days ago, I think I may have accidentally discovered what causes Chinese encephalitis."

"What? Are you serious?"

Jacob nodded. "Yep."

"That's wonderful! You're going to be a hero."

"Well, maybe."

"What do you mean?"

"Well, my business partner wants me to bury the findings. He wants me to keep quiet about the cause of the disease."

"Wait, why? Why would he want that?"

"Well because of all the good things that come from treating the disease. Like my company, the shippers, the medical professionals. It sounds stupid saying it but a lot of good is coming from the disease."

"You're right, it does sound stupid," Regan said, incredulous. "He just wants to make more money on treating the disease?"

Jacob rolled his head. "Well, yes, that's true also, but without my drug, I wouldn't be able to employ my staff, or rent the warehouse, or pay the doctors . . . ."

"Are you seriously considering keeping the cause secret so that you can make more money on the treatment?"

Jacob breathed in and thought about it for a moment. "No, no, I want to *help* people. But my business partner has a great point. If we stopped the disease, all of the good we do treating it would go away too."

"Jacob are you serious? If it weren't for the disease, all of the good that you're doing could be directed toward something else. You could be treating another disease like cancer or developing the fountain of youth or something. If you didn't have CE to fight, you could be doing good in another arena."

"But what's the harm if everyone who gets the disease gets the treatment? It's not unethical or anything. We'd still be publishing our results."

"Not unethical? Jacob, if you discovered what causes Chinese encephalitis, you have a moral obligation to tell people. You need to get on the phone with every news service in the world and blanket the Internet. I'm going to do that—this is an epidemic!"

Jacob turned away from Regan, nodding. "You're right. I know you're right. It's just . . . ."

"No, Jake, you have a duty to tell the truth. You have a duty to the people."

He nodded and looked away embarrassed.

Eighteen

Regan Matson shook her head at her thoughts as she peered out into the darkness of Laguna Madre. "I just don't get it," she blurted.

Jacob Tanner turned his head to her. "Get what?"

"This incessant drive for money. You people and your money, it's all about money to you. You couldn't care less about the people who are suffering or about social justice at all. You just want the Benjamins."

"Whoa, there, hot pants! What do you mean *I* couldn't care less about people who are suffering?"

"Because it's true. Sure, you say you want to help the underprivileged but all you people really care about is money."

Jacob smiled and sniffed a laugh. "Well, who are 'you people'? I don't know if I care to be associated with this group of miscreants and ruffians."

"You people. Businessmen, Wall Street, the corporations! "

Jacob smiled in curiosity. "Wow, you sound like my dad."

"Oh? He's probably a real smart guy."

"Yeah. So, what *is* the problem with corporations in your estimation?"

"Everything."

"Like what?"

"Well, Mr. CEO, I feel that corporations are just a legal structure designed to remove all responsibility from people in business. The law considers corporations *persons*, right? And if the corporation harms people, they can be sued or whatever, but the people that make up the corporation—the ones that actually did the harm—escape unscathed. I mean look at the gulf oil spill. So many billions of dollars wasted on clean up; so many thousands of lives and livelihoods disrupted and the

environment ruined. Why? Because the people that ran the corporation worried more about saving a few dollars than doing a thorough safety inspection."

Jacob opened his mouth as if to contest her stance but changed his mind. "No, you're absolutely right. They were completely wrong in that."

"And what about our food?" Regan said enthusiastically, getting on a roll. "The big agriculture corporations only care about making money, so they shovel this disgusting corn-fed crap down our throats that they fried in partially hydrogenated slop and put it in a bright box with a clown on it. Soon, everyone's obese and we're standing around dumbfounded as to why that happened." Regan looked to Jacob to see if he understood. "It happened because the CEOs and CFOs of those corporations cared more about money than the health of their customers."

Jacob nodded quietly.

"And the banks. Don't even get me started on the banks! You think the millionaire bankers were thinking about grandma and grandpa Tanner losing their home while they were off trading multi-trillion dollar derivatives and swaps with international corporations? Hell no they weren't."

"Yes," Jacob conceded, "it's true that many businessmen and corporations are in it only for the money and no doubt some of them hurt people, but do you think it's fair to lump *all* businessmen in the same category? Not everyone in business is dedicated solely to making money."

"Yes," Regan said bluntly. "You're all uncharitable, money-grubbing heathens." She gave a Jacob a warm smile indicating that she was kidding though her words belied that sentiment.

"Well don't hold back, Regan. Why don't you tell me how you really feel?" Jacob asked rhetorically. "But you mention charity. I wonder if you'd listen to a controversial idea." Jacob waited for approval from Regan, then continued, "I think we have the same general goal here—less poverty in the world, healthier people, more happiness, and so on—but I think we have different ways to get there. I'm assuming you think charity is the way to get to less poverty and I think that self-interest is. See, it's a

strange paradox in modern times but being charitable—in the sense of sacrifice for the benefit of others—is actually *less* charitable than being self-interested."

Regan looked at Jacob straight-faced. "What are you smoking, CEO?"

Jacob nodded and held up his hand. "Let me explain. I will assume that you agree that the point of charity isn't just to feel good about giving money to people, right? The point of charity is to actually *help* people, correct?"

"Yeah," Regan said, nodding. "You want to help people, not just to feel good about yourself."

"Okay," Jacob continued. "Right, so then the question is what helps people the most? Charity or self-interest? It just so happens that free market capitalism—the economic system based on self-interest—has helped to bring more people out of poverty than all charities throughout the history of the Earth have." Jacob lifted his right hand to imitate his words. "Charities can give money to an impoverished country, say in sub-Saharan Africa, until they're blue in the face, and not make the overall situation any better. Those people will never get out of the starvation and squalor if you just give them money. The money will just be squandered in the corrupt system. And it's even worse with forced charity—state welfare. When President Johnson launched the *War on Poverty* in the 1960s, people probably thought we'd be 'in and out' in a few years and have poverty licked by the '70s. But what has all that welfare gotten us? That forced charity never made things any better—most likely it made them worse.

"On the other hand, if you introduce a solid free-market economy based on the rule of law in one of those sub-Saharan countries, I guarantee it would lift 80 percent of the people out of poverty within a decade. It's already happened in India and China, not to mention dozens of Eastern Bloc countries since the fall of communism. Charity didn't make those countries better off, the free market did. The free market has

the miraculous effect of making everyone better off and it happens every time it's tried.

"I mean look at it; what's going to get people to stop fighting and stealing and get people working for a better life? It's not going to be our common bond of humanity—different tribes have been warring since the dawn of man. Religion and government didn't seem to stop the fighting when they were introduced into society—those institutions only made things worse. You know what's the one thing that gets people working together instead of killing each other?"

"No," Regan said with a slightly mocking tone, "but I have a feeling you're going to tell me."

"Trade! Only free-market trade between peoples allows them to get past their differences and to say, 'Hey, I may not like your religion or the way you dress or how you smell, but you make a damn fine shoe or wine or car. It's probably better that you lived.' Then, everyone's better off. That's why I say it's actually *more* charitable to not be charitable."

Regan breathed in audibly, then exhaled through a half-smile, thinking about Jacob's ideas.

He continued, "An example, when did you donate to charity last?" He waited briefly for Regan to respond.

"Um . . . ," she said thinking about it.

"Well you probably just gave money to some worthy cause to feed a couple hundred people and left it that, right?" Jacob looked to Regan's confirmation. "That's giving a man a fish. Well, when I give money to people, I do it because they are producing something for me at a job and I expect something in return. They provide me with their time and skill and I provide them with a share of the company's profits."

"Yeah, but what about when people don't know how to work? What if they don't know any skills?" Regan asked.

"Then I would teach them. It's beneficial to everyone involved if I teach them. I need a skilled employee and they need a skill—in essence, I'm teaching a man to fish for himself. And those skills can be used elsewhere to benefit themselves and—really—civilization as a whole because

the products we make save lives. Everyone wins. If I just *give* them money, I'm just giving them the fish and creating a dependent. They may eat, but they have no dignity in that. They surely don't feel like they've earned the meal."

"But what if they're sick or indigent? What if they *can't* work?"

"Well, to be honest, I think people often make excuses to take advantage of today's climate of charity. They say they got injured on the job and regardless of the severity of the injury, take the disability insurance check, and go tour the Caribbean despite their, quote unquote, disability. I actually know people like this and I don't buy it. I'm pretty sure I can find a job for almost anyone who *wants* to work."

"Well what if they don't *want* to work?"

Jacob nodded. "Then those people can choose that lifestyle, but don't ask me to subsidize that lifestyle and for God's sake don't *force* me to subsidize the lazy bums!"

Regan shook her head with a smile. "I don't know. It just seems heartless—all the people who just care about money. I mean, haven't you ever heard of altruism? You know, the virtue?"

Jacob shook his head. "Altruism is a myth."

"What? What planet are you from?"

"What is altruism? It's the practice of unselfish support of others, right?" Regan nodded at Jacob's question. "Well is anyone really unselfish? Every choice people make to support others is made because the chooser thinks it's better in general or better for them in the long run to do good for others. Even the religious zealots who give up everything to the poor do so in exchange for spiritual salvation, which, in their estimation, is a better trade, I imagine—they're profiting from the deal. A hundred thousand dollars in this world or eternal life in paradise. It's not that difficult of a decision if you believe in that. If someone was really completely selfless, he would die within weeks because he would constantly make self-destructive decisions for the so-called benefit of others. Real good he does for others when he's dead!"

Regan smiled. "You're impossible!"

"No, I'm just logical." Jacob smiled. "No, I agree, it's ugly out there, but the problem isn't self-interest. Oh, what was it Adam Smith said?" Jacob closed his eyes and rubbed his forehead in an attempt to facilitate his memory. "Something to the effect that the baker doesn't bake because he's worried about his customers' hunger, he bakes for his own self-interest. It's like my investors. All they're looking for is a return on their investment—all they care about is money as you say—but they are allowing me to create a product that will improve thousands of people's lives. Their *self-interest* is helping to save lives of others—all investors who put money into pharmaceutical companies for their *own benefit* are helping to save lives for others' benefit. And in a voluntary society, the wealthier people are, in essence, the more people they have helped."

Regan scrunched her face. "But why don't you just give away the drug if you want to really help people? I mean, you're doing well for yourself, you have nice threads." Regan eyed Jacob's suit.

"Incentives. It takes a lot of effort to invent and produce a drug. The scientists on my staff wouldn't have spent all that time and effort creating Symbalia if they weren't compensated for it and they sure wouldn't have created it if they were too busy begging for money to support themselves. When you take away the incentive to produce—the profit—you get demand with no supply—shortages." Jacob threw up his hand. "I'm sure you've heard about the drug shortages happening across the country?"

"Um, yeah, I've heard the reports," Regan confirmed.

"Hospitals don't have shortages of the new expensive drugs that companies are profiting on, they're short on the older, generic drugs that aren't cost effective to produce. Why not keep the drugs expensive and ensure we'll have them? People are still willing to pay for them at the high prices." Jacob paused a moment to let his idea sink in. "And that's my point. Patients want the drug more than the $100 they're paying for it—if it is a voluntary transaction, *both* parties are wealthier after the fact."

"What do you mean both parties are wealthier? The customers are a hundred dollars short and the pharmaceutical company is a hundred richer."

"Well, the pharma company wanted the money more than the drug and the patient wanted the drug more than the money, so both people end up with an improved situation—they are both wealthier. That's the miracle of the free enterprise system."

"But what if people can't afford $100 for the drug?" Regan asked. "Shouldn't government step in and force companies to lower the price?"

Jacob shook his head. "Well, no company is going to create a product if they're going to lose money on it forever, so if government forces lower prices, you'll just end up with no drugs. That's where the shortages come in."

Regan shook her head, then looked at Jacob with a smile. "You really believe this stuff don't you?"

Jacob smiled and nodded. "Give me liberty or give me death! Right?"

"I have to admit," Regan said leaning into Jacob. "You don't know what the hell you're talking about but it gets me really turned on to argue with you."

"Oh really?" Jacob smiled and surveyed the smooth skin of Regan's face and her plump rose lips. "I like the sound of that."

Nineteen

"So, what is it?" Regan Matson asked.

"What is what?"

"What's causing Chinese encephalitis? You said you discovered what caused it."

"Oh, right." Jacob said. "I probably shouldn't say until I'm absolutely sure. We're still testing."

Regan shook her head and looked at Jacob with her head tilted down. "You can tell me."

Jacob shook his head. "As soon as I know for sure, Regan, I'll tell you, okay?"

"Okay, but listen, you need to forget about your company Jacob. If you know the cause of the disease and can stop it, you need to tell people."

Jacob eagerly agreed with her. "No, absolutely. You're absolutely right."

"I know I am." She smiled.

"I just need a way to let my business partner down easy," Jacob said thoughtfully.

"And who is this business partner of yours?"

"Oh, I think I told you, Martin Gall."

Regan rolled her eyes.

Jacob shook his head. "I used to idolize the guy—he was a legend at Harvard, but now that I know him . . . he's just not who I thought he was."

"What? Is he an uncharitable heathen?" Regan asked with a smile.

Jacob nodded. "The guy is one of a kind. When I first met with him he told me his magic word. Want to guess what it is?"

"Please?"

Jacob shook his head and with a grin said, "No, it's 'money.' 'Money' is his magic word."

"Oh, of course."

Jacob squinted at Regan who was visibly mad all of the sudden. "Regan, do you know Martin Gall? A couple days ago, I was at his building and I saw you go in a side door there with a security guard."

"Oh?"

"Well? What were you doing there?"

Regan nodded. "I was working."

"Doing what? What is it that you do? I still don't know."

Regan took a deep breath and patted the pier. "Ah, well, it's getting late isn't it?"

"No, what are you hiding? Why won't you tell me?"

The young woman turned to Jacob and looked at him intently. "Fine, you want to know? All right, I'll tell you." She paused for a moment. "I'm curious as to what you'll say about it. I told you that this city is full of debauchery, right? Well, I'm not just an innocent bystander."

"What? What do you mean?"

"It's all pretty new to me—but I saw a good opportunity and I took it."

"What is it, Regan? Tell me!"

"Let me just say, I'm the newest member of the oldest profession on Earth . . . with a twist."

Jacob tilted his head toward her. "Okay, what's the oldest profession on Earth?"

Regan smiled. "Come on, you don't know what the oldest profession on Earth is?"

"No. Baker? What?"

Regan laughed. "No. Older than that."

Jacob's eyes widened and he stared at Regan as a realization came to him. "No," he said in a dejected tone.

Regan twisted her lips, raised an eyebrow and nodded. She wasn't happy, but defiantly proud.

"You've got to be kidding me. You?"

"I warned you about this place, didn't I?"

Jacob looked down. "Yeah, but I never thought that you . . . ."

"It's really not as bad as all that. The agency I'm with calls it a match-making service for extremely well positioned—i.e. fucking rich—men. They handpick women from modeling and acting agencies who fit their clients' specific requirements and set them up with the rich and powerful. It's basically a glorified dating service, but you're expected to meet the client's, um, desires as well as physical and mental specs."

Jacob stared at her, stunned. "I think I'm going to vomit."

"Come on, Jake. What's so wrong about it? I'm just like one of your self-interested businesspeople filling an economic need," she mocked.

Jacob shook his head and looked away. "This is different."

"The shoe's on the other foot, huh? People should be able to do whatever business they want without regulation, right? Why is this any different?"

"*You're* different."

"Oh come on. You've done online dating before right? It's just like that except for extraordinary talent. And it's strictly one girl, one client. And everyone's tested, even the clients."

Jacob stared into space for a moment, unsure how to respond, then said, "So, your client . . . is Martin Gall?"

Regan nodded and looked off into the bleak darkness of the lagoon. "I have reasons for doing what I'm doing, you know?"

Jacob grinded his teeth, then let out, "I'm sure you do."

Regan returned her attention to Jacob. "Of course, you have to promise not to tell any one. We're sworn to secrecy. I suppose, even in a place that's supposedly completely free, there's still a stigma with the whole thing."

"Do you have some sort of confidentiality agreement?"

"It's a delicate matter. You can understand."

He looked at Regan hopefully. "You said you *just* got this . . . job?"

"Yeah, he hasn't even wanted to fuck yet."

Jacob dropped his jaw and turned away from her. How could she be so cavalier about this? he wondered to himself. Jacob finally realized what Regan was telling him. His head began to spin and a knot formed in his gut. Who had appeared to be such an innocent, free spirit just an hour before had decayed into a licentious libertine in a matter of minutes. He shook his head and tried to swallow as his eyes darted around. "Um, I'm sorry, I have to get going," he managed to say.

Regan nodded in agreement. "Maybe that's the best."

Jacob stood and Regan followed. They walked down the pier silently and back to the theater.

Twenty

Jacob Tanner sat solemn in his office chair and stared at a financial report. He had been looking over the same accounting figures for twenty minutes, but the numbers weren't registering. The report showed a staggering increase in sales for his pharmaceutical, but that's not why he couldn't wrap his brain around the report. He couldn't concentrate because he kept replaying the events of his evening with Regan Matson two nights before.

When he realized that it was a lost cause to try to work, he dropped the report and hid his face behind his cupped hands exhaling loudly.

"Oh, the life of the CEO is so painful," Marc Johnson said sarcastically as he walked into Jacob's office. Marc was wearing a pristine lab coat and was using a toothpick to extract unwanted remnants of his breakfast.

Jacob lowered his hands and smiled at his own melodramatic appearance. "Marc, let me ask you a question. Say you think that you've found the one, okay, an amazing woman that has every quality you've ever looked for in someone. She's a smart, witty free spirit and probably the most beautiful person you've met."

"Sounds great, when do I get to meet her?"

"This is a hypothetical. Say you meet this girl and she's great, but she has an unbearably hideous profession."

"What, does she work in a landfill?"

"No, it's a different kind of hideous. It's morally wrong, actually."

"What?" Marc inquired, showing interest. "What does she do?"

"What if your perfect woman was a high class call girl?"

Marc broke out in laughter, then stopped, noticing Jacob was not joking. "What? Are you serious?"

Jacob nodded slowly, not smiling.

Marc moved the corners of his lip down in an exaggerated frown and considered the hypothetical. "Shit, I wouldn't care. Most women sleep around anyway. She might as well be getting paid to do it."

"Right, I forgot who I was asking—Mr. Discretion."

"Oh I've got plenty of discretion, my lad. I require all my women to have a full head of hair and at least three functioning limbs."

Jacob raised his eyebrows. "You're sick."

"That's what my shrink keeps telling me," Marc confessed before sitting down in a chair opposite Jacob's.

"So, do you have a purpose for being here or do you just want to antagonize me?" Jacob asked giving up on his hypothetical.

Marc tossed a stapled collection of paper onto Jacob's desk and announced, "It's official. There is a component in the Viper phone that, when operational and in close proximity to central nervous system cells, degrades the myelin sheath around the brain axons."

Jacob shook his head in dismay as he picked up Marc's report from his desk.

"It appears that the degradation takes some time, but after repeated exposure, the patient will suffer demyelination of the central nervous system, also known as Chinese encephalitis."

"Unbelievable."

"Actually it's quite believable," Marc contradicted. "It's happening."

"And this doesn't happen with any other phone?"

"Well, we didn't check them all, but the main producers—Blackberry, Apple, Motorola—all checked out fine. You see, every phone has what's called a D-to-A chip or a digital-to-analog chip. And most operate without flaw, but the D-to-A chips in the Viper phones are faulty and produce an extraordinary amount of low frequency radiation to which the myelin sheath is particularly susceptible. Frankly, I don't understand why this was overlooked, the flaw in the D-to-A chip must require an inordinate amount of energy."

"Shit. That's right. I remember my Viper having issues with short battery life and this must have been the cause." Jacob looked at his Viper phone, which had been switched off, then massaged the base of his neck maintaining a worried look. "I guess I need to get another phone soon."

"Yes, I would certainly recommend that," Marc agreed.

Jacob was stunned as he read over the report. "I don't get it. How the hell did this piece of crap pass any sort of quality testing? How is it one of the biggest sellers out there right now?"

"People are idiots, Jacob." Marc then remembered that Jacob had been using a Viper phone. "No offense. I mean why did you buy it?"

Jacob shook his head. "I don't know. It was a good deal and they said it was a good phone."

"Idiots . . . ." Marc repeated.

"Right. So we have our culprit, then? This is final?" Jacob lifted Marc's report.

Marc confirmed with a nod.

"We just need to find out who made those chips and get them to recall the phones," Jacob said.

"Jacob, we already know who produces the chips."

"Oh?"

"Vizor Electronics makes the chips."

"Vizor Electronics? I've never heard of them."

"No, but you've definitely heard of their parent company—Vizor Electronics is a wholly-owned subsidiary of none other than Gall Enterprises."

Jacob's mouth opened slightly as he stared at his colleague. "Son of a bitch."

"Yep. Our kind benefactor Mr. Gall," Marc said waving an index finger in the air, "makes the device that's causing the disease that we treat."

Jacob looked down in pensive thought. He gripped the armrests on his chair and shook his head, then gave Marc a skeptical look. "Marc, can I trust you?"

Marc scrunched his face. "Yeah, why?"

"Gall is going to want to suppress this. He's going to try everything. Can I count on you to back me up on this when we go public?"

Marc smiled. "I'm a scientist, Jacob. Of course you can trust me," Marc said, twisting his toothpick between two front teeth.

* * *

Jacob was walking to his car in the late afternoon when his phone rang. "Thanks for getting back to me, Berto," he answered.

"No problem, amigo," Roberto Rodriguez said, overcoming a cacophony of construction sounds around him. "It turns out my buddy who worked at Vizor knew exactly what you were talking about."

"Oh really?" Jacob said, intrigued.

"Yeah, he wants to meet you, but he said it has to be completely off the record. He doesn't want to be associated with anything you're trying to pull."

"What do you mean?"

"I don't know, man, he just seemed really worried about the whole thing. I had to keep telling him that you were all right. He was kinda freaked out about the whole thing."

"Okay . . . where does he want to meet?"

"You know where they're building the Wilberforce monument out in Locke Flats?"

"Uh, yeah, I think so."

"He'll be there at ten tonight."

"Ten o'clock?"

"Yeah, he said that way no one will be around."

"What? Why all the cloak and dagger stuff?"

"Well, this dude is kind of an oddball—fringe type. He's pretty secretive. You want to tell me what all this is about Jake?"

"Man, this is getting out of control—this thing with Gall."

"What do you mean?"

"Uh, he might not have been the best guy to go in business with."

"Just trials and tribulations, Jake. That's the nature of the beast. But it's all good. I mean remember the story of Bill Gates and Steve Jobs? Gates ripped off Apple for years but Jobs kept fighting, right? And look who's laughing last; Apple's worth nearly twice as much as Microsoft is right now. You're going to have shady business partners along the way, man. You just gotta overcome."

Jacob smiled. "Thanks, Roberto. And thanks for setting up this meeting tonight."

"No problemo, mate."

Jacob ended the call and typed "Wilberforce monument, 10 PM" in his phone calendar.

Twenty-One

The statue of William Wilberforce appeared completed, but scaffolding around the entire piece obscured it. Still, lights, which were positioned at the base of the twenty-foot statue, were operational and shone on the structure despite its state of construction. The scaffolding created dramatic shadows on the statue—almost seeming to put the anti-slavery crusader behind a mangled collection of shadowy prison bars.

Jacob Tanner saw past the steel and wood pieces to the statue itself and admired the craftsmanship. The subject was a well-to-do Englishman standing upright, but with an almost timid demeanor. In one hand, he cuffed the Bible and in the other, he let hang a pair of unfastened wrist shackles, presumably ones that were forced onto the slaves of Wilberforce's time.

The statue's surrounding landscape was finished and well manicured. Jacob imagined that once the statue was complete, that this would be a fine destination for tourists. But the grounds were empty and it seemed that there was no one around for miles. He would surely see if a car was approaching and none were.

However, Jacob was startled when a voice crept into his ear from behind him, "No one followed you did they?"

It was a low, grumbly voice, befitting a man of his seventies, but when Jacob swooped around, he found a middle-aged man wearing black-rimmed glasses and a dark gray trench coat. His hair was messy and an unkempt beard gave the man an appearance of being homeless. Lights from the base of the Wilberforce statue cast ominous shadows on the man's face.

Jacob shook his head. "No, not that I know of."

"Why are you asking questions about the Viper phone?" the man demanded.

"Look, can we ease up on the melodrama here?" Jacob asked impatiently.

"Just fuckin' answer the question," the shadowy man responded.

"Damn it. Okay, I have reason to believe that radiation from the D-to-A chip in the Viper phone could be causing an epidemic known as Chinese encephalitis."

The man paused for a brief moment then whipped out a sawed-off, slide-action shotgun from under his trench coat.

"Whoa, whoa!" Jacob yelled as he darted behind the statue. His heart began racing and his eyes bulged as he tried to discern what the man was doing. There was nowhere to run. He was entirely surrounded by open fields.

The man set the shotgun down on one of the wooden boards resting on the scaffolding. "Hey, I'm not going to shoot you!" he called out. "I just wanted to come prepared."

"Prepared for what?" Jacob yelled from behind the statue. "You don't pull a shotgun on someone you don't intend to shoot!"

"Prepared for—do you know who we're dealing with, mister?" the mysterious man shouted.

"Maybe you want to explain?" Jacob yelled out around the statue.

"Come back around here and I will," the man instructed. "I'm not going to shoot."

Jacob inched around the scaffolding. He saw the man through the wood and pipes. He was looking away from Jacob toward the empty countryside. Jacob approached the man again. "You want to tell me what the hell is going on?"

The man looked at Jacob and squinted. "That's why I'm here, right?"

Jacob stepped out into the open. "Roberto said you worked for Vizor."

"I was the lead engineer in the mobile device division. We worked on the D-to-A chip that was going to be in every Viper phone in the

country. It was going to be revolutionary—it filled the gaps in connection so no interference, no choppy connection, and perfect sound quality—we really created something special."

Jacob nodded for the man to continue.

"Well, crunch time came around and we needed to cut costs to make the device profitable so we were instructed to go with a questionable superconductor—a cheapy from China." The man began to shake his head. "I told them all along that those chips were producing too much radiation, that it wasn't safe. And it wasn't the typical cell phone frequency radio waves. No, this radiation was on the other side of the spectrum, cosmic shit."

"What are you saying?"

"There was something wrong with the design. The chip did all the fancy shit we wanted, but it was leaking radiation like a sieve."

"What did you do?"

"I told everyone that it wasn't going to work, that we couldn't use that design. But word came from above that we were going with the cheaper design." He shook his head again. "They just didn't listen."

"You said word came from above. From who?"

"Well, I got the command from my veep, but I went to the president of the company himself. I knew this was going to be big."

"The president? You mean Gall?"

"Well, as a matter of fact. I spoke with the president of Vizor. His name was Daniels. But Daniels was on my side and, he did say that *he* got his marching orders from someone above *him*. I can only imagine that meant Gall."

"Damn," Jacob said looking down. Suddenly a rage formed in the pit of Jacob's stomach and moved up. Gall knew about the radiation? He knew about it? Jacob then came to the realization he had been dreading. "That son of a bitch killed my sister."

"What?" the man asked.

"Nothing—look, do you have any hard proof of this? Proof that Gall knew about the radiation?"

"Well, after I made a huff about the D-to-A, they canned my ass. And since there is no labor regulation here, I couldn't claim wrongful termination. Everything I had on the subject—files, emails—they were all confiscated by Vizor. But there was an email exchange, I am sure of that."

"Emails from Gall?"

The man nodded. "You can bet your ass that there are some dirty little secrets in Martin Gall's inbox that he don't want anyone to see."

Jacob slowly started to nod. "I bet you're right."

"If someone was willing to risk it, he could sack Gall's office and come up with some serious dirt about this. But only a fool would risk that. The man is more powerful than the president of the United States. He's got more money than the Sultan of Brunei and a security force bigger than some countries' armies."

Jacob stared at the man. "Well, you might be looking at just that kind of fool."

The man shook his head. "I'm warning you, pal. Don't even joke about that. They did me a favor by just firing me. They got the whole system working for them. It's like the Russian mafia with these guys only, it's legal here, cause there ain't no laws. And what's more, they got people in the government—big time politicians. The whole system's on their side."

"But people are dying! Innocent people," Jacob protested.

"Well, do you want to be one of them?" the man said as he took his shotgun and placed it back in his scabbard.

"I'm prepared to do what it takes to stop CE."

"Man, you got a death wish. Take my advice, pal. Just leave it alone."

Jacob looked down then scanned up the scaffolding toward Wilberforce's face, his heart starting to pound again. When Jacob looked back to the man, he was gone. Jacob flinched and looked around the statue and the nearby fields. He spotted the man walking into the misty darkness toward the west.

*I saw sitting in this House of Dust a priest and a servant,
I also saw a priest of purification and a priest of ecstasy,
I saw all the priests of the great gods.*

Twenty-Two

Jacob Tanner fidgeted and bounced his right leg as he waited in Martin Gall's front office. When the executive burst out of his office, he didn't notice Jacob, who then jumped up and called out, "Mr. Gall!"

Gall quickly turned to Jacob then continued on to the elevators. "Tanner, how goes it?"

"I'm good—"

"Take the elevator down with me," Gall said, not letting Jacob finish. "I got a Gala to put on, but you can have a minute of my time on the ride down. I won't even charge you," he joked.

Jacob walked behind Gall and waited as the elevator approached their floor. "It's about CE and its cause . . . ." He waited to see Gall's reaction, which was half interest.

"Oh yeah," Gall said paying more attention to the elevator button than to Jacob. "What about it?"

Jacob hesitated, then said, "I have reason to believe one of your products causes CE." He scrunched his face and braced for a violent reaction from Gall.

Gall looked at Jacob with a suddenly intent stare. The elevator arrived with a ding and the doors opened. Gall tilted his head toward the opened doors and put his hand behind Jacob's back.

"Is that so?" Gall asked with a concerned tone.

Jacob nodded as they entered the elevator car and Gall pressed the button for the lobby. "The D-to-A chip in the Viper phone. It releases radiation and causes the myelin sheath in the nervous system to deteriorate." He waited for a response from Gall, but received none, just a concerned look. "Mr. Gall, we have to do something. We have to stop it."

Gall nodded thoughtfully, then looked at Jacob. "Okay, I will. First thing next week I will look at your paperwork—the Viper you said?"

"Yes, but Mr. Gall, with all due respect, we have to do something now. People are dying out there."

Martin Gall looked down in conscientious reflection, and then looked back at Jacob. "Okay, Tanner. You're right. But can we just hold off until after the gala? I've been working so hard on this that I'd hate to see it ruined on account of some bad news. What do ya say?" Gall put his hand on Jacob's arm in a warm gesture.

Jacob nodded. "Okay, sure . . . thanks."

"Oh, no need to thank me, Jacob," Gall said as the elevator came to rest and the doors opened again. "It's the right thing to do." They walked out of the elevator. "You're coming tonight, right?"

Jacob confirmed with, "Yeah, I'll be there."

"Sounds good. See you there." He hurriedly walked out of the building and into a car waiting for him. Jacob stood in the middle of the lobby and watched with a strained smile.

* * *

The Gall Enterprises Gala had always been one of the largest charity events of the season when it was held in New York, but since relocating to South Texas, Martin Gall felt compelled to raise the bar to draw the various donors from the rest of the country. Gall designated the year's proceeds to go 100 percent to the Noble Creature Fund, a conservation fund created to help support manatee populations in North America. The gala was to be held at the newly constructed Gall Aquarium on the water in the Acton sector of Ur.

Jacob Tanner shifted uncomfortably in his rented Tuxedo as he waited for the beautiful and glistening woman in front of him to be photographed on the red carpet. Producing an uncertain look, Jacob confided in his friend Roberto Rodriguez, "Man, I hate these things."

"What are you talking about?" Roberto answered. "This is the biggest party in town."

"That's what I mean. These galas are supposed to be these great benefits, but I think it's just an excuse for all these rich people to party."

"Hey, you're not going to turn down free caviar and fine wine are you?"

Jacob shook his head then looked at the red carpet in front of him. "How did we get in this line? Are we supposed to wait or do we walk past?"

"Don't you want to be in *Cosmo*, Jakey?" Roberto said smiling at the inattentive photographers.

Jacob had a million things on his mind, not one of them was getting into the events section of a women's fashion magazine. "Nobody wants to take pictures of us, Berto. We're nobodies in this crowd. Let's just get inside."

"Speak for yourself, Jake." Roberto straightened his suit jacket and walked around Jacob to stand next to the beautiful woman posing in front of them. The woman took a moment to see what man dared interrupt her photo opportunity.

"Was that an earthquake, darling," Roberto asked the sequined woman as he pointed confidently at the photographers, "or did you just rock my world?"

"Do I know you?" the glamorous woman asked maintaining her posed smile for the cameras.

"No, but did you just fart? Because you're blowing me away."

The woman arched her head back in an exaggerated, boisterous laugh and the photographers went wild, flooding the red carpet with flashes.

"Oh, there's more where that came from, darlin.'"

The woman turned to Roberto. "You're kinda cute." The woman then took Roberto by the arm and led him past the two stocky security guards into the aquarium's main atrium, leaving Jacob. Jacob smiled at

his friend ahead of him and slowly followed him but was stopped by one of the security guards.

"Excuse me. Only guests with passes can enter," the sturdy guard informed Jacob along with a forearm blocking the intruder's midsection.

Jacob smiled and pointed to the vanished Roberto Rodriguez. "What about him?"

"He's not of any concern right now, sir. Please step away from the door."

Jacob reached into his suit jacket and pulled out his tickets to the gala and presented them to the security guard.

The guard looked at Jacob through squinted eyes, then looked at Jacob's passes. "Okay." He stepped aside and led the way into the atrium with his hand.

Jacob gave a fake smile and walked past the security guard into the sprawling atrium filled with elegantly dressed members of America's elite business class and high society. He gazed up at the soaring glass and steel roof that arched above and tried to identify the classical piece that a string quartet was performing nearby. He surveyed the crowd and spotted Donald Trump surrounded by three beautiful women, Warren Buffett surrounded by a circle of associates, and several other businessmen whom Jacob recognized.

One such man was Arun Kula, the president of Universal Steel and the founder of the charter city of Ur. He was a thin but strong looking young man of East Indian descent, his light brown skin signifying his heritage. His five-inch-long hair arched around his face and flared slightly at the tips and his tailored tuxedo was worn expertly. Everything about the man was exquisite, Jacob thought. The way he stood, like a hero in a cartoon, to the way he held his wine glass, masculine yet with class. There was something very James Bond-like in the figure, Jacob thought.

From what Jacob had heard of the man, all the attention he was receiving by the group of people around him was warranted. Arun was the only son of Rajesh Kula who had founded Universal Steel, a multinational steel behemoth; he had attended Oxford when he was sixteen and

graduated in under three years, after which he went on to receive three doctorates at MIT and Cal Tech in economics and engineering and used those degrees to produce numerous inventions such as virtual currency and a sophisticated artificial intelligence application. Somehow along the way, Arun Kula had found time to become a superb concert pianist as well. Jacob was skeptical, however. He had heard great things about Arun Kula, but he had also heard great things about Martin Gall. Was Kula an unscrupulous businessman just like Gall?

Jacob meandered his way through the crowd to join the group Kula was entertaining or simply overhear the successful businessman speak.

A man among the five patrons surrounding Kula posed a question when Jacob got within earshot of the circle, "But Mr. Kula, when you see around the globe all the strife and the malnutrition and the complete failure of people to redistribute the wealth on their own . . . when you see so few *haves* and so many *have-nots* . . . when you see such greed in the face of such need, didn't you ever have a moment of doubt about your preferred economic system—about capitalism?" Before Arun Kula could answer, the questioner added, "And whether *greed* is really such a good thing?"

Arun Kula straightened his already erect posture and answered in a proper, Oxford-educated English, "To be sure, it is a good question and one everyone should ask himself or herself. But tell me, is there some society that doesn't run on greed?" The question was rhetorical as Kula continued, "I suppose by your referencing capitalism, you should prefer the opposite—socialism—but everywhere in the world that socialism has been tried it has come down to the great masses serving the greedy interests of the elite few who are at the head of the party. There is no less greed in socialism, it simply manifests itself at the top of the pyramid of government, that is all."

The same questioner followed up with, "But don't you feel that we, as a society, must provide for those in need? Shouldn't we ensure that everyone has the basic necessities like food and shelter and health care?"

"I do, but you are begging the question of how best to provide for those needs." Kula paused briefly to reflect on something he had read, then spoke, "There was a Soviet fighter pilot—Belenko I believe was his name—who defected to the West and on his first trip to the United States he visited a typical grocery store and he thought it was artificial—a phony. He thought the CIA had designed it as a showcase. There were thousands of products, plenty of fresh produce, and no lines of hungry people. Belenko thought it was fake because this type of thing was unheard of in Soviet society. Under socialism, scarcity is the rule. Under the free market, abundance is the rule."

"I've heard of this story," another person added. "Belenko bought a can of food that was labeled 'Dinner' and went back home and cooked it up with some potatoes and garlic and enjoyed his meal. Later, a friend came over and asked if he had adopted a cat and Belenko said no. Evidently the guy had bought a can of cat food and eaten that for dinner! He said it was better than the human food back in the Soviet Union!"

Some in the crowd chuckled at the story.

"That is true," Kula confirmed dryly. "If you attempt to ensure the abundance of something by authoritarian dictate, you almost always ensure its scarcity. Such is the inevitable downfall of every socialist community."

"Well, how about the Amaurot sector here in Ur?" Another questioner asked. "Isn't that socialist?"

"Amaurot is a noble experiment, to be sure, and it has qualities that no major socialist society has had and that is freedom. Whereas in all major socialist countries, the system is forced on its people, in Amaurot, the system is voluntary—the people there *choose* to live under socialism. Still, I'm afraid Amaurot will also devolve eventually into a greedy elite controlling the masses as well. *Every* socialist society contains greed. Do you reckon the Soviet Union was free from greed? Do you reckon communist China was free from greed? It's not that greed is *good*, in and of itself as some capitalists will have you believe, but that it is unavoidable. It is neutral. It can lead the horrors of fascist domination when unbridled,

and greed—the natural interest to improve one's lot in life—can lead to unmatched prosperity when accompanied with the concept of Natural Law."

"Natural Law?" the first questioner repeated.

"But of course, Natural Law, the idea that all human beings are born with inalienable rights to life, liberty, and property. If one respects the Natural Law, one can be as greedy as his heart desires and it will only benefit humanity because his greed will never inhibit the existence of another. Respect of the Natural Law means there is no coercion and all transactions are voluntary. When a society is based on this principle, it will be accompanied with unlimited prosperity, as you see here in Ur. As you know, the only man-made law here is *vulnero nemo*, or harm no one—coerce no one. It is the first society on earth to adhere strictly to the Natural Law and no others."

"The first? What about America?" one guest questioned.

Kula nodded. "Yes, early America was very close to adhering to the principle. In fact, some of the original colonies were much like Ur is today—completely free, in adherence with the Natural Law. But, while the foundation of America was rooted in Natural Law, the Constitution did indeed allow for some people to coerce others."

"What people? The Constitution allows nothing of the kind."

Kula smiled. "My friend the Constitution allows Congress to tax the people. What is taxation but monetary coercion backed by the threat of force?"

"What? You would have no taxes in the entire country?" Someone asked. "How would you pay for defense, or roads, or education?"

"Look around my friend," Kula said with a wave of his hand. "All of this was built without taxation or regulation."

A question came from another tuxedoed gentleman standing before Arun Kula, "Mr. Kula, the wealth disparity between the rich and poor in this country is getting out of control. I mean, we're up there with countries like Venezuela and Mexico. Don't you think we should do something about that?"

Arun Kula pursed his lips and bowed his head slightly to deflect the comment. "Let me ask you a question to answer your question. Would you prefer there be no disparity in wealth but everyone be relatively poor, or would you prefer a vast disparity with everyone better off?"

"Can't we have both?" the guest asked.

"Unfortunately no. When you force equalization of income, you restrict the inventive, entrepreneurial nature of people and the inevitable result is universal poverty. However, when you allow people to make great sums of wealth, you unleash the creative power of industrialists and everyone prospers as was seen in nineteenth century America."

The man replied, "Well, but there are people dying of hunger in the streets and meanwhile you have people like yourself—no offense—who live lavish lifestyles with wine and women. It's just not fair."

Kula pondered the man's statements. "Sir, no one in this country starves to death, I assure you. You would have to go to far more impoverished countries to see that. But let's assume that the poor in this country do suffer, what would you have done to remedy the situation?"

"Well, we should tax people like you. Ninety percent should go to help the poor."

"And you sir, I assume you make a decent wage, what should your tax rate be?"

The man shook his head, "Well, I'm fine paying my thirty percent. But the truly rich should pay more."

"Sir, to a starving individual in the Democratic Republic of Congo, you would look like Croesus himself. You are truly rich to 95 percent of the population. Why shouldn't you have a 90 percent income tax as well?" The question was rhetorical and Kula continued, "You see wealth as an evil that needs to be vanquished in order to provide for the poor, but if you steal money from the wealthy long enough, there should be wealthy no more."

"Well, isn't that the point?" the man asked.

Kula stared at the man intently. "Is it? Tell me, sir, who would support your poor after you vanquished all the wealthy? You see wealth—

capital—as evil, but without it, there would be no production. It is stored wealth that has brought civilization out of the despotic, brutish Iron Age and allowed humanity to flourish as it has. You eat the wealthy, sir, and it will be your last meal."

The group nodded and sighed as they digested Kula's words and Jacob Tanner saw his opportunity to interject himself into the conversation. "What do you think of Martin Gall, Mr. Kula?"

Kula looked at the new face. "Well, he sure knows how to put on a good party, does he not?" Kula asked with a forced ounce of humor.

"But what about ethics? Do you think all businessmen adhere to the Natural Law?" Jacob asked firmly.

"I don't believe we've met, mister . . . ?"

"My name's Tanner, Jacob Tanner."

"It's a pleasure Mr. Tanner." Kula paused to collect his thoughts, then explained, "It is a fine question that and I will answer with an analogy. In nature, there are the saints and the scavengers. In the animal kingdom, there are bowerbirds, which are really quite magnificent creatures that build elaborate bowers—or nests—including amazing hut-like roofs with pillars made of twigs, beautiful collections of flowers, shells, stones, and berries. If you're ever in New Guinea, I do recommend that you make an excursion to see them, they're really quite marvelous. Those are the saints."

"And the scavengers?" Jacob asked.

Kula shook his head. "The other type of bird is the common vulture. A magnificent, large bird by sight until you view their disgusting scavenger tendencies. Vultures have exceptionally corrosive stomach acid that allows them to digest putrid carcasses infected with Botulinum toxin, cholera, and anthrax bacteria."

"So, which one is Gall?"

Kula smiled. "I will let you decide that for yourself."

Jacob smiled and looked admiringly at Arun Kula. He reached out his hand toward Kula and they shook. "It's a pleasure to meet you Mr. Kula."

"Likewise," Kula responded. "Now, if you'll excuse me gentlemen," Arun Kula said and turned to leave the circle.

The group of people dispersed and Jacob stood contemplating Kula's ideas with a calm, thoughtful smile.

Twenty-Three

A cocktail server walked by Jacob with a tray full of sparkling wine flutes, one of which he gently accepted without the server stopping. After a couple sips of champagne, Jacob shook his head at the thought of how much wealth was represented in the room in which he was standing.

"There aren't many places where I'm less noticeable than any number of men," a sultry voice layered with a think foreign accent said.

Jacob looked to his left where a beautiful young woman stood. She wore a glittering blue gown and her hair was up in an intentional tangle. She looked strikingly familiar and, as Jacob surveyed her profile, he recognized the star of Cirque de la Lumière.

"You're Madeleine Pichette," Jacob said pointing his wine flute in the performer's direction.

She returned a smile and tapped her glass to his. "The one and only."

"I saw you perform the other night. You were amazing!"

"Merci bien, monsieur. It is an amazing show. I am glad to be a part of it," she said with pouting lips. Jacob recognized her accent as French.

"You know, a friend and I were debating the theme of the show. I understand it was very abstract, but I think there was a real meaning behind the performance and I was just wondering your perspective."

"Bien sur," Madeleine confirmed, "but of course. Monsieur Chavrout is *all* about meaning."

"Yes, yes. So tell me. What idea did *your* character in particular represent?"

Madeleine looked up and smiled at a debonair man walking toward her with a devious smile. She looked at Jacob to answer before her

companion was close enough. "Love, of course," she said batting her eyes at Jacob. "I played love."

The debonair man stepped in between Madeleine and Jacob and began walking her away. "À tout à l'heure!" Madeleine called to Jacob over her shoulder as the couple left him alone in the middle of the atrium.

Jacob resisted a smile and nodded his head. "She was right," he whispered to himself. He looked to the marble floor and shook his head. She, he thought. Good thing *she* wasn't going to be there that night.

At that moment, Jacob heard the collection of attendees erupt in a cheer. He looked up and saw a small group of five people entering the gala. Leading the pack was the gregarious and confident Martin Gall, the host of the extravagant gala. The crowd surrounding the newcomers applauded and welcomed them, focusing on the main benefactor, but Jacob's attention was drawn to the woman on Gall's arm. With a rush of shocked adrenaline, his focus was glued on the stunning beauty of Regan Matson. Jacob's heart sank as he watched her compliment the sophisticated man to her side with smiles and waves toward the crowd. She was dressed in an elegant, form-fitting white dress with flowery ruffles surrounding her neck.

Jacob's wine flute slipped out of his hand and crashed on the marble floor as he took a step backward. Immediately, a server was at Jacob's heels cleaning up the mess he made and Jacob maneuvered around the cleanup.

It felt like a swarm of bees had invaded Jacob's mind. Should he confront Gall now? Should he reveal Regan's occupation to the crowd? He couldn't think. He couldn't breathe.

Martin Gall and his company shook hands and greeted nearby attendees and Jacob looked around for something to do to look busy. He found no one and as Gall's entourage inched closer, the powerful executive spotted Jacob.

"Tanner, you made it!" he exclaimed. "This is the guy," Gall told the crowd around him, "that is saving the world from the dreaded Chinese encephalitis epidemic." He reached his hand out to shake Jacob's and

Jacob reluctantly complied. The group all honored Jacob with smiles and congratulations. "What's the matter, Tanner?" Gall continued, "Couldn't find a date?" Gall laughed at Jacob's lack of companion.

Jacob swallowed then eyed Regan. She stared back at Jacob with cold, unemotional eyes. Jacob then turned to Gall. "There was no one that fit my high standards."

Gall laughed. "Well, I hope those standards work out for you, pal. Hey, I want you up on stage later when I talk about Symbalia. That shit is great PR for us." He patted Jacob on the shoulder and walked past him.

Jacob watched Regan as she followed Gall. She did not look back at Jacob.

* * *

Jacob Tanner turned around amidst the crowd of finely dressed gala guests, then turned around again. He needed an escape. He pushed through several guests and made his way to a secluded hallway that led away from the central atrium. A velvet rope closed off the end of the hallway. On it rested a sign declaring that the area was closed to guests. Jacob looked behind him, saw no one, then unhooked the rope from a ring on the wall and slid behind it into the unauthorized area.

After a couple turns and a half-flight of stairs, Jacob found himself in a completely empty and dim smaller atrium hanging over a lighted, shimmering blue pool. On the other side of the pool was a wide panoramic window opening up to the dark Laguna Madre.

Jacob walked to the edge of the atrium overlooking the pool and rested on the metal railing. He gasped as he spotted a giant form gently gliding through the water in the pool eight feet below him. It was a stunning 10-foot-long gray manatee and Jacob was instantly drawn into the strange-looking but elegant creature. Its flippers serenely waved and propelled it forward, then the large mammal floated to the top of the pool and took in some air through its snout.

Voices from where Jacob had entered the secluded atrium broke his trance with the manatee. He flinched then ran behind a nearby pillar. Jacob could not see the approaching men, but as the voices grew louder, it became clear to whom they belonged: Martin Gall and Peter Driesel.

"Man, I wouldn't tap that with *your* dick, Peter," Gall was heard saying as they approached.

Peter responded with a dry, "Thanks Marty."

"Fuck, man, lighten up. It's a party."

Martin Gall led Peter into the atrium and over to the railing above the pool. He pulled out a small wooden step from under the railing and climbed up two steps so that his legs were leaning against the metal bar, towering over the pool.

"Now, this is why you build a fucking joint like this!" Gall announced as he unzipped his pants and exposed himself. Peter turned away with slight annoyance. Gall began urinating, creating a loud splash in the water below. "I mean, who gets a pisser like this?"

"You're a class act, Marty, you know that?" Peter said sarcastically.

"Ah, you wish." Gall looked down at the floating manatee in the pool. "Just look at that fucking thing. What the hell is it? It looks like a giant gray turd." Gall chuckled as he finished his physiological business. He stepped down off the ladder, zipped up, and put his hand on Peter's shoulder.

"Did I tell you that fucker Tanner wants to break up my little goldmine?"

Jacob clenched his teeth, listening to the two from behind the pillar.

Peter shook his head. "What does he want to do?"

"He wants to pull the Viper because of some bullshit safety issues."

"What safety issues?"

"Oh, he says it causes some disease."

Peter was quiet for a moment then said, "What does he want to do, a recall?"

"I don't know. I mean what the fuck? We're making a killing on this and Symbalia."

"What are you going to do?" Peter asked.

"What do you think I'm going to do? A recall would just cost too much. And I'm not going to let some two-bit entrepreneur get in the way of billions. He's going to need a lot more than words to stop me, the little fucker."

"Marty," Peter said quietly. "Aren't you ever afraid you're actually going to do some real harm at some point?"

Gall lifted his index finger and shouted something unintelligible at his colleague. "Stop right there, Peter. The minute you start thinking about the poor helpless fuckers at the bottom of the pond is the moment *your* ship starts to sink. You think I got to where I am thinking about the bottom feeders? Fuck no! It is a dog eat dog world, Peter, and if you don't eat up, you're going to be the one getting eaten."

After an intense stare, Peter broke the ice. "Speaking of eating, those vegetarian spring rolls down there looked excellent."

"They better be. I paid a shitload for them!" He patted his colleague on the shoulder, then motioned back to the hallway from which they came. As they walked away from the pool, Jacob could hear Gall say, "So, what do you think of that bitch I dragged here tonight?"

"Who, the redhead?" Peter asked as they left the small atrium.

"I think I found a good one, Peter. I think she wants to play."

"Oh really?"

"Yeah, I wanted her to look good tonight, but I can't wait to get her back and really fuck her up."

A faded laugh was heard from Peter and Gall as they walked back toward the gala.

Furious rage overcame Jacob. He gnashed his teeth and clenched his fists. After the voices diminished into silence, Jacob erupted from behind the pillar. He swung his hands in the air and whispered obscenities. He stood in the middle of the small empty floor and thought with his hands on his hips.

* * *

After returning to the gala minutes later, Jacob saw Martin Gall leading a group up the stairs to a small platform in the middle of the atrium. Regan followed the group and Jacob rushed to her side, placed his hand on her arm, drawing her attention to him.

Her face showed disappointment but Jacob ignored her unwillingness to communicate.

"Don't do it," Jacob whispered.

Regan pursed her lips as she walked up the steps. "What?"

"Don't go with him! You don't know what he's capable of."

Regan shook her head and turned away from Jacob as they both made their way onto the platform.

Twenty-Four

"And how about the music, huh?" Martin Gall called out to the crowd of gala attendees, who responded with a round of applause. "I've yet to hear a better string quartet in my life!" Gall said turning his head back to the collection of musicians on the stage to Gall's right.

Jacob Tanner was hidden behind a collection of gala attendees also on the stage. Through the people, Jacob kept an eye on Regan Matson standing next to Martin Gall at the podium, her wavy auburn hair complementing her feminine profile. Her backless dress revealed the even complexion and fit form of a professional model. Such a waste, he thought.

"And the food? Have you tried the delicious chocolate fountain yet? You all should get there before I can make it to that corner of the room," Gall quipped with an exaggerated grin. The crowd responded with polite laughs.

"But in all seriousness, this event isn't about the music or the food, or even you lovely people, believe it or not. This year's installment of the Great Gall Gala is all about the appreciation and preservation of that noble creature, the West Indian Manatee. That's what this event is about and that's the cause to which this beautiful building, the Gall Aquarium, is dedicated.

"Now, I'm no oceanographer, but I was told that these amazing creatures—the West Indian Manatee—once migrated all the way to the Texas coast and right up to Laguna Madre beyond those walls," Gall explained pointing behind him. "That's why I'm pledging, along with all the proceeds from tonight's gala, three percent of all future ticket sales

from this facility to the Noble Creature Fund until we can reestablish the natural migration patterns and return the manatees to Texas!"

The crowd erupted in an encouraging ovation and Martin Gall smiled at the well-dressed patrons.

"You know," Gall continued, "they give us businessmen a bad rap for just being money-grubbing Scrooges, but that couldn't be further from the truth. The average net worth of you all is well above most small countries . . . trust me, I researched my guest list well," Gall joked and received a warm chuckle from the crowd. "You've all done very well for yourselves in business and investment. But that's why you all are here in the position to do something for a worthy cause, save these manatees!"

The crowd applauded again.

"No, we businessmen don't always just think of only ourselves. For instance, I've recently gone into business with a remarkable man, Jacob Tanner, who developed Symbalia—a drug that treats that terrifying epidemic that I'm sure you've all heard about, Chinese encephalitis. Now, I've never been a proponent of importing my goods from China, but I think everyone's against *this* particular import." Some muted laughs were heard in response to the awkward joke.

"Together, Mr. Tanner and I are going to save thousands of lives." Gall turned around. "Where is Tanner? Tanner?" He spotted Jacob on the stage behind a few other colleagues and reached out his arm as Jacob maneuvered toward the podium. "Get up here." Gall put his arm around an apprehensive Jacob Tanner and reeled him in toward center stage.

"Here he is folks. The man behind Gall Enterprise's new wonder drug, Symbalia!" The atrium thundered with applause.

Gall attempted to continue with his speech, but Jacob had leaned in and muttered some unintelligible words over Gall. The two exchanged a look, Gall's of denial and Jacob's of worry, then Gall started again, "This is the man that will save hundreds of thousands of lives in the next few years, mark my word."

Jacob's mind was a flurry of doubt and confusion. He was standing next to a man who had deliberately risked the lives of thousands—

perhaps millions of people—all to increase his profits. Here was someone who had no scruples in his business dealings. He was a vulture. Jacob looked out to the crowd and realized the amount of wealth and power that it represented. He had to say something. He had to make a stand— for all the little people, for the sufferers of Chinese encephalitis, and for his sister.

Jacob quickly stuck his neck out and spoke into the microphone, at first producing an unexpected explosion of sound on the atrium's speaker system, "But all the credit can't go to me, Mr. Gall, you deserve much of the credit for getting us off our feet here in Ur when others had rejected the business as too risky." Claps were heard throughout the crowd as Gall nodded at the praise, but Jacob continued, "None of this could have been done without you. In fact," Jacob's voice elevated, "the disease wouldn't have even existed if it weren't for you because . . . well, because one of *your* products actually causes the Chinese encephalitis."

The entire crowd produced a confused murmur. They stared at Jacob and Gall, waiting for some sort of punch line.

"That's right—" Jacob said but was interrupted.

"Ah, you're such a kidder!" Martin Gall said with an exaggerated grin while trying to push Jacob away from the podium.

"No, it's not a joke. And you know it, Mr. Gall. You gave that authorization for the defective D-to-A chips. You caused the disease, Mr. Gall. Let's all give Mr. Gall a round of applause!" Jacob said into the microphone and aimed an intense stare at Gall. Some people in the crowd, unaware of what was going on did clap.

"All right," Gall was heard over the microphone as he waved for security to take Jacob away. "That Tanner! Always got something up his sleeve!" he addressed the crowd again.

A security guard secured Jacob but he repeated his warning, "Martin Gall caused Chinese encephalitis, people!"

"Right, and I created the bird flu too," he laughed, "and one of my favorites, the common cold!" A few people in the crowd released their discomfort with uncomfortable chuckles.

Jacob walked through the crowd and turned his head to see Regan Matson who was staring at him with a concerned look. The security guard pushed Jacob off the stage through dozens of people and out of the atrium.

* * *

"You can't keep me here," Jacob Tanner told his captors. The tuxedoed executive stood on a pier that jutted out from the Gall Aquarium complex. None of the elaborate architecture from the front of the building was visible, just the service bay and loading dock. Two short and stocky security guards in matching blue blazers and grey suit pants stood between Jacob and dry land. Jacob eyed a sewn-on badge on the left breast of the blazers that read "Keynes Aegis." At the other end of the pier was the dark blue emptiness of the Laguna Madre at night.

"You're welcome to leave this pier," one of the security guards informed Jacob with a nod to the end of the pier. "But, you're not going that way." The guard pointed behind him toward land.

Jacob huffed and paced around for a minute until he saw a small group of people walking toward the pier from the Aquarium. It was Martin Gall with a thick brown cigar clenched between his teeth. He was followed by a short bespectacled man and another security guard.

"You had to fuck it up, huh Tanner?" Gall shouted as he marched down the pier toward Jacob. "You had to open your big mouth?"

Jacob stood defiantly and ignored Gall's question. "You're not going to get away with this, Gall."

"The hell I'm not," Gall said as he stepped into Jacob and blew cigar smoke into his face. "We talked about this, Tanner. Everything's going as planned." Gall made a line with his hands in the air.

"Bullshit! People are dying and we . . . can stop it. I am going to stop it."

"You pathetic son of a bitch. You have no idea what you're up against, do you?"

"What? You and your little army of Oompa Loompas? They're not going to stop this. This is about principle."

A smile crept over Martin Gall's face as he popped the cigar back between his teeth and he slowly reached his left arm around Jacob as a sign of reconciliation. Jacob hesitatingly let him.

"Tanner, Tanner, Tanner. There are more things in heaven and earth than are dreamt of in your philosophy."

Jacob scrunched his face and looked at Gall quizzically before Gall suddenly swung his fist into Jacob's gut. Jacob buckled over landing on his hands and knees and coughed at the concrete pier. The environment began to swirl around Jacob as a rush of blood and adrenaline overcame him.

"You just declared war, Tanner," Gall said leaning in to his victim. "Now, if you're not out of this city by noon tomorrow, I'm gonna personally string you up and feed your intestines to my pet fucking alligator. And don't think I'm fucking around!"

Martin Gall leaned back and kicked Jacob in his face, knocking his head upwards with an explosion of blood. Jacob lunged over and fell off of the pier. To Jacob, the fall seemed like an eternity. He twisted and turned in the blackness of night and for a moment he forgot about the pain in his gut and his bleeding nose. He was in a semi-conscious peace.

The lagoon water hit Jacob like a block of ice smacking his face and the rest of his body. It thrust his body into revulsion and, submerged, he contorted to get his bearings and gasped for air as he returned to the surface like a wet dog. His heart was pounding and he heard a loud piercing noise in his ears.

Gall regained his composure on the pier, straightened his jacket, and eyed Jacob who was flopping around in the water. "Give him a couple minutes, then fish him out," Gall instructed his security personnel then walked up the pier and into the darkness.

CHAOS
AND
KINGDOM

PART 3:

THE BEAST AND DRAGON ADORED

Father, let me have the Bull of Heaven
To kill Gilgamesh and his city.
For if you do not grant me the Bull of Heaven,
I will pull down the Gates of Hell itself.

Twenty-Five

The room was completely dark save a dim spotlight directed on Regan Matson. She stood erect in the same figure-hugging white dress she wore at the gala. The floral ruffles around the V-neck of the dress created dramatic shadows under the direct light from above.

Suddenly, the towering figure of Martin Gall emerged from the darkness of the surrounding space. He kept his right hand behind him and used his left hand to gently move over Regan's forehead, then down the side of her face. He pushed her flowing hair behind her ear and glided his hand to the back of her head where he clenched a fist full of her auburn locks.

Regan opened her mouth and took in some air in a nervous gasp. Her eyes were glued on the stone-faced Gall who surveyed Regan's feminine lips and neckline.

Gall moved in for a forceful kiss and, maintaining his grip on her hair, he slowly revealed a flawlessly polished six-inch knife with his right hand. Regan's eyes widened at the startling sight.

Pulling her head back, Gall brought the sheer metal blade to Regan's cheek, causing her to fearfully inhale as if she was in danger of drowning. Regan's eyes bulged and her pulse quickened as she watched the reflective metal inch closer to her vulnerable skin.

Gall slid the blade down Regan's soft, flawless cheek, marking a red line in the skin, but not piercing it. Regan remained absolutely still and silent as Gall watched himself drag the knife down to her chin line and neck. The knife slithered down Regan's chest between the canyons of fabric from her dress.

In a flash, Gall slashed outward and Regan cried out, but stopped herself. Gall had sliced Regan's dress, causing the fabric at her shoulder to fold over. He threw the knife off to the side with a clang on the concrete floor, then gripped the dress and pulled it down away from Regan's body. He shredded the dress with a ferocious rip, leaving her completely bare in the spotlight.

Regan swallowed and lifted her head to attempt to maintain some dignity as she stood nude like a goddess statue.

"Don't move," Gall whispered. He disappeared into the darkness.

Regan's chest moved in and out rapidly as her breathing increased.

Gall returned holding a black leather strap connected to red rubber ball. He dragged the ball down Regan's face and stopped at her mouth, which was tightly closed. She carried a sour look of disgust and Gall recognized her sentiment by smiling.

"Are you angry?" he asked.

She didn't answer but stared at Gall accusatorially.

"Good," he said, assuming her answer.

He pried open Regan's mouth with the leather and rubber apparatus and she acquiesced, lowering her jaw and taking the red ball between her lips.

After a moment, Gall smiled. "Not for you," he said then pulled the piece out of her mouth. He handed the leather strap to Regan and slowly fell to his knees.

* * *

The buzz and the howl of machinery echoed through the construction site in the early morning sunlight. Jacob Tanner raised his arm to cover his nose and mouth with his shirtsleeve as he walked toward a group of swarming laborers. He tried to spot Roberto Rodriguez but the air was so bad and there were so many other workers on the site that it was an impossible task so he stayed put where he seemed to be out of the way.

To Jacob, it looked like Roberto's team was constructing the foundation for a high rise, but he knew that it was instead a ramp to an underground highway. He enjoyed the sound of construction and the smells of the building site, but his mind was weighed down by fear, uncertainty, and doubt.

"You dang asshole." A voice shouted at Jacob from twenty feet away. Roberto wore a suit and a construction helmet and once he was within striking distance, threw an additional hardhat at him, which he caught instinctively. "What the hell do you think you're doing? You trying to start a war with the second most powerful person in the city—no the country?"

Jacob put the hardhat on slowly and frowned. "You saw it?"

"I was there, remember? Hell yes, I saw it. And it's all online too. They're calling you emprasario loco—the pharmaceutical director who had a little too much of his own drugs, man."

"You're kidding me," Jacob said, almost as a question.

"Dangit, Jake. You're actin' like a damn fool and you're making me look bad too. I mean I was the one who introduced y'all in the first place!"

Jacob threw his hands in the air. "What happened to your usual pep talk, Berto? Where's the go-get-em mentality?"

"This is different, man. Now you're running your mouth off like you're insane. And at the Gall Gala of all places, like you're a drunken fool!"

Jacob looked at his fuming friend. "Bert, I wasn't making that shit up. Gall signed off on a defective product that is making people sick. I'm not going to just sit by and watch as people die!"

"What defective product?"

"It's a chip inside the Viper phone. That's what's causing the epidemic everyone's talking about."

Roberto looked at his friend silently for a moment. "Shit, Jake. You serious?"

"Yes! That's why I went off up there on stage."

"Yeah, but there are other ways to go about this, Jake. You don't have to make a dang scene at the biggest event of the year in this town."

"This couldn't wait, Berto. I couldn't find a better time. I need to expose this. I need to take Gall down. And I could use your help."

Roberto paused to look around his construction site shaking his head. "I got three men ditch this week, I got problems with my steel supplier, and I'm a month behind schedule. I don't need this extracurricular shit, Jacob."

Jacob hesitated before slowly nodding. "I understand Berto. You're a busy man. You've got a lot of responsibilities—"

"Not to mention, Jake, you're talking about going up against the second most powerful man in the city if not the country."

Jacob said nothing but looked at his friend hesitatingly.

"You want my advice?" Roberto asked rhetorically. "I say you high tail it out of here before you cause any more damage."

"And forget about all this? Bert, people are dying!"

"Well, what the hell do you think you're going to do about it? You don't have any connections. You're broke as hell. Shoot, you got nothin'," Roberto said with a headshake.

"That's why I need your help, Bert."

"Man, I'm just trying to keep my head down and run my business. I got a wife to think about. I don't need all this CSI Miami nonsense."

"So, it's like that, Roberto? After all these years?" Jacob said deflated.

Roberto looked down at Jacob disappointed.

"Seriously?"

"All right, you want my help?"

Jacob nodded.

"You want to know the only way you can beat the number *two* guy in town? You go to the number *one* guy."

"Who's that?" Jacob asked with a slightly hopeful tone.

"Arun Kula. He's the guy that created all this—he's the vision behind Ur. He's brilliant, he's filthy rich, and he's the most principled man I know. If anyone can help you, he can."

Jacob nodded. "Okay, right. Where can I find him?"

Roberto pointed away from his construction site. You see that tall building over there with the big antenna? That's the Archon Building. His office is up there."

Jacob patted his friend on the arm. "Thanks buddy."

* * *

"I'm sorry, but there is no space available in Mr. Kula's schedule today," the sophisticated receptionist said with a regretful tone. "In fact, he's booked solid through the month."

"You don't understand, Miss, but this is a matter of life and death! There is a madman in this city who's producing a product that is killing people!"

The receptionist smiled but shook her head. "Uh, I'm sorry, sir. I can take your name and phone number and try for something next month . . . ." She left the statement open-ended as in a question.

Jacob looked up from the receptionist. "No, no. That's too late."

"I'm very sorry," the receptionist said.

Jacob nodded and turned to walk away.

Twenty-Six

"Bobby," Martin Gall barked as he snapped his finger at his personal broker. When Bobby turned around, Gall pointed toward his office doors and looked down, concentrating on the voice coming through his cell phone. Bobby stood up and walked out of the office. "Close the door," Gall added and Bobby complied.

"People are talking," the voice on the other line said. "That outburst at the gala last night didn't help."

"Don't worry about it, I'm on it," Gall said confidently.

"I don't think you understand what's at stake here, Martin."

"The fuck I don't. I've got billions riding on this."

"Then I expect this to go away immediately."

Gall pursed his lips and hesitated momentarily before responding. "Look, I said I'm on it didn't I? I already got a guy on it. Either Tanner disappears or I'm going to make him disappear."

"Do it now, Martin," the voice responded. "The sooner the better."

"Yeah, okay." Gall squinted and a grin crept across his face. "My girl Allie upstairs is getting hungry. It might be time for a feeding."

* * *

"Thank you for calling the Federal Bureau of Investigations suspicious activities hotline," the pleasant, pre-recorded feminine voice on the end of the line said. Jacob Tanner listened patiently. "We've recently upgraded our hotline to a 24-hour, automated service to better serve you. If you know your party's extension you can say it at any time. Please tell me what your tip is regarding."

The voice went silent and Jacob enunciated clearly, "Corporate crimes."

"You said, 'Go home'. Is that correct?"

Jacob answered the automated question. "No, I said, 'Corporate crimes.'"

"I'm sorry," the pre-recorded voice said. "I didn't understand that. Can you rephrase your question?"

"Yeah, Viper phones are causing Chinese encephalitis and Martin Gall is trying to cover it up," Jacob said, raising his voice.

"You said, 'Domestic Terrorism'. Is that correct?"

"No! I want to report corporate crime!"

"Okay, transferring you to Domestic Terrorism . . . one moment."

"What?" Jacob whispered, exasperated. "No, back!"

After a brief pause, another automated voice—a male's—said, "Thank you for calling the FBI Domestic Terrorism hotline. To better serve you, please select from the following options . . . For the ten most wanted terrorists, please press one. For seeking terrorism information, please press two. For cyber-terrorism, please press three . . . ."

Jacob pulled the phone away from his ear and hit the star button. "Go back," he yelled into the phone, then listened.

After a pause, the pre-recorded voice said, "Please make a selection or press zero to leave a message."

Jacob shook his head, then pressed zero on his phone.

"Thank you for calling. Good bye," the voice said.

Jacob released an exaggerated grunt of frustration and threw his phone on the floor in front of him. Then, Jacob jumped as a knock at his apartment door broke the silence. He pushed off from his leather sofa and ambled toward the door. Who in the hell? He wondered.

He leaned into the peephole and saw a fidgeting Regan Matson through the small magnifying glass. Jacob straightened his posture and exhaled through a frown. He closed his eyes as another knock reverberated through the apartment. Jacob turned the deadbolt lock and pulled open the door.

Regan Matson wore a casual black dress and carried a large leather purse. She gave him a forced smile and after a brief hesitation asked, "Hi. Can I use your shower?"

Jacob scrunched his face. "I'm sorry?"

"It's a long story. Can I come in?" She looked down the hall outside Jacob's apartment and then back at Jacob.

"Sure," he said and moved out of the way to allow Regan to walk in.

Regan immediately stepped into Jacob's apartment and set her bag on the floor next to bar stools, which lined a kitchen counter. Jacob lightly closed his door and followed Regan in.

"I wasn't expecting you," Jacob said with a low tone.

"We need to talk," Regan said straight-faced.

"About what?"

"Was that true what you said up there at the podium?" she asked with an intent look. "Is that what you were talking about the other night on the pier?"

Jacob nodded. "My scientist confirmed it that day. Gall's D-to-A chip in the Viper phone puts off a dangerous amount of radiation and degrades the myelin sheath around your brain cells," Jacob said waving his index finger at his head. "That's what causes CE and I have reason to believe that Gall signed off on it himself."

"What do you mean?"

"I think Gall knew that these chips would be dangerous, but he went ahead with it anyway."

Regan squinted and shook her head. "Do you have any proof?"

"Proof he knew? How about a disgruntled former employee?"

Regan continued, "Okay, we need to get a statement from this employee—video preferably—and we'll need your scientific report about the Viper phone, then we need to get this on the top media outlets immediately."

Jacob nodded, then mocked, "Okay, I'll just call up Stone Andrews on the phone and ask him to mention it tonight on his broadcast."

"Jake, I'm serious." Regan was not smiling.

"Well, I'm sorry, but I don't know how to get a story on the national headline news. It's not really that easy."

Regan paused before looking Jacob in the eyes and speaking slowly. "I have a confession to make."

Jacob squinted at Regan. "Okay."

"I'm not what you think I am."

"Okay," he repeated.

"I'm a journalist working for the television news magazine *Face the Facts*."

Jacob jutted his head toward Regan and squinted. "Come again?"

"Look, I told you I was a working for a high end dating service and that was partially true. I'm working on a story for *Facts* about Ur's seedy underground. I'm sort of undercover, you could say." Regan made an awkward smirk.

"I don't get it. Like a cop?"

Regan nodded. "Well, sort of. I'm an investigative journalist."

"So, you're not *really* a call girl?"

Regan laughed. "No, no. I'm doing it for the story."

"Well, that's good to know." Jacob looked to the floor and his body followed his stare as he walked toward his sofa. He sat down gently in the sofa then turned up to Regan. "I . . . I don't know what to say."

"Jake, I only told you those things because I was playing a role. My goal is to uncover the news—to tell the truth."

Jacob moved his head backward. "So, you *lie* in order to tell the *truth*? You don't see anything wrong with this picture?"

"It's not really a lie . . . ." Regan hopped over to Jacob and kneeled down in front of him, taking up his hands in hers. "Jacob, I know this sounds crazy, and you probably won't believe anything I say at this point, but you have to trust me now. This story—the one about the phones— this is big, bigger than any story about the seedy underground in some über-capitalist city. This is corporate corruption on an epic scale. This is massive, unadulterated fraud. I mean . . . this is outright murder! I can get this story out there, but you need to tell me what's going on."

"Regan, *I* don't even know what's going on."

"Well, you said your scientist tested the phones right? Do you have those results?"

Jacob slowly nodded. "Yeah, I think so."

"Okay. And you said that Gall knew about the defective phones—that he signed off on them?"

"Well that's what this guy said."

"What guy?"

Jacob put his right hand to his forehead and closed his eyes briefly. "Um, some guy that my friend knows. He used to work for Vizor—the company that made the device. I had to meet him out in the middle of nowhere and he was really sketchy—he brought a shotgun!"

"Proof, Jacob. Did he have proof?"

"No, he said he didn't have proof. He said that there was an email exchange about it."

"With Gall? About the defective device?"

"Yeah," Jacob confirmed.

"Okay, so we need to get into Gall's inbox," Regan said easing away from Jacob and looking around in thought. She raised her eyebrow and after a moment's thought, she added, "I'll get the email from Gall's machine. You just need to get me the report from your scientist. I can have a story just in time for this Sunday's *Face the Facts*."

"Really? That soon?"

Regan nodded. "Yes. This is really big, Jake."

Jacob tightened his face as he looked at Regan.

Regan patted Jacob's knees and bounced up. "I'm just going to have a shower but we should get to work as soon as I'm done."

Jacob smiled. "You're so . . . bizarre."

Regan shook her head, "Uh, it's a long story." She turned and pointed down a short hallway to what looked like a bedroom. "This way?"

Jacob nodded and watched her slip into the bedroom and turn the corner into the bathroom. A mirror in the bedroom projected a view of the bathroom and of Regan as she reached behind her and unzipped her

dress, uncovering her bare, slender figure. Jacob widened his eyes at the sight and swallowed involuntarily. She turned around and Jacob could see a number of clearly defined red marks on her back.

He flinched and stood to walk toward the bathroom when Regan called out, "Hey, I wasn't lying to you the entire time. I *was* really starting to like you. There are a lot of really fucked up people in this world and you're not one of them. I hated having to act that way at the gala."

Jacob pursed his lips and nodded silently, unsure what to believe. "Oh?"

"Yeah, I don't even mind that you're a capitalist pig and hate poor people," she joked.

"Funny."

Regan closed the door to the bathroom and Jacob could faintly hear the sound of water moving through the pipes to the shower.

Twenty-Seven

Jacob Tanner raised his hands to his shaking head and breathed heavily. He paced back toward the beige leather sofa in his living room and collapsed on it, arching his head over the cushions. He was in a confused, pensive haze when he looked up and noticed a man in a black suit walking toward him from his front door.

That's strange, Jacob thought. The man did not look familiar, though he had a distinct appearance. All of his physical features were light—pale skin, white hair, light blond eyelashes. His eyes had pinkish rings around them. He had what doctors called achromia or albanism.

"Good evening," the stranger said softly and politely. "The door was unlocked." He motioned behind him toward the front of the apartment.

"Can I help you?" Jacob asked, scrunching his face. His hands surveyed the surface of the sofa around him.

"Yes," the albino said, then paused and stood in his place pointing toward his shoes. "Are shoes all right? Inside, I mean?"

"What can I do for you?" Jacob asked, ignoring the intruder's question.

"Are you Jacob Tanner?" the man inquired softly while taking black leather gloves from his back pocket and putting them on.

"Yes. Who's asking?" Jacob demanded.

"That is of no concern, Mr. Tanner. Is anyone else here? In the apartment?" he asked pointing to the floor.

Jacob reflexively looked at Regan's bag, which was five feet from the intruder on the floor. "No," Jacob lied. "Look, I'm going to have to ask you to leave." He flinched to get up but stayed seated as if under a spell by the intruder.

The man looked at the bag on the ground, then around the apartment. The rest of the apartment seemed quiet and still. "Now, Mr. Tanner, you don't want to be rude to your guest do you?" The man unleashed a .32 caliber Beretta Tomcat handgun with his left hand from his rear belt strap and a 3.5-inch suppressor with his right hand.

Jacob's heart began pounding as he witnessed the intruder screw the suppressor onto the handgun, making the small gun appear enormous. All senses were heightened. He heard the menacing sound of metal on metal as he fidgeted in his place, then immediately flung himself behind the sofa and landed awkwardly knocking over a potted plant.

"Now, now, Mr. Tanner, let's be civilized," the intruder said. He quickly finished screwing in the suppressor and aimed at the sofa where he judged Jacob's chest to have been. "There's no need to make this a barbaric hunting exercise."

He fired a lone round and the bullet pierced the sofa and shattered the ceramic plant pot that Jacob was resting on. Jacob blurted out a terrified scream and rolled over, then scampered across the room behind a large wooden armoire.

The smell of gun smoke and heated metal quickly filled the air in the apartment and Jacob sniffed it in with quick breaths, his heart pounding at a frightening rapidity. The room began to spin.

The intruder slowly paced around the sofa and when he was satisfied that his victim could no longer escape, he inched toward the armoire.

"Civilized, Mr. Tanner. Try to remain civilized." He stepped around the armoire, a safe distance from a potential counterstrike from his victim.

Jacob's lips quivered and his face lost all its color as the intruder raised his gun. Jacob shut his eyes and nodded, resigning himself to his fate. He was going to die.

Jacob contorted his face in a violent twist as his impending doom neared.

He heard the cold click of the Beretta's hammer, then clunk.

Clunk? Jacob thought to himself. He opened his eyes and saw his assailant, unconscious and falling toward him. Behind the criminal was a tense Regan Matson wielding a thick Teflon frying pan. She was dripping wet and wearing a white bathrobe.

"Holy shit!" Jacob shouted. He allowed himself to breath again.

"Did I kill him?" Regan screeched.

Jacob jumped at the intruder and grabbed his gun, then patted him down to ensure there were no other weapons on his person. There were none.

"Get his wallet!" Regan blurted.

"Does he have one?" Jacob asked as he checked. No wallet. "Quick grab the duct tape in my kitchen drawer."

Regan ran to the kitchen and searched the drawers.

The intruder shifted in his unconscious state and Jacob jumped back and raised his hands as if the man was a poisonous snake. The albino lifted his head and before Jacob could think, he came down hard on the man's forehead with the butt of the Beretta. The man collapsed again, blood emerging from his skull where Regan had struck him before.

Regan returned with a roll of silver duct tape and Jacob traded the gun for the roll. She held the gun confidently with one hand, aimed away from the assailant and Jacob, and she closed her bathrobe with the other hand. Jacob bent down to tie the criminal's wrists together with the duct tape. The tape screeched as Jacob pulled a piece out and wrapped it around the wrists of the unconscious man.

"Oh," Regan blurted, "do his feet too."

"Right," Jacob said shifting down to the prisoner's feet.

"What are we going to do?" Regan asked with an unsteady voice.

"I don't know, call the police?"

"There are no police, remember?"

"Right. Well, who's in charge?" Jacob asked.

"No one's in charge. Everyone's in charge of their own security."

Jacob finished wrapping the criminal's ankles together with the tape and looked around. "Well, whoever was in charge of security in this building failed miserably."

"That's an understatement," Regan agreed.

Jacob moved along the prostrate body and patted him down. He felt a bulge in the man's inner jacket pocket—a wallet.

Jacob pulled the wallet out and asked, "Who the hell would bring a wallet to a hit?"

Regan shook her head as she looked intently at the wallet. The wallet contained a heavy brass badge with a three-dimensional eagle design at the top and a small frieze design of a fist holding a hammer in the middle. Below the eagle, a gold font read "Special Officer" set on a blue background and around the middle it read "Keynes Aegis."

"What is it?" Regan asked.

"Security badge for Keynes Aegis. It's one of the big security firms here."

"A *private* security firm?"

"Yeah," Jacob said pensively.

There was no other identification or money in the wallet. Jacob put the wallet in his pocket and continued his pat-down but found nothing.

"We need to get out of here," he said.

"Where?"

Jacob stood and looked Regan in the eyes. "Arun Kula."

Regan shook her head. "Arun Kula? The hotshot businessman? Isn't he one of Gall's buddies?"

"No, no. Kula is of a different breed, Regan. He's our guy."

Regan turned away with a hum of uncertainty. "No, we need to get you into the hands of the FBI or something."

Jacob shook his head. "No, trust me. Arun Kula's our guy. We'll be safe with him."

Regan raised the gun in the air. "We'll make sure of it."

Jacob's eyes bulged.

"I need to get dressed, then we'll leave." She turned toward the bedroom but Jacob pulled her back by her hand. "Wait." He brought her body towards his and firmly kissed her lips. "Thanks for saving my life."

Regan smiled. "Any time."

Twenty-Eight

Regan Matson came out of the bedroom dressed in tight blue jeans and a dark blue sweatshirt she had come in and turned toward Jacob Tanner's apartment door. "You ready?"

Jacob was slow to answer. "Yeah."

"Wait. What if there are more like him out there?" She pointed at the unconscious man, bound at his wrists and ankles with duct tape and lying on Jacob's floor twenty feet behind them.

"Right. They may be looking for us," Jacob said.

"Do you have a fire escape or something?"

Jacob nodded then turned 180 degrees to the windows on the opposite side of the apartment. Through the translucent window coverings, the iron skeleton of a fire escape revealed itself in the dusk light. Jacob took Regan's hand and ran to the window, opened it, and climbed out onto the platform. Regan followed suit and in the process waved around the Beretta handgun, startling Jacob.

"You want me to handle the piece?" Jacob asked.

Regan smiled confidently. "Daddy made me take two months of firearms training in Montana when I was a kid. I think I can handle it."

"Wow." Jacob raised his eyebrows. "Next you're going to tell me that you're a CIA operative or something instead of a journalist."

"Well, I do moonlight as a ninja sometimes." Regan smiled and headed down the fire escape stairs.

Jacob shook his head not knowing what to believe any more and followed Regan down six flights of stairs then down the ladder to the sidewalk surface below. When he landed on the concrete he looked in the

direction of the front of his apartment building and noticed a clean-cut man in a suit leaning on a car and smoking a cigarette.

"Let's go," Regan said and pulled Jacob's hand in the opposite direction.

"Right, the Archon Building." Jacob said hurriedly.

Jacob looked back and made eye contact with the smoker, who spotted him, flicked his cigarette onto the street and ran around to the driver's side of his car.

"Uh," Jacob blurted, "do you know a short cut by any chance? We're about to have company."

Regan looked back to see the man's car screech around the corner and speed toward them.

"Shit!" she shouted.

She and Jacob picked up their pace but the man's car was soon even with them. The car's passenger-side window lowered and Jacob saw a swarthy, dark-skinned, European-looking driver staring at him. While trying to keep an eye on the road, the driver reached into his suit jacket and pulled out a handgun.

"Gun!" Jacob yelled and Regan immediately turned down an alley yanking Jacob's arm to follow her. The car slowed down and stopped 20 feet past the alley but a car behind him prevented the driver from backing up. The man threw the car into park and jumped out to the sounds of honking by other drivers. He ran around his car and into the alleyway but there was no sign of his prey.

The man slowed up his run and inched forward through the alley. He scanned the area around him, figuring it was unlikely the couple had reached the other side so quickly and he calculated the few places they could have taken refuge. Quieting his steps and breathing, the pursuer made his way to the dumpster. With a brief pause and a deep breath, he lunged to the other side, holding his gun out in front. Startled by the absence of his victims he quickly turned and scanned the alley once again. He inched his way to a large pipe and then on to a brick protru-

sion, rounding each object, leading with his gun, expecting to find his prey. They had disappeared.

All the man heard was a thump before he blacked out. Jacob Tanner had been hiding in a recess on a nearby building's fire escape and after the assailant walked by below, he jumped down putting the force of his entire body weight into a fist blow to the man's skull.

The man collapsed to the ground flinging his gun down the alley and Jacob landed awkwardly on his feet.

"Shit!" Jacob yelled out in agony. "I think I just ruptured my spleen!"

Regan Matson lowered the ladder of the fire escape and joined Jacob on the ground. "You'd make a pretty good spy yourself, Mr. CEO."

Jacob shook his head as he went to collect the man's gun. "Not sure I'd pass their physical. I've just about shit my pants seven times in the last thirty minutes."

* * *

Jacob and Regan hurried through the glass doors of the newly constructed Archon Building in the city center of Ur. Suddenly a high-pitched alarm signal went off and flashing lights flooded the area. A security guard ran to the couple with a pistol trained at Jacob's chest and yelled, "Freeze!"

Jacob and Regan stood still and raised their hands slowly as another security guard ran to join the first. We must have passed through a metal detector, Jacob figured, and that set off the alarm.

"Jacob Tanner?" the second guard demanded from Jacob.

"Yes?" Jacob complied. "How did you—?"

"And Regan Masden?" the same guard projected toward Regan.

Jacob looked at Regan. "Masden? Not Matson?"

Regan peeked over to Jacob, trying to keep an eye on the guard. "Yeah, sorry. Another fib."

The second security guard patted Jacob down and from his jacket pocket pulled the gun he had taken from his assailant just minutes before.

He then patted Regan down and pulled the Beretta with suppressor from her sweatshirt pocket.

"We know everything folks. We have video of everything," the second security guard said securing the weapons.

"So, you know what happened? That they were trying to kill us!" Jacob blurted his questions.

"Yes sir. Mr. Kula would like to see you."

"What a coincidence," Regan said with a smirk, "because we'd sure like to have a few words with him."

"Follow me," the first guard said turning toward the elevators.

Jacob and Regan followed the guard and Jacob asked the second guard, "So, did you have metal detectors in the doors? Is that how you knew we were armed?"

The guard shook his head. "No, it's a biometric scanning system— facial recognition. The scan matched your ID with the two people who were involved in an incident in an alleyway six blocks away."

Jacob moved his head back and raised his eyebrows. "You have cameras back there in the alley?"

"On most roads and thoroughfares, they do, yes," the guard confirmed.

Jacob lowered his brow in confusion.

Regan asked under her breath, "Ever heard of civil liberties?"

The group walked past curious onlookers to the elevators and the guards took Jacob and Regan to Arun Kula's office on the top floor of the building.

Twenty-Nine

Arun Kula strode into the conference room like a bullet train and his calm demeanor belied his feverish quickness. He was followed by a quiet assistant. Both the founder of Ur and his assistant were expertly dressed in fine Italian suits.

There was no introduction and no small talk. Arun Kula simply began speaking in his refined English, "Mr. Tanner. Ms. Masden. We have been working with Shield Security Systems in this situation to minimize any further disturbance. The man who pulled the gun on you in the alleyway is Jonas Smalls. His record in Ur was initiated two months ago. Prior to that he resided in Philadelphia, Pennsylvania, mainly working odd jobs. It's unclear why he relocated here. He has no official employment record at this time."

"And what about the albino in Jake's apartment?" Regan blurted.

"Are you referring to the apartment in the Grand Ur Hotel?"

"That's right," Jacob replied.

"Unfortunately our security forces do not maintain jurisdiction at the Grand Ur Hotel."

"So? What does that mean?" Regan asked impatiently.

"Shield Security is not responsible for the security at that particular property and they rarely share intelligence with other security firms."

"I don't understand. A man tried to kill us there," Regan said, confused.

"Surely, you're aware of the way in which security is organized here in Ur? There is no overarching police authority here—each property owner is responsible for their own security."

"Right, so who's in charge over at the Grand Ur?" Jacob asked.

"A firm called Keynes Aegis," Kula answered.

Jacob flinched. He looked at Regan who returned the stare. He maintained his eyes on Regan but pulled out the albino's wallet from his pocket and handed it to Kula.

Arun Kula accepted the wallet, opened it up and read the badge within. "Where did you get this?"

"We found this on the first man who tried to kill us," Jacob replied. "The albino."

"There is no badge number," Kula noted. "Did he have any other identification?"

Regan and Jacob both shook their heads.

"Who runs Keynes?" Jacob asked.

"Keynes Aegis is a subsidiary of Gall Enterprises," reported Kula.

"Of course," Jacob sighed.

"Do either of you know why these men should wish to harm you?" Kula posed.

Jacob Tanner looked at Regan, who was silently observing Arun Kula, then turned to the executive himself. "Mr. Kula, I believe Martin Gall sent those goons to have me killed."

Arun Kula hesitated, then peered at Jacob. "That is a substantial accusation, sir."

"Well, after what I witnessed last night, I wouldn't put anything past that man."

"I see." Arun looked intently at Jacob and calmly stated, "Let us start at the beginning. What is this all about, sir?"

Jacob took in a deep breath to release an extraordinary amount of tension that had built up over the past hour. He collected his thoughts, then looked up to Kula. "I have evidence that one of Gall's products—a chip in the Viper phone—is making people sick with a disease called Chinese encephalitis and I think Gall intends to cover it up. I think he wants to kill me to stop me from getting the story out."

Arun Kula thought about the accusation for a moment. "Well, this is certainly something. I shall file a report with Burnett & Jones and submit a story to the local news wires immediately."

Regan spoke up, "With all due respect, Mr. Kula, this story is bigger than the local news wire. I work for the international news magazine show *Face the Facts*. We're going to run a story on that program this Sunday."

"Of course," Kula said with a nod. "You said you have evidence?"

Jacob added, "My lead scientists wrote up a report on the Viper chip and we think Gall knew about the defective product but decided to launch it anyway. We still need to break into Gall's email to get that evidence, though."

Kula opened his mouth momentarily before saying, "Sir, there is a flaw in your plan."

"What's that?" Jacob pondered aloud.

"There is only one law in this city and that is *Vulnero Nemo*, or harm no one. If you were to break into Mr. Gall's office, that would constitute harm, no?"

Jacob nodded disappointingly but Regan leaned her head toward Kula, incredulous. "You're joking right? These guys tried to *kill* me and Jacob. Gall is complicit in an epidemic that is harming thousands of people and he's trying to cover it up." Regan was flushed. "And you're worried about us stealing a measly email?"

"Well, such an act would constitute a violation of property rights and theft," Kula explained.

"Yeah," Regan confirmed as if to say, "So what?"

"That would be harm, Ms. Masden. It would be logically contradictory and, as a result, morally repugnant to propose to help one group of people by harming others." Kula asked calmly.

"If you can save thousands of people by copying a measly little email, that is not morally repugnant!" Regan protested.

"I think you'll find that your style of rationalization has led to all of the crime, war, and destruction throughout history. No one plans on

doing harm for harm's sake. It is always done with a greater good in mind. What you are defending, Ms. Masden, is the concept of necessary evil, which does not surprise me considering your father."

"My father?" Regan blurted. Jacob squinted at Regan at the mention of her father.

"Let's leave him out of it, okay?"

Kula continued, "Very well. It appears that *you* support the concept of necessary evils. I, on the other hand, do not."

"With all due respect, Mr. Kula," Regan said, shaking her head, "you're spouting off a bunch of philosophic mumbo jumbo and we don't really have time for philosophy right now. We need to stop an epidemic."

"Yes, time is of the essence, indeed," Kula agreed. "Still, you entered Ur under the agreement of *Vulnero Nemo* and I expect you to hold to it."

"What and just sit by while Gall kills thousands?" Regan was furious.

"Of course not, miss," Kula denied. "But you must work within the concurrent system of *Vulnero Nemo* to achieve your ends."

Jacob nodded his head in agreement but Regan contested Kula's command. "But Mr. Kula, your system is broken. There was a man in Jake's apartment attempting to put a bullet into his skull! Does that fall into your system of *Vulnero Nemo*? There are people running around with guns trying to kill us in *your* city. Jake wouldn't be here right now if I didn't knock that guy out who was trying to shoot him. What? Do you think I should have *let* the guy shoot Jake?"

"Certainly not miss," Kula denied again. "If you are in immediate danger, the use of force in self defense is most certainly warranted."

"Well, call this self defense, then," Regan complained.

"Unfortunately, theft of any kind cannot be realistically considered self defense. You must trust in the system, miss. Under *Vulnero Nemo*, Ur has the lowest crime rate of any city of its size and we're proud to boast that there have been no murders within our borders. I see that record is still alive."

Regan looked away. "Barely," she scoffed.

"Nonetheless," Kula continued, "it remains the case. I do not wish to do nothing. We have already filed reports with Burnett & Jones regarding the safety and corruption concerns with Keynes Aegis, which will dramatically reduce confidence in their products, and we've ensured Jonas Smalls will be excluded from nearly every property under the Shield Security Systems jurisdiction, including all roads."

Jacob interjected, "Look, Mr. Kula, I believe in Ur. I believe in what you're doing here but we need your help. We need your help to stop Gall and save thousands of lives. Tells us what we can do."

Kula nodded. "Certainly, you should pursue the story on Ms. Masden's news magazine program but I should expect that you also pursue legal recourse as well."

"Legal recourse? How?" Jacob inquired.

"You should open a case in the *dikasteria*—the judicial system here in Ur."

"Great, you want us to *sue* a mass murderer?" Regan asked with more than a hint of mockery.

"But of course. The judicial system here in Ur is remarkably efficient and effective. I will put you in contact with a legal firm that will assist you on a pro bono basis if you'd like."

"You're not going to sic the dogs on them?" Regan asked, incredulous.

"I'm not sure I understand your meaning, Ms. Masden," Kula said.

"Are you going to go get Gall? Arrest him with your security forces?"

"Until Mr. Gall is convicted of a crime in a court of law, it would be a crime to even attempt such an enterprise. If you are concerned about security, you are both free to stay here in my building until the trial is finished. I can have you set up in apartments if you'd like." Kula noticed some apprehension still on Regan's face. "I assure you that you will be perfectly safe within this building under the umbrella of the Shield Security Services—they are unparalleled."

"People are dying and you're offering us a lawyer and a hotel room?" Regan said, incredulous.

Kula analyzed Regan's face for a tense moment, then spoke, "Would you like me to set you up with rooms?"

Jacob turned to Kula. "Yes, thank you Mr. Kula, that is more than generous of you. We'll take you up on your offer."

"Very well. I'll have my assistant set you up immediately."

With that, Arun Kula turned and walked out of the conference room, leaving Jacob and Regan staring at each other with uncertainty.

* * *

Regan Masden and Jacob Tanner walked toward the exit under a massive colored glass sculpture, suspended under the tall ceiling of the Archon Building lobby. It was a stunning work of art, but their attention was elsewhere.

"Please tell me you're beginning to see my side on this," Regan, who had changed into a simple, flowing green dress and heels, said. "Without laws, people like Gall will do whatever it takes to increase their wealth. They will steal, cheat, and murder their way to more money. They turn into animals."

"No, don't you see? Sure, there are evil people here—there are evil people everywhere. But that's why they have this *dikasteria*, the court. It will allow us to tame the animals."

Regan shook her head. "Jake you don't know Gall. He's not going to let a little court system get in the way of billions."

"Look," Jacob said intensely, "I see your point, but I believe in what Kula is doing here and I know he's right when he says we can beat Gall in court. We just have to let the system work."

"That's great, Jacob, but I'm not going to sit around and wait for the *system* to kick in. You may feel fine staying locked up in this building and waiting while some half-baked judicial system slaps Gall on the wrist, but I'm not. I'm going to go get this story."

Jacob put his arms around Regan and pulled her close to his frame. "Don't do this. It's too dangerous."

"I'll be fine."

"Well, if you're going, let me go with you," Jacob said, unsure of himself.

"Look, Jacob Tanner, those goons are trying to kill *you*, not me. Gall has no idea I'm with you and I'm the only one that can get into his office. I need to do this alone."

Jacob shook his head and looked away. "You're a stubborn one."

"Okay, so it's the D-to-A chip by Vizor and you're saying Gall signed off on it? What am I looking for in an email? Who would he have approved this with?"

"Uh," Jacob put his right hand to his forehead and squinted, trying to remember what the man had told him at the Wilberforce statue. "I think his name was Daniels—the president of Vizor Electronics."

"Okay, got it." She smiled as she slowed her pace before they got to the doors leading into the night's darkness. "Wish me luck!"

Jacob nodded. "Hey—" he grasped Regan and brought her back to him. "What was that about when Kula mentioned your father? What did he mean?"

Regan shook her head. "Oh it was nothing."

Jacob lowered his head. "Regan, he acted like he knew your father."

"No, he doesn't know my father. I'll tell you later—okay? Wish me luck."

"Be safe."

Regan nodded and kissed Jacob firmly and compassionately on his lips, then turned and walked out of the lobby glass doors into the evening air.

In the Forest of Cedar, where Humbaba dwells,
Let us frighten him in his lair!
Let us slay him so that his power is no more!
Let me start out, I will cut down the cedar,
I will establish forever a name eternal!

Thirty

The doors to the elevator parted and Regan Masden stepped into Martin Gall's dim front office. Through a window adjacent to Gall's door, she saw that the lights in his office were off. The entire office appeared to be completely empty and a check on the office door handle confirmed as much. It was locked.

Some businessman! Regan mocked to herself. Who goes home before midnight?

She surveyed Gall's assistant's desk. Perhaps there is a key in her desk? Regan sat down in the assistant's chair and moved her hands over the empty leather desk blotter. Her eyes darted to the desk drawers, which she hurriedly opened and sorted through.

Regan sifted through papers in the filing section of the drawers but nothing looked worthwhile. She closed the drawers and sat back in the chair.

Without warning, Regan heard the door handle to Gall's office depress and the door creeped opened. Regan's bulging eyes honed in on the person exiting Gall's office—a beefy security guard who was leaving.

"Jermaine!" Regan yelled. "Thank God!"

Jermaine eased out of the door and fluidly locked it behind him, then turned to Regan. "What were you doing in Martin's office?" she asked in a friendly but overtly suspicious tone.

"Just doing my rounds, sweetheart. What are *you* doin' here? You know Mr. Gall ain't here."

"I know. I wanted to surprise him," she said sauntering over to Jermaine.

"Oh yeah?"

"Yeah, it's kind of a secret. Can you let me in?"

Jermaine stood straight and looked down at Regan who had put on a seductive air. "What you mean? Let you in the *office*?" He gestured to Gall's door.

Regan nodded. "It's really important," she said dragging her right index finger down the lapel of Jermaine's jacket.

"Girl, you know I can't do that," he said in a matter of fact manner.

"Really?" Regan frowned. "Not just this once?"

"I'm sorry. You have to come back in the morning."

Regan pouted and looked up at Jermaine with her best puppy dog eyes.

"That shit ain't gonna fly, girl," Jermaine said shaking his head.

Regan nodded. "Okay," you want to play hardball? You know what I do right?"

"What you do?"

"Yeah, for Mr. Gall?"

Jermaine shrugged. "Yeah, you a ho."

"Ah!" Regan yelped and playfully slapped Jermaine on the chest.

"What? You a ho," Jermaine repeated. "I ain't judgin.'"

"Fine. Listen, if you let me in," Regan said as if telling Jermaine a secret, "I'll give you a freebie."

Jermaine rolled his eyes. "You crazy."

Regan could see she was getting to him. "I'm serious," I just need five minutes in there, that's it."

"Funny, 'cause that's all I need for my freebie." Jermaine laughed at his self-deprecation. "So when do I get this . . . freebie?"

"Not now, I need to have the place to myself to get ready for the surprise. You can have it Saturday night. How does that sound?"

Jermaine squinted his eyes and curled his lips. "You pulling my leg?"

"Well, I've always had a thing for big strong men," Regan said moving her hand over Jermaine's chest.

"You know I could get fired?" Jermaine asked rhetorically, shaking his head. He turned to the door and pulled out his key chain complete with thirty keys.

"You're the best, Jermaine. You're not going to be sorry!"

"Sure I'm not," Jermaine called her bluff as he opened the door to Gall's office. "Five minutes then I'm pulling you out of there."

"Perfect!" Regan jumped up and kissed Jermaine on the cheek before bouncing into the office and closing the door behind her.

She ran to Gall's computer terminal and slapped the space bar on the desktop computer to awake it from sleep mode. The screen illuminated but Regan was distraught to find a text box with a flashing cursor in it. The system required a password.

Hunched over Gall's computer terminal, Regan typed, "password1," in the text box and hit enter. The monitor shook off the attempt and emptied the text box to allow for another try. She began typing in everything she could think of that a man like Martin Gall would use as a password, "Gall," "MartinGall," "Gall#1," "Imthebest," and the system rejected them all.

Regan let out a grunt of frustration and shook her hands in the air. She looked up to help her think, then back at the computer terminal. What's the password, she thought. The magic word? She smiled and typed in, "money," then hit enter.

She was in.

The background changed to an image of gold bullion and icons began popping up on the screen. She clicked the "email" icon, which launched the system's email application. From the looks of the many recent emails that appeared after the application loaded, it appeared that what she was looking at was Gall's main account.

She typed, "Daniels," in the search box and hit enter.

A list of emails popped up. Regan scanned the email titles. None looked promising. She typed, "D-to-A" in the text box and hit enter again. Only a few emails loaded based on that query and one was from Billy Daniels of Vizor Electronics.

She clicked on it and scanned the email quickly. At the top of the email chain, Regan read, ". . . continue with production . . . ," and ". . . costs outweigh potential risks . . . ." Below in the email chain, she caught, ". . . problem with the D-to-A chip . . . ," ". . . high levels of near-gamma-ray frequency . . . ," and ". . . to immediately cease production on these chips or risk serious damage to users." It was exactly what she needed.

Startling her, Regan heard a ding from the elevator doors through Gall's office door.

Martin Gall was blabbering on his cell as he stepped out of the elevator and approached the door to his office. "Don't give me that Leslie. I don't want excuses, damn it!"

Inside Gall's office, Regan scrambled. "Shit!" she whispered. She quickly forwarded the email to her work address and waved her hands in the air impotently as the computer slowly processed the forward accompanied by a rotating hourglass icon.

Martin Gall pulled out his keys from his pants pocket and slurred, "What did I say, Leslie? I know he can get the job! But can he do the job?" Gall's keys slipped out of his hand and hit the floor causing him to swear violently.

Regan acknowledged the sent email, then closed the program and put the computer in sleep mode. She danced around nervously waving her hands in the air. She spotted a leather whip hanging on a nearby wall with a gold plaque situated underneath and deflated at the thought of what she had to do.

Outside, Gall picked up his keys, fumbled for the right one, and put the office key in the slot.

"Mr. Gall," the deep voice called out. It was the security guard Jermaine, who had appeared behind Gall. The executive turned around to see Jermaine walking toward him. "How was the meeting sir?" Jermaine asked casually.

"I killed it, as usual," Gall said wryly.

"Well, congratulations, sir."

Gall scrunched his face in confusion as opposed to gratitude and opened the door to his office.

Inside, he was startled to find the elegant nude shape of Regan Matson resting on his chair with her legs crossed on his desk. The even, warm tone of Regan's flesh was evident in the dim moonlight that poured onto her body through the large window behind her. Her well-formed breasts sat perfectly aligned on her chest and separated by the dark, meandering leather whip, which was wrapped around Regan's body in sensual curves.

Gall coughed. "Regan! Damn. I wasn't expecting you . . . so soon."

"I wanted to go above and beyond the call of duty."

Gall let a smile creep over his face as he closed his office door behind him. "I don't know if I deserve it," he said slowly. "I've been a very bad man."

Regan gripped the whip handle, which was resting on her pelvis and returned the smile. "Yes, you have."

Thirty-One

Gary Javert was like a brainless authoritarian, the young assistant Nicholas Debbs thought to himself. Why did he want him to report like this every day like a little lap dog and why did he go along with it? Nicholas knocked on Gary Javert's office door at the FDA headquarters in Silver Spring, Maryland, early the next morning.

"You're late," Javert snapped. He was eating a bagel with cream cheese and spoke through a mouthful of half-chewed goo. "Come in."

Nicholas shrugged as he walked into the cold office. "There was a ten-car pileup on the Beltway. Traffic was backed up for miles." He stared blankly into the air in front of him. "I think there were fatalities."

"We don't have time, Mr. Debbs," Javert explained between chews. "Updates, I want updates."

Nicholas looked at a legal pad of paper in his hand, which contained his notes and began slowly, "Well, first and foremost, the Senate HELP committee is set to have a hearing on extending the HEAL America Act to Ur. That's in two weeks."

"Yes, yes, very nice. Have they requested me?"

"Well, they would be remiss if they failed to get testimony from such a prominent figure in the FDA. I'm sure your pending promotion may be a factor."

"I am simply a humble public servant," Javert said with a faux humility. "And what of the generic version of Symbalia?"

"Yes, anaxavir. They will be shipping later this week."

"Oh, very cool. What more?" Javert asked through another mouthful.

Nicholas frowned. "Well, I'm holding in my hands a warrant for the arrest of one Jacob Tanner of Bentonville, Arkansas."

A smile crept over Gary Javert's face as he slowed his chewing. With a loud swallow of food, Javert flapped his hand toward Nicholas to bring him closer. He took the piece of paper from Nicholas's hand and quickly surveyed it. "Ah," he let out, "yes, yes . . . misappropriation of federal funds . . . ." After a brief analysis, Javert nodded. "This is good. This is very good."

"Of course, there is a problem," Nicholas started to clarify.

"Oh?"

"OCI has the authority to arrest Tanner with this warrant, but our best intel has it that he currently resides in the special administrative zone of Ur, Texas."

"So, what? Let's go get the scoundrel!"

"Well, theoretically, we could go in after him, but we would need warrants for each of the properties that OCI entered."

Javert squinted his eyes. "Come again?"

What was the use of conveying all this information? Nicholas wondered silently. Why was this slob in any position to order him around? "Well, there is no federal or state or even municipal land in Ur. Even the roads there are privately owned, so we have no authority to even drive in Ur without permission or a warrant. He is, for all intents and purposes, untouchable."

"What?" Javert coughed. "That's certifiably absurd. How uncool— what kind of confounded sociopath devised a system like that?"

Nicholas huffed. "Sir, that's the agreement according to Title nine-thirty-four 'A,' which Congress approved three years ago."

"That is unacceptable—what do they mean we have no authority?"

"That is the law, sir, our hands are tied."

Javert nodded and thought about the situation, letting his eyes wander around his desk. "Well," he hummed, "that could take a year!" He lifted his left hand almost as surrender.

"It's not officially a lost cause, however," Nicholas offered.

"What do you have in mind?"

"We could lure him out of Ur."

Javert squinted and peered at his assistant. He hummed, "And how would we accomplish such an act?"

"We could initiate some sort of business deal—"

Without allowing time to consider Nicholas's suggestion, Javert interrupted, "No, it'll never work." And after some thought, he added, "Well, we could talk to family members, friends. Get them to talk some reason into him."

Debbs pursed his lips and nodded.

Javert let a grin creep over his face. "Like the old honey trap!"

"Yes, exactly. Except it's nothing like a honey trap," Nicholas clarified.

"Good," Javert said looking up to Nicholas. "Look up family members, friends down there. Get them on the phone and let's try to work something out. The sooner the better."

"Right. I'll have Gloria get on it," Nicholas said.

"No," Javert contradicted his assistant. "I want you on this."

Nicholas shrugged his lips and dryly said, "Whatever you say." He turned around to leave Javert's office.

"Little brat," Javert said under his breath then turned back to his unfinished bagel.

* * *

Jacob Tanner looked nervously at his cell phone that was sitting on the office desk in front of him. There were no messages and no missed calls. The phone read "7:15 AM."

"Are you late for something?" the brunette asked, slightly miffed. She wore a form-fitting, gray skirt suit with a sheer white blouse underneath. Her eyes were difficult to make out past the reflection on her Gucci eyeglasses, but Jacob could tell they were cold and business-like. Her hair was pulled back tightly and held up with two simple metal hairpins at

neatly arranged angles. Everything about her was structured and neat. Her office and desk followed suit without one paper out of place.

"No," Jacob said with a shake of his head. "Sorry, I'm just waiting for an important call."

"Should we reschedule?"

"No, Anne. Let's continue."

"Look Mr. Tanner, I may have a vagina, but I do deserve your respect and full attention."

Jacob widened his eyes and looked stunned. "I didn't . . . ," he said stymied.

"Do I have your full attention?"

Jacob smiled. "Yes, yes, of course."

"Here's the deal Mr. Tanner," Anne Gold said dropping a stack of papers on her desk. "You can sue Gall Enterprises for harming your sister with the D-to-A electronic device. You can also sue as part of a class action against Gall for endangering the public. But you should be forewarned, the legal system works a bit different here than on the outside, I'm not sure if you're familiar." She looked to Jacob for confirmation.

Jacob shook his head. "No, I'm not familiar."

The attorney sat back in her chair and released the papers in her hands. "Okay, here's the executive summary. The judicial system in Ur is called the *dikasteria*. It's modeled after the one in Ancient Athens in which all citizens participated as judges, though here, participation is completely voluntary. There are currently 5,200 judges in the system. When someone files a suit with the *dikasteria*, the case is randomly assigned to a single judge from the list of all judges. The selected judge has the option to hear the case, dismiss it, or recuse himself from the case. If he accepts, the case will go to trial and the judge will decide and assign damages."

"How long does that take?"

"It's all very quick—a few days to a week."

"That's it? And then we have a decision?"

"Correct. One thing, however, the *dikasteria* is a loser pays model—"

"A what?"

"You might have heard of it called the English rule, but really, it's the policy for most of the world outside of the United States."

"Okay. How does it work?"

"Loser pays means the losing parties in the litigation must reimburse the winner's legal costs including attorney fees. The idea is meant to avoid low-merit lawsuits like the ones that are so common throughout the rest of the country."

"Oh I'm familiar with low-merit lawsuits. Last year I won a case against my company by some scam-artist who claimed Amelior made him sick. He wanted 90 million. I won the case but that was after $100,000 in legal fees."

"How unfortunate," Anne said without a hint of compassion. "If that case was presented here, the plaintiff would have had to pay your fees."

"Gotcha," Jacob said.

"This is a very important point, Mr. Tanner, because if I decide to represent you on a pro bono basis, you will still be responsible for the damages and legal fees should your case lose."

Jacob nodded. "I understand. Is there any recourse if we lose? Can we appeal?"

"Yes. If your case loses, you can file for appeal, which will be sent back to the *dikasteria*. On first appeal, three judges will be assigned to decide the case and there would be a retrial. With each successive appeal, the number of judges increases and, theoretically, so does the accuracy of the judgment. But of course, the more appeals a case sees, the higher the stakes are with regard to damages and legal fees. The longer a case goes through appeals, the greater the penalty and payout."

"What are we talking about here?"

"Legal fees?"

"Yes," Jacob confirmed.

"My last case netted $775,000 in legal fees. And that was on top of the damages awarded."

Jacob's eyes bulged and he tilted his head back. "Shit."

"Would you like to proceed, then, Mr. Tanner?"

Jacob thought about it. He took a deep breath and exhaled audibly. "I don't know."

"Why, Mr. Tanner? Do you have reservations about me as counsel?"

"No, no it's not that—"

"Look, I'm going to make myself clear. I'm not taking you on as pro bono work because I'm not qualified to charge for my services or anything of the sort. My acceptance of your case is on a strictly professional basis and my ability to litigate is far superior to any associate at this firm and even to several of the partners."

Jacob breathed in deeply. "Anne, can I be honest with you?"

Anne was not impressed by the question. She drooped her eyelids while maintaining a stare and did not respond.

"I have collateral—equipment for my company, which is worth a quite a bit, but I'm up to my eyeballs in debt right now to pay for it. And this lawsuit will hopefully stop a dangerous man who is hurting thousands of people, but it will also have the effect of completely eliminating demand for my product. Either way, I'm going to be broke after this trial. I can't afford to pay for this lawsuit. I can't afford to lose." Jacob shook his head.

"Well, we all have our problems now don't we?" Anne asked dryly.

A grimace came over Jacob's face. "Just hypothetically speaking, what would happen if we were to lose and couldn't pay?"

Anne averted her eyes as she considered the question. "Well, there is precedence. Some non-profits have been established to help losers in such cases. Otherwise you can consider payment options or a work-settlement."

Jacob raised his eyebrows.

"Look, Mr. Tanner. How much does this trial mean to you?"

Jacob breathed in heavily, then exhaled. "Anne, this trial means everything to me. I believe in freedom—I believe in this city."

"What you're willing to stake on this claim?" Anne rephrased.

"I'm willing to stake my life on this."

"Well, then. We'll have to make sure not to lose, I guess," Anne said in a mocking tone.

* * *

Jacob was sitting on his bed in the furnished apartment that Arun Kula had arranged for him and held the receiver of a landline phone to his ear.

"No, Marge, I can't come in to the office," he said.

"Did you hear, Mr. Tanner?" Marge Sorenson asked excitedly. "They nullified our patent and they released a generic version of Symbalia."

Jacob deflated. "No I hadn't heard that." He brought his right hand up to rub his forehead. "When it rains it pours!"

"What's that?"

"Nothing."

"No one can figure out why they did that, Mr. Tanner."

"It's because we're not under the FDA's thumb anymore Marge, that's why."

"I don't get it, Mr. Tanner."

"Sorry, but I really can't explain right now, Marge" Jacob stated tersely. "Look, can you just please send those files to me?"

"I already did," Marge Sorenson said, defending herself. "They should be to you by now."

Jacob tapped on his new phone's screen and navigated to the native email application. It loaded several new messages, the first one being from Marge Sorenson. Jacob tapped on the email and then on the attachment entitled "Effects of Radiation by Vizor D-to-A Chip on the Human Nervous System."

The attachment opened to a report of the findings by the Axelaris laboratory describing the causal link between the D-to-A chip in Viper phones and Chinese encephalitis. Jacob pressed his lips together in a slight smile.

"Mr. Tanner? Are you there?"

"Yes, Marge. I got your email. Thank you. Listen, you said you couldn't find Marc Johnson?"

"No, Mr. Tanner. I haven't seen Mr. Johnson since last week."

Jacob frowned and hummed.

"Tina said she saw Mr. Johnson talking to a pretty little Latina girl the last Wednesday on his lunch break and we think he might have skipped along down to some cabana on the south of the Gulf of Mexico." Marge giggled.

"But you haven't heard from him at all?"

"Nope."

"That's very strange, don't you think? I've tried his cell phone, probably five times."

"I can try Mr. Johnson's apartment."

"Could you?" Jacob asked.

"No problem. You want to tell me what this is all about?" Marge inquired.

"Marge, I'm sorry. It's really better if you didn't know."

Jacob heard a hum on the other line. "I sure hope you know what you're doin' Mr. Tanner."

"Me too, Marge. Me too. Talk to you later."

"Okay. Bye now."

Jacob ended the call and checked the time on his phone. It was 9:15 PM. Still no missed calls and no messages. He shook his head and whispered, "God, just let her be okay."

Thirty-Two

Lying down, Jacob tapped the screen on his phone. It displayed the time, "3:29 AM," in bold white figures on a colorful background. The bright numbers burned his tired, bloodshot eyes, but he couldn't sleep. Where the hell was she? he thought.

Like a lightning bolt, reverberations from a rap on the apartment door filled the air. Jacob jumped in his bed and threw his covers off. He ran to the door and peered through the peephole. He saw Regan Masden waiting outside of his door, her head turned to her right. She reached up to knock the door again, but Jacob unlocked and opened it.

"Thank God. I was so worried about you." Jacob reached out to embrace Regan, who was caught off guard by Jacob's extended arms. She obliged him with a quick embrace, but didn't look at him.

"Did you get the report on the D-to-A chip from your scientist?" She asked abruptly.

Jacob looked at Regan intensely as she walked past him into the living area of his apartment.

"Regan, what happened? Where have you been? I thought they had taken you hostage or . . . worse."

"I was working on the story," Regan said nonchalantly. "So, did you get the files?"

Jacob nodded. "I sent them to your email."

"Good. We're going to need them."

"So, you're all right? Everything's fine?"

Regan lifted her shoulders and extended her hands as if to push Jacob away. "Will you quit with all this third degree? It's kind of annoying."

Jacob turned his head and squinted at Regan. "Did I miss something here? What's going on?"

Regan averted his gaze. "No, it's just that *you're* acting like we're married or something. We're not married."

Jacob nodded and pursed his lips. "Well, I apologize for being concerned that someone I care about may have been murdered!"

"Oh, come on, big boy, I was *working!*"

Jacob rolled his eyes and lifted his hands toward Regan. "That's right, you were working. So, did you see Gall while you were *working*?"

Regan squinted her eyes at Jacob. "As a matter of fact, I did."

Jacob exhaled through his nose and he nodded. "Regan, you can't just run off like that without telling anyone where you went."

"Hey, I'm a big girl. I can take care of myself."

"But you can't just do whatever you want."

"Oh no?" Regan looked at Jacob amused. "Whatever happened to live free or die, huh? I thought you were all about individual freedom."

Jacob released some of his intensity and swallowed before responding. "Well, when other people are involved, you have to consider them too."

"Jesus, you sound like a girl," Regan said turning away from Jacob. "If you want to know something, why don't you just ask me?"

Jacob nodded. "All right. Did you sleep with him?"

"Let's just say, I got the job done. I got the story."

"Did you sleep with him?"

"You know what? This is getting a little weird. I don't know what you think this is between us, but you're acting way too possessive. I just met you."

Jacob pulled closer to Regan and took her in his arms. "Regan, I see a fire in you that I haven't seen in anyone else I've met and I know you see something in me. We can do this together—we can bring down Gall and save thousands of lives. I just want you to tell me what happened." Jacob's intense stare softened Regan's cold demeanor. She tilted her head and made a subtle smile. "Did you sleep with him?"

Suddenly, Regan hardened again. She withdrew from Jacob's arms and averted Jacob's stare. "I can do what I want, Jake."

Jacob curled his lips and gave Regan a dull look. "Right."

"Don't give me that, Jake. It's not that big of a deal."

"Not that big of a deal?" Jacob shouted. "Regan, you're . . . you're a whore! No, you're worse. Whores do it so that they can eat. You do it for . . . for a freaking story!"

Regan pursed her lips and flared her nostrils as she stared down Jacob, who immediately scrunched his face and shut his eyes.

"I'm sorry—" he blurted opening his eyes.

Regan pushed past Jacob. "Fuck you. I'm leaving."

"I didn't mean that. I'm sorry."

"You can watch the story on *Facts* in two days," she said waving her right hand carelessly in the air as she stopped toward the door. "Good luck with your stupid little lawsuit," she mocked, flinging her hand in the air.

"Regan, don't do this," Jacob called after her but before he could stop her, she had escaped around the front door and slammed it shut.

After a moment of anxious pacing in the apartment, Jacob burst through the door and ran down the hall to the elevators. She was nowhere to be seen. Jacob frantically punched the elevator down button repetitively and looked up at the floor indicator. He heard a ding behind him and rushed on to the elevator.

A minute later, Jacob was rushing though the vacant lobby toward a fleeing Regan Masden.

"Regan, wait!"

She kept walking and pushed through the glass doors of the building.

Jacob ran toward the glass and suddenly realized he was wearing only a white T-shirt and white boxer shorts. A security guard stationed to the side of all the doors stood up from his stool and eyed Jacob with suspicion.

Jacob followed Regan outside and called again, "Regan, wait!"

She didn't stop. "You better go back inside CEO. There are dangerous people out here trying to kill you."

Jacob looked around. The entire area was empty and silent aside from a sprinkler that fed nearby landscaping. Regan's heels echoed through the business park's thick early morning air. Jacob ran in front of a marching Regan and gently held her from walking further.

"You know what?" She asked rhetorically. "Maybe this is better. People like you and me shouldn't mingle. It's bad for the gene pool or something."

"Look, Regan. I need you . . . for this lawsuit."

Regan looked at Jacob with a raised eyebrow. "You need me for the *lawsuit*?"

"Yeah. I need you. And you need me for the story. Why are you doing this? We can help each other."

"Listen, I don't need you. I don't need anyone. I'm going to go finish my story . . . by myself. And you can finish your lawsuit by *yourself*. Now, you need to go back inside before those crazy people come after you and hurt you. We need you living so that you can keep producing drugs . . . and saving lives." Regan tried to produce a smile but her wrinkled brow expressed worry. She reached her arms around Jacob and embraced him. "Good bye," she said and then walked past Jacob without another word.

Jacob stood in the middle of the empty office park and watched Regan Masden walk into empty darkness.

Thirty-Three

Michelle Torres walked off the set of the *Headlines Now* news program in a hurry. She had received an urgent call from her friend before she had gone on air, but had no time to answer. She was worried that something had happened. Was she okay? Michelle wondered.

She rushed through the studio hall toward the green room. The show's producer, Sam Barnes, walked into Michelle's path and gave her a sarcastic grin and nod. "Lookin' good up there, Torres."

"Shut the fuck up Sam," Michelle replied tersely, not looking at her superior and walking around him.

Sam Barnes laughed off the antagonism and winked at his suddenly successful on-air talent as if he was fine with her verbal abuse.

Michelle threw open the door to the green room and immediately tore into her purse, which contained her phone. She navigated to her friend's contact page and tapped "CALL." As the phone rang, Michelle sprawled out on a firm, squared sofa nearby.

"Michelle," the voice on the other end of the line exclaimed.

"Regan, girl. What's up? You scared me with your message." Michelle asked in a concerned tone.

"I've got something working down here in Texas."

"A story?" Michelle exhaled and deflated, rolling her eyes. "Shit girl, I thought you were in danger or something. What are you on to? The prostitution ring?"

"It's bigger than the call girl story, Michelle, really big."

"Well they say everything in Texas is bigger," Michelle added.

"I'm putting together a story for *Facts* right now and I want to hand it to you before it breaks. I know you're anchor now and I want you to

mention it on *Headlines* the same time we break it on *Facts* tomorrow evening."

"What is this about?"

"Well, you've been reporting on the CE epidemic right?"

"Chinese encephalitis?" Michelle asked.

"Yes. That's the one. Well, people are saying that mosquitoes are causing the disease, but that's all wrong. That's not what's causing CE at all."

"Fuck, Regan. What is it?"

"Look you have to keep this on the down low until we break it."

"Of course . . . ."

"Okay, you know those super high-tech phones that came out a few years back, Viper?"

"Yes . . . ," Michelle said with an inflection as if it was a question.

"A chip in the Viper phones is releasing an unprecedented amount of radiation. That's leading to the deterioration of the myelin sheath in the nervous system. It's the phone that's causing CE."

"Oh my God, Regan you're shitting me." Michelle pulled her phone away from her ear and viewed the logo on the top of the phone. It was a sleek, rounded design of a head with two teeth and an italicized logotype that read, "VIPER." "What phone did you say caused CE?"

"The Viper phone. I'm trying to get evidence here that shows Martin Gall—you know the big shot capitalist?"

"Yeah, yeah, yeah," Michelle acknowledged after putting the phone back to her ear hesitantly.

"Well his company produces the chips and I'm gathering evidence that shows he actually knew about it. Oh, and get this . . . Gall is working with someone here in Ur producing the medication used to treat the same disease. They're trying to cover up the cause so that they can make more money on the cure. They're making a killing."

"Those fucking greedy bastards," Michelle said shaking her head and staring into space.

"It's big, Michelle," Regan agreed.

"Who's the other guy?" Michelle asked.

"What, the business partner?"

"Yeah, the one with the drug?"

Regan paused and thought about keeping his name secret, then blurted, "His name's Tanner. Jacob Tanner."

"Never heard of him."

"He's a nobody," Regan said tersely. "So, will you get something on air about it if I get you the story?"

Michelle thought about it for a second. She had no power to control what went on air—there was a strict process that took place before the news got to her teleprompter—but she could talk to her producer Sam Barnes and work something out, she thought. "I'll see what I can do. When can you get me the story?"

"I'll be done tonight."

"Good. I'll keep an eye out for it."

"Thanks, Michelle. You're the best."

"I know I am, sweetheart," Michelle smiled and ended the call.

Thirty-Four

"And we're back with Nobel Prize winning economist, Michael Finney," the talk show host announced over a roar of applause from his studio audience. Jacob Tanner looked up from his papers to watch. The host continued, "Now, in your book you quote Adam Smith, who said, 'By pursuing his own interest he frequently promotes that of the society more effectually than when he really *intends* to promote it. I have never known much good done by those who affected to trade for the public good.' In other words, spare me the do-gooders."

The guest, Michael Finney, sat on the opposite side of a table from the show host and smiled as he gave his answer, "That's absolutely right. No one does any good when they *affect* to trade for the public good. I mean you get all these multi-national corporations who march down to Washington—you don't think they say, 'Look, you should vote me a big windfall of a million dollars because I'm a great guy and I deserve that.' No, they say, 'Give me this money or else the good, middle-class people in Kansas and Illinois and Oregon will suffer if you don't.' So, you have two kinds of people in this situation, right? The do-gooders consist of two types. You have the honest, sincere ones who actually want to help people and they inevitably end up being the front men for private interest that they would never knowingly support."

The talk show host interjected, "What's an example of that?"

"Well, for instance," the economist replied, "an example of that is the nineteenth century Ralph Naders who got the Interstate Commerce Commission started. They were sincere—they thought that the railroads were monopolies and they were charging too much because there was no chance for competition, so we have to get the government in there to

eliminate that exploitation of the consumer. But who benefited from it? The ICC was set up, the do-gooders went on to their next reform, and the railroads infiltrated the ICC. And they used the ICC to keep out competition, to raise rates, not lower them, and in the twenties, they extended the control of the ICC to trucking because that was the most dangerous form of competition to the powerful railroad companies. So those well meaning reformers—not because they were bad people—but they ended up being the front men for special interests—the exact special interests that the original reform meant to curb. And you see that over and over again in the history of this country."

"The government became an agency to help existing companies maintain their power?"

"That's absolutely right. Regulation doesn't stop monopolies, it encourages them. Now, let me put it this way. There's an old saying, if you want to catch a thief, you send a thief. If you want to stop a businessman's monopoly, the only way to stop it is to send in another businessman. The most effective anti-monopoly regulation government could initiate would be free trade—to open up the markets."

"Okay," the host said, "we have a question from the audience. The screen showed a woman from the audience stand up and speak into a handheld microphone.

She spoke in a soft voice with a subtle accent, "Hi, I learned hair-braiding skills at my home country in Africa and when I came here to America I was able to support my two children selling that service. But government shut my service down because I didn't have a cosmetology license. I looked into getting the license but it requires 2,000 hours of instruction. I cannot afford such training."

The show host turned from the audience member to his guest. "Two thousand hours of training in order to braid hair legally?"

Michael Finney shook his head. "It's absolutely appalling. No wonder we have such high unemployment. This nice lady was making a decent living braiding hair for people who," he put up his hand and continued, "I presume thought your service worthwhile? This is simply the case of

a government board made up of so-called cosmetologists who want to keep competition out. They force you to take this expensive training so that there would be less competition—"

"And," the audience member added, "the 2,000 hours of training does not even cover African hair braiding."

The audience murmured.

"It's absolutely ridiculous. It used to be one in 20 workers needed a government license to do their job, now it's one in three. And really, the occupational licensing laws hit the lower class, minorities, the elderly, who want to start a new career and they just help the entrenched companies that want to keep out competition."

The talk show host looked down to gather his thoughts, then turned back to the economist. "Okay, so, I'm just going to keep hammering this question. How do you stop them? How do you stop the exploitation of the companies? How do you prevent the slave labor and the price gouging?"

Michael Finney grinned enthusiastically and shook his head. "You don't stop it by increasing government authority, that's for sure. Lord Acton once said that, 'Power corrupts and absolute power corrupts absolutely.' And that is certainly true with government. Once you grant a certain class of people the authority to regulate others, they will inevitably take advantage of that authority. Yes, you can prevent the exploitation, but the answer is freedom, not more government."

"You don't think government works at all, then, I take it?" the talk show host asked.

"Well, just look at the track record. Name just one thing that the government has set out to do that has worked. The war on poverty? Trillions of dollars spent and we still have poverty. The war on drugs? Trillions of dollars spent and millions incarcerated and we still have the problem. Encourage home ownership? Trillions squandered and a massive housing bubble later, home ownership is down. The Fed wanted to keep prices stable. What happened? Our dollar is worthless compared to what it was. War on terror? Our troops are still in wars in the Middle East and every so often someone sneaks a gun or a bomb onto an airplane.

The war on terror hasn't worked either. Since World War II, I can't think of a single government action or program that has accomplished what it set out to do."

The cameras switched to another audience member, a young man with glasses. His T-shirt contained a cartoon depiction of the state Missouri holding hands with cartoon depictions of Kansas and Illinois. The caption read, "Missouri loves company." The young man cleared his throat and asked into the microphone, "What about the money changers—the people who just make money on money and other people's toil?"

"They don't exist," Michael Finney responded.

"Well, the bankers and such," the questioner added.

"Everyone who makes money does so because they have a product that someone else wants. In this case, the product they have is stored wealth—wealth that they have earned but haven't spent. Some people require large amounts of stored wealth to open a restaurant, for instance, and bankers give them that product for a specific price. They make money just like anyone selling a product; only their product is stored wealth. The only people who make money out of nothing is the Federal Reserve governors, who, in their infinite wisdom, find it fit to print money at various times out of thin air. Real bankers lend stored wealth that they have earned."

"But," the questioner continued, "what about the bankers who leverage their assets 100 to one? Don't they need to be regulated and stopped?"

"No. In fact, I believe the market would adequately address that risky behavior if it *weren't* for government regulation. Let me ask you— why do you think those banks make such risky gambles and leverage themselves so extensively?"

"Because of the competition—because other banks are doing it, so in order for them to survive, every bank has to do it."

"No, they do it because there really is no risk. They get deposits from people like you—why do you put your money in a bank—why do

you feel safe depositing your money in a bank that leverages 100 to one? Why aren't afraid you'll lose your deposits?"

"Well because my money is guaranteed by the FDIC."

"Right, and if your money wasn't guaranteed by the FDIC, would you put your money in such risky banks?"

"No."

"No, you would find a bank that observes sound banking practices. You see government regulation has created moral hazard in the banking industry and allowed banks to make such absurd transaction. And when those banks fail, they are bailed out by the American taxpayer, creating even more moral hazard."

The talk show host turned to his audience and announced, "He has an answer for everything. Professor Finney, ladies and gentlemen. We will be right back." The show faded out to the sound of applause.

Jacob hummed as he reflected on the professor's idea but dramatic advertisement bumper music for the news magazine *Face the Facts* commanded his attention. The ad was a flurry of abstract red and blue graphics connoting excitement and prestige. The astute and grim-looking host of the show, Thornhill Brooks, came into view in the ad, then flashed away after his name was announced.

"Could your next phone call be your last?" A masculine announcer declared over a symphony of dramatic music. Video in the commercial showed slow-motion stock footage of a woman picking up her cell phone in a dark room with stark lighting.

"Tonight, *Face the Facts* will tackle the question that has been haunting us since the dawn of the age of technology, 'Are our cell phones killing us?'"

The announcer continued while a high definition video of a posing Thornhill Brooks moved gently across the screen, "Join Thornhill Brooks for an hour of groundbreaking journalism about an everyday device that will shock you."

Jacob Tanner's eyes widened, then he nodded as the advertisement ended. "She's actually doing it," he whispered to himself then returned to

the papers in front of him. He had been going over Marc Johnson's findings regarding the defective D-to-A chip in the Viper phone when his phone rang. He reached for it after a brief hesitation.

"Mr. Tanner?" the terse, female voice pronounced on the other end of the line.

"Yes, this is he."

"Anne Gold here with Providence and Moyer."

"Ah, yes, thanks for the call."

"We had our first hearing on the case with the selected judge."

"You're kidding, already?"

"I don't kid, Mr. Tanner. I told you that the process works quickly here."

"Well?" Jacob asked anxiously.

"The case was thrown out by the judge."

"What?" Jacob said, instantly livid.

"Well, technically, he just expressed doubts about our case, but said that if we went forward, he would have to throw it out. He claimed that there was insufficient evidence for the case and, quite frankly, I don't blame him."

"No, no, no, what do you mean? It's all right there in the report. The D-to-A chip in the Viper phone degrades the myelin sheath. That device causes CE! What more evidence do you need?"

"Respectfully, Mr. Tanner, that report was created by a small and insignificant lab—yours—and that's the main reason why the judge threw out the case."

"What do you mean?"

"He discounted the report because it came from a company affiliated with the accused. Since you had done business with Gall Enterprises, he said that there was a conflict of interest with that report. And since that report was the basis for the lawsuit, he claims that there is insufficient evidence."

"No, wait. That doesn't make any sense. We're not on the same side as the defendant. We're the insider—we're the whistle blower!"

"Regardless, Mr. Tanner, that is where we stand. What do you wish to do?"

Jacob looked around the conference room while he gathered his thoughts. "I don't know. What are my options?"

"Well, you can continue with the suit as is and hope for the best."

"Or?" Jacob said, unhappy with that option.

"You could withdraw your suit. At this point there are no monetary damages and the opposing counsel will not seek reimbursement for fees. If you press on, however, they could easily come back with countersuit damages that you would have to pay if your case failed."

"What if I get another scientific report backing my report—more evidence?"

"That's an option, of course, but you'll have to step on it. The case is going to trial tomorrow."

"Tomorrow?" Jacob screeched, shaking his head. "That's not enough time."

After a momentary pause, Anne Gold offered another solution, "We could, of course, force trial and assume an appeal."

"Refresh my memory on how that works."

"An appeal would send the case to a three-judge panel. We can, of course, introduce new evidence on appeal."

"Right."

"And this current judge would be excluded from the three-judge panel."

"Right." Jacob paused. "To be honest, we need to win this now. I can't stand to be hiding here in the Archon Building forever."

"Well?" Anne asked impatiently.

"Well, what?"

"How do you wish to proceed Mr. Tanner?"

"Let's do it. We've got to."

"All right, Mr. Tanner. I'll need you to be ready tomorrow at eight. We'll convene at the dikasteria building then."

Thirty-Five

"Could you please change the channel, miss?" Jacob Tanner asked the bar tender in the Archon Building lounge indicating the flat screen television above the bar.

She was in her mid-twenties and wore a friendly smile and her hair up. Her name tag read "Melody" and her voice matched her name as she sang, "Sure thing honey. What would you like to watch?"

"*Face the Facts*. They're breaking a really big story tonight."

"Oh really? What's it about?" the bartender asked as she reached for the remote control and aimed it at the television.

"You know that disease that everyone's talking about these days?"

"Oh yeah," Melody said turning back to Jacob. "Chinese Ensipolagraphy or somethin'?"

Jacob nodded. "That's it. Well, we've figured out what causes it."

Melody's jaw dropped and her eyes widened. "No! Really? What is it?" Melody exclaimed as a nearby bar patron turned toward Jacob to listen in.

Jacob nodded toward the TV, which showed commercials. "How about I let Thornhill Brooks explain?"

"Oh, now I'm really intrigued!" Melody said turning back to the screen. "This is exciting!"

"Excuse me," a man sitting at the bar to Jacob's right interrupted. He wore a loose-fitting gray jacket over a white shirt with the top two buttons undone. "Are you talking about the feature story tonight on *Face the Facts*?"

Jacob looked at the stranger and nodded. "Yes, they're breaking the story about Chinese encephalitis."

"Is that the story about the phones? They're killing people or something?" the man asked.

"As a matter of fact, we have discovered a link."

"I knew it! Those newfangled computers ain't nothing but trouble." the man said. "I knew I should have never bought that damn thing."

"Well, it's not *every* phone. But yes, it's pretty scary."

Just then, Roberto Rodriguez walked up to Jacob and slapped him on the back. "Boy, you are crazy. Anybody ever tell you that?"

Jacob turned around in his bar stool and let a slight grin come over his face. "Hey Berto. Thanks for coming."

"Hey, you said this was important, so I came."

"Well, thanks."

"But seriously, I thought you'd be clear outta town by now."

"Yeah, well, I have to take care of some things first."

"Jake," Roberto said seriously, "what are you doing, really? I heard you almost got yourself killed. I seen the tape of the surveillance video!"

"Oh really?"

"Yeah, man. I told you not to mess with that dude Gall."

"What can I say? I can't just stand aside and watch innocent people get sick and die." After a brief silence, Jacob continued, "Hey, by the way, do you think you can get me a security escort tomorrow morning?"

Roberto nodded and sat down in the stool to Jacob's left. "Uh, yeah, I think I can set something up with Triple 'S'. What for?"

"I'm suing Gall so I'm leaving the friendly confines of this here Archon Building and heading to the dikasteria building."

"You carrying cash or something?"

"No, I just want to make it to my trial alive."

"No problemo, buddy. Just let me know when you need it."

Roberto ordered a beer from the bar tender and fiddled with a coaster that was in front of him on the bar. "So what is this all about, Jake?" He motioned to the television.

"It's coming down. They're breaking the story about Gall," Jacob said pointing to the television screen, which was still airing commercials.

"Who?"

"*Face the Facts*. It's on next."

"Seriously?" Roberto asked. "How many kidneys did you sell to get on the most popular show on television?" Roberto chuckled.

Jacob looked at the screen. "I knew somebody who works for the show."

Roberto turned toward the television also as the flashy news magazine graphics of *Face the Facts* exploded across the screen. The familiar dramatic theme music accompanied the intro and Thornhill Brooks's visage was shown looking down on the viewers in an authoritative pose.

"This is *Face the Facts* with Thornhill Brooks," the announcer proclaimed. "And now, your host, Thornhill Brooks."

The well-dressed, middle-aged man sat on a stool in the middle of a studio stage with stark lighting from below as the camera panned into his face. "Tonight," Brooks addressed his audience in a stately manner, "you were expecting *Face the Facts* to present a shocking exposé on an electronics company that is endangering the lives of millions of people."

A crowd began to form around Jacob and Roberto in the bar area. All eyes were on Thornhill Brooks.

"What we weren't expecting was to find evidence that tells a different story. While the electronics company in question appears to be, in fact, innocent of any wrongdoing, that's not the case for its accuser."

A photo of Jacob Tanner appeared on the television screen and Jacob's eyes widened as the room began spinning. He heard the clanking of silverware and sensed people looking at him. "Is that you?" Melody asked with a concerned whisper.

Thornhill Brooks continued in a gruff, authoritative voice, "His name is Jacob Tanner. Several years ago, he sold the nation on his wonder drug, Amelior, which he claimed to cure a host of medical conditions. Tanner was going to be the next hero in the medical profession—an American Louis Pasteur. Or was he? As it turns out, Tanner was more P. T. Barnum than Louis Pasteur. His wonder drug turned out to be nothing more than a placebo—a sugar pill—and its purveyor, a charlatan. At the

time, Tanner claimed that, quote, 'if you believe it works, it really does.' The FDA then pulled the drug due to its false claims. Now, after years of legal trouble, that same businessman—called a snake oil salesman by many—is behind the only drug that treated the terrifying disease, Chinese encephalitis, until the FDA recently revoked the patent for Symbalia. Jacob Tanner . . . business innovator or medical scam artist?"

Jacob gripped his chest in which he felt a confiscatory pressure around his heart. He tried to block out his surroundings and the surrounding people talking about him.

The television showed Thornhill Brooks shifting in his stool to direct himself toward a new camera angle. "Tonight we visit with a former employee of Mr. Tanner's that will shed light on this controversial man."

The camera panned to the left and followed Thornhill Brooks to a pair of simple leather chairs that were bathed in spotlight. Brooks took the chair on the right; the other chair was occupied by Jacob's Scientific Research Director, Marc Johnson.

Jacob's jaw dropped as he took in the meaning of what he was seeing. "That bastard," Jacob whispered.

He watched as Marc Johnson answered Brooks's questions. "It was really a shame," Marc said. "Aside from having simple false and utterly unscientific views on pharmaceuticals and the medical profession in general, the man was completely driven by one goal and one goal alone, to make money. He didn't care about the science or industry protocol and he sure as hell didn't care about federal regulation." Marc's words became foggy noises to Jacob as he drooped in his bar stool. "At one point," Marc continued, "Mr. Tanner wanted me to change the ingredients of an FDA-approved pharmaceutical just to cut down on costs."

"He wanted to make Symbalia a placebo," Thornhill Brooks presumed.

"All he cared about was money," Marc Johnson said as the camera panned in on him.

"Astonishing," Thornhill Brooks gasped.

"You all right, buddy?" Roberto asked. Jacob did not answer.

* * *

"This is bullshit!" a furious Regan Masden shouted at the flat screen in the control studio of the Washington D.C. offices for *Face the Facts*. She paced the dark, soundproof room packed with technicians and producers, all watching the live recording.

"Now Regan," an elderly man with soft, pudgy skin said, pleading with the furious woman, "this is still your story, you'll still get credit—"

"I don't want credit for this crap. This is a lie! This is bullshit!"

The man tilted his head down. "You know better than that, Ms. Masden. We don't lie here on *Face the Facts*."

"You corporate . . . lackey! I would have thought that out of everyone here, Benny, you would be on my side!"

Benny Newman ran his left hand through his thinning gray hair and let out a deep breath from his wrinkled face. "I like you Regan. You have fire and principle. But sometimes it's unwarranted. Sometimes, you have to just pay the piper."

"What the fuck does that mean? Pay the piper?" Regan shouted. She received looks from the technicians. "I risked my life on this story and you're protecting Gall—why? Because he's a fucking sponsor?"

Benny Newman shook his head as if to disagree.

"Really, Benny, why? Why are you protecting him?"

Benny retorted defensively, "Because he's the largest shareholder in this company—he owns 51 percent—that's why!" He raised his voice to match Regan's.

She slowly nodded and stared at the show's executive. "And that's the price of truth, huh? Fifty-one percent?" She shook her head and looked around. Everyone was staring at her.

Regan took a deep breath to compose herself. "You are a disgrace to the profession," she said calmly to Benny Newman, held her head up, and walked out of the studio.

"Regan! Don't walk out of here!" Benny called after her but received no response.

* * *

In the *Headlines Now* studios in New York, Michelle Torres stood in the doorway of Sam Barnes in a defiant stance.

Barnes sat back in his chair at his desk. "*Facts* isn't airing the story either, sweetheart."

"Don't sweetheart me jackass," Michelle Torres countered.

Barnes's smirk turned fowl. "Look, Michelle, I've been taking your crap for weeks now. If you don't buck up, you're going to find yourself doing bullshit human-interest stories for the local news in Paducah, Kentucky. You hear me?"

"Why pull the story, Sam? Huh? It's been fact-checked a dozen times. It could be the biggest story of our lives and *we* could break it."

"No one's breaking this story, Michelle. This isn't from me. It's from upstairs." Sam Barnes accompanied his words with a point upwards. "It is too important—there are bigger players involved here than me or even Martin Gall, Michelle. You don't want to fuck with corporate on this."

Michelle shook her head and squinted at the aging executive. "Bigger players than Gall?"

"Don't ask questions, Michelle, just read the script. If you fuck this up, you won't have a job in the morning, I promise you that."

Michelle looked away from Sam Barnes, turned around from his office, and walked away.

Thirty-Six

"I have some good news, Mr. Tanner." Anne Gold said as she walked Jacob Tanner to the courtroom for their trial.

"I could use some good news," Jacob said, dejected.

"It turns out your company's report on the Viper phones wasn't the only one. Burnett & Jones filed a disclosure brief following the release of the Viper phone two years ago. They condemned the phone for resale citing unhealthy radiation levels."

Jacob smiled. "So, that's it? We have our proof?"

Anne nodded. "This should help our case, yes."

The two arrived at the assigned room and found opposing counsel already there. It didn't look like a courtroom to Jacob Tanner. It was more a glorified conference room with nice furniture. He and Anne each took a seat down the table from the other attorneys and eyed the empty seat on the opposite side of the table presumably designated for the judge for the case.

Jacob squinted at Anne. "Who is our judge by the way?"

Anne pursed her lips. "A man named Peter Driesel. A businessman—"

"Wait, Peter Driesel? I know that guy."

"*You* know him?"

"Yeah! He's the one that introduced me to Gall. He's that bastard's associate!" Jacob was infuriated but Anne showed no visible response and the other counsel did not respond verbally though it was clear they had overheard Jacob. "Talk about a conflict of interest!"

Just then, Peter Driesel rushed into the conference room. He wore a tailored Italian suit and a crisp white shirt with cuff links. He flipped through several documents pertaining to the case in a manila folder but

managed to address the group simultaneously, "Thank you all for being here this morning."

Jacob shook his head as he watched Driesel sit down without acknowledging anyone in particular.

"Although, I must say that I'm disappointed to see the lack of evidence presented by the prosecution since the preliminary hearing. You could have saved us all this time by withdrawing your claim." Peter said looking at Anne Gold.

Anne replied, "Well, Peter, to be honest, we're more interested in justice than saving time and if you're too busy for your civic duty, perhaps you should have recused yourself from this case altogether."

"I'm never too busy for my civic duty, Anne," Peter said with a wink as he adjusted himself in his seat opposite the two sides in the dispute.

"I'm glad to hear that." Anne said.

Peter winked at Anne, then looked down at his papers and began explaining the case. "The central question here—in fact, the only question in any legal case in Ur is whether harm has been done—whether the single law of the land has been compromised. In this case, the plaintiff claims that he—or a relative—has been harmed by a subsidiary of the defendant, Gall Enterprises. We are here to settle that matter once and for all."

"Unless there's an appeal?" Jacob added.

After taking a moment to think about it, Peter nodded. "Correct. Unless there's an appeal."

The next few minutes that transpired filtered through Jacob Tanner's mind but was lost in a sea of disillusionment and confusion. He watched and listened as his attorney presented the case against Gall Enterprises based on the evidence. His glazed eyes watched a disinterested Peter Driesel nod and accept the information mechanically. Then he watched as the defending counsel presented their side. Driesel again accepted the information mechanically. Driesel wasn't interested, Jacob perceived. He had already made up his mind.

Soon, it was over.

"Thank you for your case," Peter said to Anne and Jacob. "The Burnett & Jones audit certainly bolsters your case. As we all know, Burnett & Jones is a fine company with a great reputation here in Ur, but one thing that strikes me with this case," Peter said nodding at Jacob, "is that this may not be the proper jurisdiction in the first place. It's true that Mr. Gall runs his operation here in Ur and you're here, Mr. Tanner, but the victim of the supposed harm—your sister—never lived here and . . . ," Peter reviewed a piece of paper in front of him with sales figures on it then continued, ". . . yes it appears that none of the alleged defective Viper phones were even sold here in Ur. Now, if you end up pursuing this case, I suggest you consider the proper jurisdiction for it—perhaps in a US district court? Some place where the alleged harm was actually committed."

After a pause, Peter continued, "Now, I'm ruling in favor of the defendant here."

Jacob squinted at Peter Driesel and fumed silently. Did he set me up? Jacob wondered. He led us to believe that the case rested on the audit, but Driesel knew all along that he was going to throw out the case. It was an absurd, biased judgment from a friend of the defendant. Jacob couldn't believe that such cronyism could be allowed to happen in such a supposedly free society. Wasn't the idea of Ur to get rid of the corruption and the injustice? Jacob wondered. Ur was no better than the rest of the country and perhaps, it was worse.

Peter raised his hand to point to the defendants' counsel and asked them, "Do you wish to charge the prosecution for fees incurred in preparation and during the trial?"

One of the attorneys at the opposite end of the table nodded. "Yes, your honor."

"What is your countersuit demand?" Peter asked.

The attorney replied, "Three hundred thousand."

Anne Gold and Jacob Tanner erupted with verbal protest. "What?" Jacob exploded with a guffaw.

"That's preposterous," Anne said looking at Peter.

The defendant's attorney handed Peter an invoice, which he perused. After analysis, Peter looked at the defendants. "This does seem a bit inflated, counsel."

"We are not some public DA's office, Peter," the attorney said smugly, "your honor."

"Damages are set at $161,000," Peter said tersely, then looked at Jacob. "The prosecution will be expected to pay these fees within thirty days or be held in contempt of this court."

"That's outrageous," Jacob protested.

Ignoring Jacob's complaint, Peter continued in a businesslike fashion, "Justice has been done."

"Justice?" Jacob screeched. Anne put her hand on Jacob's forearm. "You call this justice? This is like a playground for grown ups in which the big shots all bully up on the little guys like me. When I first got here, I thought you had it all figured out. This was a free-market paradise, but that's just a smoke screen. This place is more corrupt than the outside. This isn't justice. This is a joke."

Peter collected his things in preparation to leave.

Jacob continued, "So, that's it? This is supposed to be the remarkable system that will save civilization? You've got to be kidding me! Unbelievable!"

Peter stood up to leave but paused. "Mr. Tanner," he said, "this system is helping to create the most advanced and productive civilization on Earth. It is by far the most equitable I have encountered in all my travels across the globe. If you don't like it, you are welcome to leave this city and never come back. We will not miss you."

Jacob pursed his lips but held his tongue. His face grew red and he fumed as the defending counsel left the room. Peter Driesel broke his stare with Jacob and walked out of the room as well, leaving Jacob and Anne alone.

* * *

Outside of the dikasteria building, Jacob looked into the sky in hopeless desperation. Anne Gold shrugged and offered her condolences, "Mr. Tanner, I have to apologize. I have failed you. I'm not sure why it's so difficult for me to express that, but, there, I said it."

"He set me up," Jacob said, still looking at the sky.

"How do you mean?" Anne asked.

"He wanted me to go through with the case so that the defendants could countersuit."

Anne hardened her face. "Mr. Tanner, I don't think that's the case. I simply was too focused on the scientific report. I wasn't even considering jurisdiction."

"What a crock," Jacob said, shaking his head in frustration.

"I know it's of no consolation, but I'd like to buy you a drink . . . if you'd like."

Jacob looked at Anne and scrunched his face. "Um, thank you. I do have a question. Driesel said that Ur was the wrong jurisdiction to present our case because there were no defective Viper phones sold in Ur."

"Yes . . . ."

"Why would that be, do you think?" Jacob inquired in a defeated tone.

"Yes, well, I'm assuming that's because the Viper phone failed the Burnett & Jones audit. I believe they identified the flaw in the product and condemned it for resale. No retailer in Ur would have sold the product without Burnett's approval. Again, I should have known the case would be thrown away. I failed you."

Jacob said shaking his head. "So, my question is why were the phones sold outside of the Ur? Don't they have similar auditing outside of Ur? An FDA for cell phones?" Jacob mocked.

"Well, I know that cell phones must go through an approval process with the FCC regarding information processing, but I'm not sure if there's any regulation regarding the safety of the device. I can look into it."

Jacob nodded then put his hands over his face and rubbed out the tension. "I just didn't realize it would come back to bite me so bad." He shook his head and looked to the sidewalk. "One hundred and sixty thousand . . . ."

"Yes." Anne had nothing more to say on the subject. "Well, what are you going to do now?"

"Well, I'm going to wait here for my security escort."

"No, I mean about the case."

"I don't know. I guess the case is completely dead here in Ur?"

Anne Gold turned her eyes down to the cold concrete at Jacob's feet. "I hate to admit it but yes."

Jacob shook his head and stared in the distance, fuming. "I can't pay the fees. I don't have the money . . . ."

"So . . . ?"

Jacob turned his eyes to Anne, then looked past her down the street.

A rush of adrenaline jolted Jacob's body and he jumped in place. What looked like several security guards were walking toward him from a small SUV a hundred yards away. Emblazoned on the hood of the SUV was a shield logo and the words "Keynes Aegis." One of the security guards stared intently at Jacob, whose heart suddenly started pounding in his chest.

"Mr. Tanner?" Anne asked noticing Jacob's lack of attention. "What are you going to do now?"

Maintaining his stare on the security guards bearing down on him, Jacob stumbled away and answered Anne, "Run!"

Thirty-Seven

The midday sun beat down on the central thoroughfare of Ur as Jacob Tanner turned back once more to the pursuing Keynes Aegis guards who ran past a confused Anne Gold. Jacob picked up his pace and began running in the opposite direction.

"Mr. Tanner! We'd like to have a word with you," the lead guard called out toward Jacob. Once the guard saw that Jacob was out of reach, he turned and directed two others into a black SUV with the Keynes Aegis logo, then began to run after Jacob himself.

All Jacob could think to do was run. He exploded down the sidewalk of the Ur city center, nearly knocking over an elderly lady with a rolling cart.

"God, sorry!" he yelled out trying to keep the lady on her feet as he kept moving.

He heard a car charging up from behind so he turned on a dime around the street corner.

The SUV screeched to a halt and took the turn, driving up onto the sidewalk around a light post and back onto the street with a cacophonous thud. Bystanders squealed and frantically jumped out of the way as Jacob shouted for them to clear out.

Suddenly, a rusty, military-issue Jeep tore around the corner in front of Jacob and rammed the pursuing Keynes Aegis SUV head on with a thunderous crash. Jacob paused momentarily to gather what had happened and stared wide-eyed for a split second before stumbling away from the scene.

Gunshots were fired from the SUV, which punctured the air bags that had deployed, but they weren't aimed at the Jeep, whose driver

was backing the vehicle up and turning around toward Jacob. The Jeep pulled up to a dazed Jacob Tanner who turned to look at the driver. It was Roberto Rodriguez.

"You said you needed a security escort, man?" Roberto yelled. "Ask and you shall receive! Get the hell in here!"

"What are you nuts?" Jacob shook his head and hurriedly jumped into the moving vehicle, which had smoke seeping out from under the hood. Jacob angled himself into the open Jeep window and into the passenger seat.

"Great timing," Jacob said to his friend once he was situated in the passenger seat.

"I saw those bastards on the monitors over on the job site and knew they were up to no good so I high-tailed it over here as fast as I could."

"Yeah? Where's the cavalry?" Jacob said eyeing the black SUV, which had started up again and was trailing the Jeep.

"Man, we don't have any money. We had to cut back on security during this last push for the tunnel."

"They're after us again," Jacob said looking in the rear view mirror.

"Don't worry. I'm taking you up North. We got some Triple 'S' security at our checkpoint and there's a whole battalion of federal agents camped out there."

"What? Why?"

"Not sure," Roberto replied slowly concentrating on the road. "But you'll be safe there."

Jacob didn't reply but looked in the passenger-side rear view mirror and noticed the SUV losing ground on Roberto's Jeep. They were going to be home free.

* * *

As Roberto's Jeep barreled toward the northern checkpoint on the border of Ur, a sign stretching across the state road read, "You are now entering the United States of America." A moment later, Roberto drove

up to the border, which was represented by a five-foot-wide cement line in the pavement and parked the Jeep, staying on the Ur side.

Jacob scanned the checkpoint area, which was full of what looked like U.S. federal agents stationed just past the border. He opened the passenger-side door and stepped out onto the pavement. A quick look behind him spotted the Keynes Aegis SUV sputtering toward the checkpoint.

"You better get your butt over there," Roberto implored, referring to the area with federal agents. "They'll protect you buddy."

Jacob began walking toward the federal agents when a man stepped out from around a black truck with the words "Office of Criminal Investigations" displayed in bold white type on the side. The greased-back hair and robust waistline of the man was familiar to Jacob. When the man smiled and revealed a sliver of a canine tooth, he was unmistakable. It was Gary Javert. Jacob froze in his steps.

"Mr. Tanner," Javert announced. "Thank you for turning yourself in. As you know, you will be taken under custody and offered our protection once you cross back over into our jurisdiction."

"Custody?" Jacob wondered aloud.

"Surely your associate informed you?" Javert asked, motioning to Roberto. "We have a warrant for your arrest."

Jacob looked back to Roberto. "What's going on Berto?"

"Man, it's for your own good, Jakey. You were in over your head."

Jacob slouched and clenched his chest, slowly shaking his head. "You too, Berto? You too?"

Behind Jacob, the smoking SUV drove up to the checkpoint line and one of the guards stepped out of the car. He walked around to the front of the SUV and observed the scene in front of him.

There was nowhere else to run, Jacob thought. It was either face the private army of Keynes Aegis in the lawless charter city of Ur or give himself up to federal control. He had to submit—to give up to the government agents. After all, being arrested for a crime he didn't commit

was better than being killed by a rogue security agency in a city where anarchy rules.

Jacob looked down and took the few remaining steps across the border out of the special administrative zone and two OCI agents jumped into action, securing their prisoner by his arms.

"Jacob Tanner, you are under arrest for the misappropriation of federal funds and attempting to defraud," one OCI agent said as the other secured Jacob's wrists behind his back. "You have the right to remain silent. Anything you say can and will be used against you in a court of law. You have the right to speak to an attorney. If you cannot afford an attorney, one will be appointed for you. Do you understand these rights as they have been read to you?"

Jacob nodded and blurted, "Yes," when it was clear the officer wanted a verbal response.

The OCI agents directed Jacob past Javert to the back of the black OCI truck. Javert smirked and calmly stated to no one in particular, "Here endeth the lesson."

Assistant Inspector Nicholas Debbs shook his head at his superior's braggadocio. He turned to Jacob and offered a hand to help him into the truck. "You understand why we're doing this, right?"

Jacob did not answer. Debbs followed Jacob and the agents into the truck as Gary Javert toddled to an unmarked car nearby.

"Jakey boy, I'm sorry," Roberto called out to an invisible Jacob Tanner. He pressed his lips together when he received no response. The OCI agents shut the swinging back doors closed and the truck pulled away. Roberto watched as it sped off in a northeastern direction. He turned around and observed the Keynes Aegis guards as they traded terse words. Two Shield Security Systems guards stepped out of the checkpoint guardhouse and joined Roberto as he walked toward the other guards.

Roberto looked over the smoking Keynes Aegis SUV, which had a mutilated front grill and a crunched hood. He smiled. "Did you have a little accident boys?" He chuckled as he pointed at the damage. "Are you sure that's road-worthy?" He then walked over to his Jeep, climbed in, and drove back to work.

CHAOS
AND
KINGDOM

PART 4:
KIN OF BEASTS

The skies roared with thunder and the earth heaved,
Then came darkness and a stillness like death.
Lightning smashed the ground and fires blazed out;
Death flooded from the skies.
When the heat died and the fires went out,
The plains had turned to ash.

Thirty-Eight

Loose equipment rattled in the back of the Office of Criminal Investigations prisoner truck, which was transporting Jacob Tanner to the regional office in Houston. Jacob was seated on a side bench next to an OCI officer wearing a black bulletproof vest and opposite FDA Assistant Nicholas Debbs, who was reading a folded newspaper with a pensive, melancholic look.

Jacob eyed Nicholas and twisted his lips, then said, "Well, if anyone should be looking glum, it's me."

Nicholas turned his eyes to Jacob but gave no response.

"What are you reading?" Jacob tilted his head and looked at Nicholas's newspaper.

Nicholas put the paper down. "The obituaries. They tend to raise my spirits."

Jacob smiled at the bizarre answer. "Is it working?"

Nicholas turned his eyes to Jacob and curled his mouth in the shape of a smile. He thought about it, then addressed Jacob. "You know, it's not like I'm happy about this part of my job. I don't like arresting criminals."

"What a coincidence, because I don't like getting arrested!" Jacob said happily. "Maybe we can just call this whole thing off?"

"Nice try," Nicholas Debbs said dryly. "You received millions of dollars of FDA money and ran off to that special administrative zone, clearly in breach of FDA policy, labor regulation, and . . . common sense to be quite blunt. You have defied the system and, unfortunately, there has to be a sacrifice for that defiance."

"The system . . . ," Jacob repeated as if he were in mocking awe. "Is that the same system that punishes the productive people in society and facilitates criminals like Martin Gall?"

Nicholas Debbs raised his hands in surrender and shook his head. "I don't know—am I supposed to know who that is?"

After a pause, Jacob sniffed audibly and shook his head. "You know . . . it *is* the system and you're just a cog. You may think you're doing something good here by arresting me—you may think you're helping the people—but you're not. You're just helping one person, the bad guy." He shook his head and looked around the back of the truck. "You're just a tool—a tool in the hands of some corporate special interest."

"A tool, huh? Can I be the hedge clippers?" Nicholas asked sarcastically.

Jacob nodded. "You joke?"

"Man, I'm just a regular guy with a nagging girlfriend and a hefty car payment. I'm just trying to do my job."

"That's exactly my point!" Jacob exclaimed, eyes bulging at Nicholas. But he shook his head after failing to connect with him. "You're just blindly going along in this system . . . this overarching bureaucracy that your predecessors have created. It's not helping people—it's actually *hurting* them."

Nicholas defiantly shook his head. "Yeah, we're the real bad guys. Is that what you are trying to tell me? Government is the problem? You know what life would be without us, Mr. Tanner—without the government?" After a silent pause, he answered himself, "It would be chaos. It would be people killing each other for scraps of food, slave labor, and worse. Dogs and cats sleeping together—mass hysteria! It would not be life as we know it at all, instead, it would be a horrific existence trapped in the barbaric state of nature. They have a place like that, it's called Somalia. I want to help this overarching bureaucracy that you decry in order to save humanity from its natural tendency toward utter savagery. What's wrong with that? You know it's bad enough without people like us trying to help others, we have to deal with your type who's bent on getting rid

of the government that we do have. True, you may not be able to do quite anything you wish—you cannot kill people or rape and pillage—but in return for giving up those antisocial behaviors, you get civilization. Is that too much of a price for civilization?"

Jacob did not answer.

"You see we have this sort of remarkable system that, believe it or not, satisfies everyone quite neatly."

Jacob squinted at Nicholas Debbs. "How do you mean, 'satisfies everyone'?"

Nicholas continued after a huff, "Well, everyone seems to be quite happy in this system, except for maybe malcontents like yourself."

Jacob posed to Nicholas, "You and the special interests are happy, maybe. Not everyone."

Nicholas smiled. "Wow, aren't we ungrateful? Wasn't it your company that received $12 million from the government to produce your drug? Idiocy, I can handle, but hypocrisy, no thanks." He lifted his newspaper again to continue reading.

Jacob shook his head. "I had no choice. With all the regulations you guys dump on us, it's impossible to be profitable as a small company. You either need to be the size of Johnson & Johnson or make only widely used drugs."

"Like I said, everyone seems to be happy except for you."

"Not everyone."

"No, I mean everyone," he said dropping his paper again. "Sure, there are special interests that lobby the government to influence legislation and favors, I don't argue that. Why *wouldn't* they lobby for help from the government? You certainly did. And yes, it's true, politicians take their legal bribes and perks from the special interests because those politicians are better off with those perks than without. Then they discern and apply public policy based on their ever-wise judgment and public servants like myself enforce that policy to the best of our ability all in accordance with the social contract. And the more laws and guidelines

we establish for a better society, the more of us public servants are needed within the system. So you see, everyone is happy under our system!"

Jacob tilted his head and frowned. "And what about the people? The *people* aren't happy in this system. They make up the majority of this system but yet they get the shaft every time because they're too small individually to stand up and make a difference. No, it's the lobbyists and the politicians and the public servants," Jacob said the last words sarcastically, pointing at Nicholas Debbs, "that benefit from the system and they do so at the expense of the people. We're the ones that have to foot bill for each political favor that benefits the special interests. And we're the ones that suffer when the FDA holds up a drug for five years in the approval process. We're the ones that go out of business and have to lay off a dozen workers because we're not allowed to make manufacturing improvements after some bureaucrat waved his magic wand over in Washington DC. The people aren't happy in your system, they are getting screwed! That's the point."

"No, I actually think that the people are the *happiest* group in our system! You see, the people don't have to deal with the mundane details of governance and paperwork and the big decisions the politicians make. They don't need to pay someone to pave their roads, or worry about their security, or put out their own fires and can instead just sit back and watch *Glee* and *Grey's Anatomy* and fiddle with their iPods while the government takes care of them from cradle to grave. And the cost of that care is so low per person, that there's absolutely no benefit in them trying to change it. Why would they? Why struggle to change the system when the price is so high and benefit so low?"

The kid was right, Jacob thought. People were happy in the system or at least they were so used to their standard of living that they couldn't care less that some extremely undeserving people were getting rich at their expense. He was right, but that thought infuriated Jacob.

"That's a disengaged citizenry," Jacob shot back. "You can't think that's a good thing. Just because something bears an insignificant cost

per person, doesn't mean it is the *right* thing to do. It doesn't make it just, right?"

"Mr. Tanner, if the people wanted a different system, they would ask for it. I mean, who elects the people in power, after all? The people do. It appears that the people, as you call them, are perfectly happy with the way the system operates too."

Jacob shook his head. "But even then, each voter has such little impact on the election that it doesn't make sense to put much effort into learning about the candidates. And I think if they were really given a choice outside of Tweedle Dee and Tweedle Dum every four years, they could actually do some good, but voters are given two versions of the same brand. They're given Pepsi and Diet Pepsi, not anything close to the glass of fresh water that they need and deserve."

"Well, if you're willing to discount the concept of democracy itself, then I have no answers for you. Man, everyone seems to be happy with the system except for you. You need to either get in line with the other Pepsi drinkers or you'll find yourself dying of thirst. But that's what's happening now isn't it?" Nicholas drew his eyes to the steel handcuffs shackling Jacob's wrists.

Jacob nodded as he silently fumed. "So that's it, then? Agree with the system or go to jail. That's basically what you're saying."

"Agree with the *social contract* or go to jail," Nicholas corrected.

"Whatever. Agree with this contract or go to jail. What's the difference? It's still just the use of force."

"But you act like there's an alternative. There isn't. The use of force is inevitable. Either you can choose force in a capitalist, lawless realm like the place you just escaped from or you can choose force by legitimate means—government—and the democratization of force. Absolute freedom is not an option unfortunately, Mr. Tanner. Absolute freedom is a fairy tale. Instead, we must all choose between legitimate and illegitimate force. Kinda sucks, doesn't it?"

A fire burned in Jacob's chest as he stared silently at the young FDA assistant. It was true, he thought. Everyone was making logical, economic

choices in the current American system. Each player in the game, the lobbyists, the government officials, the public workers, and even the people were all making rational, economic decisions, yet the majority of the people involved—the general citizenry—were being used and abused. They were trading freedom for convenience. The people ostensibly had the most power out of all the players in the system due to their numbers but they were being pushed around by the rich and powerful.

Why? Jacob thought. Why would the most powerful contingent put up with a system that took advantage of them? Why?

Perhaps it was because the alternative to the current system—the purely free-market society of Ur—was as much of a failure as well, Jacob thought. Ur was anarchy—a place in which the big boys had even more power over the little guys than in the broken corporatist system of the greater United States. The system of overbearing government was bad, but it seemed that the absence of overbearing government was worse.

Maybe that's just the natural course of things, Jacob thought to himself. Maybe the rich and powerful would always come to dominate the poor and meek, no matter how much freedom and openness there was. And the poor and the meek were stuck with getting diseases like Chinese encephalitis so that the rich and powerful can make more money. It was unjust, but the kid was right, there was no alternative.

A glum look had returned to Nicholas Debbs and Jacob turned away from him. He shifted in his bench to get comfortable for a long ride.

Thirty-Nine

The pretrial detention cell wasn't that bad, Jacob Tanner had thought to himself when he had been directed to it. It was clean, it had a fresh coat of paint, and he had it all to himself. It wasn't what he had imagined jail being like at all. No menacing thugs or crooked security guards and it was even cleaner than his old factory in Arkansas. Most importantly, Jacob felt safe. There were no crazed lunatics trying to kill him in the detention center. It was strange to consider, but there were actually benefits to being in prison, Jacob thought.

The detention center also had a fairly good collection in its library. Jacob was pleased to find classic economic books *Human Action* by von Mises and *Free to Choose* by Friedman. But what caught his eye on his first trip to the library was *The Epic of Gilgamesh*, a tattered 1920s edition of one of the oldest of humanity's stories. Jacob was lying on the bottom bunk bed mattress covered with a thick, gray, wool blanket reading *Gilgamesh* when a guard knocked on the bars of Jacob's cell with a loud clank from his nightstick.

"Lucky you, Tanner, you have a visitor," the guard said.

Jacob dropped his book and looked up at the guard without moving his prostrate body.

Minutes later he was being escorted into a concrete gray holding cell with a table and two metal chairs. The guard sat Jacob down and eyed him as, a moment later, Regan Masden followed them into the room, also escorted by a prison guard.

"Regan," Jacob let out in a disappointed sigh.

Regan Masden carried an unsure look as she sat down in the remaining free chair across a metal table from Jacob. After a brief, tense silence, she softly said, "Hi."

"Hello."

"They said you were in here on remand."

"The judge refused bail—said I was a flight risk since I had spent time in Ur." Jacob's tone was devoid of energy.

"So you're stuck in here until the trial? You poor thing."

"I'll survive. The food's all right . . . no one's trying to kill me. It's no Guantanamo, that's for sure."

Regan stared at the peaceful Jacob. "Don't tell me you've resigned yourself to this." She looked around the holding cell. "You haven't given up have you?"

Jacob gave Regan a stern look. "Look, why did you come here?"

Regan firmed her lips and looked down, gathering her thoughts, then said, "Will you hear me out? I know all of this looks really bad, but I want you to know that I'm on your side."

Jacob nodded in mockery. "Oh, you don't have to tell me. Your actions prove it. Like when you ran off that night when I needed you for our lawsuit? Or when you ran a story on *Face the Facts* that indicted *me* instead of the real criminal, Martin Gall? Oh, you don't have to tell me you're on my side, Regan. You've already proved that beyond any doubt."

"You have to believe me, Jacob, I had nothing to do with that story. They screwed me on that story!"

Jacob shook his head but did not answer. He just stared at Regan, disappointed.

"Jake, I wanted to run my story—our story—more than anything but those weasels Newman and Brooks buckled because—guess who—Gall is a controlling shareholder in the company. *They* sold out, Jake, not me."

"Why are you here?"

"I want to take down Gall—"

Jacob burst out laughing. "How the hell do you plan on doing that?" He looked at her with disbelief. "Gall's got the media in his pocket as you've clearly demonstrated. He's got my lead scientist out there slandering *me*. I'm in a federal correctional facility thanks to the FDA, which Gall probably has in his back pocket too along with the president probably and the rest of the country. Good luck trying to take down one of the most powerful men on the planet, Regan."

"Jake, listen. This story about the defective phones is going to break one way or the other. They can't suppress the truth forever and I think we can leverage the story to fix this mess."

"It's not going to happen, Regan. It's hopeless."

Regan let a grin creep across her face. "Hopeless? Is this coming from the guy who said *nothing* is hopeless? Is this coming from the guy who took a hardened criminal and turned him into his best employee? Who actually healed people with a chalk pill? The guy who discovered the cause of the deadliest epidemic in modern times? Jake, you were right. *Nothing* is hopeless. We can do this!"

Jacob hesitated for a moment, then smiled at Regan's enthusiasm. "What do you have in mind?"

"Well, I've done a little snooping and you won't believe what I've found out."

"Oh?"

"Yeah. It turns out that your friend in the FDA, Gary Javert, has set up a Senate hearing about extending FDA authority to Ur. It's the type of thing that all the media outlets are forced to cover, so it will be highly visible. Javert's going to testify, obviously, but guess who else will be there?"

Jacob tossed up his hand. "Martin Gall?"

"That's right."

Jacob tilted his head backwards in surprise. "I was just kidding."

"No, Gall is going to testify as well. I think this is our chance to confront that bastard once and for all and tell the world about the Viper phone and CE."

"How are we going to do that?"

"You're going to testify before the Senate also."

"Me?" Jacob raised his hand to his chest.

"Yes, you."

Jacob couldn't hold back a chuckle. "How—?"

"Well, the senators on the committee must request the witnesses but Javert is going to give them recommendations and Javert is going to recommend you as a witness."

Jacob angled his head and squinted at Regan. "He is? Why would he do that?"

"Well, let's just say he might be compelled to. You see, in my snooping I found out something about Inspector Javert."

"Yes . . . ?"

"Under law, the FDA does not review the safety of cell phones or mobile devices, but they can take action if any product is shown to have hazardous levels of radiation."

"Okay . . . ."

"Well, the case was brought to the FDA two years ago when the Viper phones were first released. The FDA ignored the case and, in essence, provided a stamp of approval for the phones."

"No kidding?"

"And can you guess whose office approved the phones?"

"Gary Javert's."

Regan nodded. "Javert was in charge of the REP division of the FDA when this occurred—the division that handles radiation emitting products."

"Very interesting."

"Isn't it?" Regan asked rhetorically. "I'm going to have a little chat with Javert and see if he doesn't want to keep his role in all this under wraps."

"By getting me on the witness stand? Well, that sounds good. How do you plan on getting a meeting with Javert?"

Regan smiled. "Well, Mr. Tanner, you're still speaking with a producer for one of the most prestigious news magazines in the country. I've been know to get into a lot more difficult places with my cameras."

"And what if he doesn't want to talk to you? What if he says the hell with your threat?"

"Well, if all else fails, I happen to know someone on the HELP Committee."

"The HELP Committee?" Jacob asked.

"The Health, Education, Labor, and Pensions Committee. That's the one holding the FDA hearing next week."

"You know someone on it? A senator?"

"Let's just say I know some pretty important people."

Jacob shook his head. "Well, no one could ever accuse you of being dull, Regan, that's for sure."

The two shared a silent, amiable stare before the prison guard called time.

Regan slowly stood up and thought for a moment. She pursed her lips then blurted, "I'm sorry."

Jacob smiled but said nothing and watched as Regan turned and left the cell.

Forty

Regan Masden threw open the door to Gary Javert's office and led her film crew in with a flurry. A stoutly cameraman carrying an elaborate camera pushed through the doorsill and a technician followed, carrying a heavy-looking black case.

Javert was startled and looked up from a paper on his desk. He stared wide-eyed at the intrusive journalist. "What's the meaning of this?" he demanded authoritatively belying his shock.

"Inspector Javert, I'm Regan Masden, producer for *Face the Facts*. I have some questions regarding your role in a defective consumer product that's endangering millions of lives."

"You can't just barge in here like this unannounced! Into my office? What do you mean by this?" Javert flinched and leaned forward to stand up but couldn't manage to get out of his seat. He eyed Regan's credentials, a plastic cover holding a paper badge, held by a black lanyard. The camera equipment looked professional and the assistant was wearing an official *Face the Facts* polo with the show's insignia on the left breast. These people were legitimate, Javert assessed.

"Rolling," the cameraman said calmly, training the camera on Javert.

Regan strode toward Javert and slammed a dossier down on Javert's desk, drawing his eyes. "March fifth, two years ago, your office signed off on a defective product that has gone on to cause the Chinese encephalitis epidemic that has killed hundreds of people."

Javert's eyes bulged and he flared his nostrils as he stared intently at Regan, stunned by the accusation. He slowly looked down to the manila folder she had laid on his desk and opened it.

"Go ahead," she said. "It's all right there."

Javert skimmed the front page of the dossier and shuffled through some other pages. He looked up—first to the camera then to Regan. He offered a phony, uncertain smile, then returned to the papers in his hands.

"This . . . this was my office?"

Regan nodded, her accusatory stare weighing on the federal agent. "That's *your* signature!"

Javert coughed and cleared his throat, then shifted in his chair. "I'm sure there's an explanation."

"The explanation is that you let a critically dangerous product slip under your nose."

Javert cleared his throat again with an abrasive cough. "Um, can you please give us a moment?" The ambiguous question was directed at the cameraman and the producer.

Regan turned to her crew. "Wait outside." The two men nodded and left the office. With the click of the door latch, Regan turned to Javert and smiled. "All right, Inspector Javert."

Javert sat back in his chair, keeping his grasp on the report in front of him. He looked Regan over in an attempt to assess her intent. "What is it that you want, miss?"

"I'd like to make a deal. I have something you want and you have something I want."

"Oh really?"

"You're set to appear before the Senate HELP committee next week and you need a good reason to extend the HEAL America Act to cover the charter city of Ur."

"I'm listening," Javert said with a straight face.

"You also want to clear your name of this cell phone debacle." She pointed to the report Javert was holding and paused momentarily, then summarized, "You need a scapegoat."

"And you have one for me?"

"Gall Enterprises . . . ." Regan waited to see Javert's reaction, but he gave none. "Gall Enterprises is one of the largest conglomerates in

the country—with assets and various holdings, it ranks fifth. And it is based in Ur. One of its subsidiaries produced those defective products in question and I have evidence that incriminates the CEO, Martin Gall himself. He knew about the danger of his product, but okayed it anyway for increased profit."

"Typical," Javert said quietly. "So, it's Gall Enterprises that's really at fault, not me. Why don't you just run your story on Gall?"

Regan nodded. "Gall is a majority stockholder in the parent media company that runs *Facts*, so my producers won't let me run the story on Gall. However, there's nothing stopping me from running a story on a negligent FDA inspector."

Javert pursed his lips and silently fumed. "What is this? Blackmail?"

"Look, we both want the same thing here—Gall's head on a platter. I just need something from you."

"And what would that be?"

"I need you to drop the charges against Jacob Tanner and instate him up as a witness in this hearing."

Javert stiffened his spine. "Impossible."

"Oh?"

"I can't do a thing about that case. Those are federal charges."

Regan turned slightly toward the door. "Such a shame. Aren't you in the running for Inspector General? This whole mess won't look very good for you, will it?" She opened the door slightly and called to her crew, "Hey guys?"

A grimace came over Javert's face. "No wait!"

Regan closed the door but not all the way.

"Perhaps we can work something out," Javert said meekly.

"Yes?" Regan asked, turning back to the inspector.

Javert stood up and put his hands in his pockets. He looked to the floor as he paced around his desk.

Regan watched as Javert considered the options.

Javert looked up and gave Regan a smile. "Yes, yes, I see it now. Reformed businessman supports the FDA. He will support our cause will he not?"

Regan nodded. "His goal will be to indict Martin Gall for his crimes. You can twist that whatever way you'd like."

"Good, good. You have a deal, then."

* * *

The next day, Jacob Tanner was being escorted down a hall in the federal facility in Butner, North Carolina by a correctional officer. "You're a free man again, Mr. Tanner" the officer called out. "I don't want to see you back here as a repeat customer, now!"

Jacob nodded. "Oh, you don't have to worry about that." He pushed through a dilapidated steel door and into the bright spring sun. He ran down the concrete steps leading to the entrance and toward a public bus that was pulling away. The sign above the windshield on the bus read, "Washington D.C."

The bus was in worse condition than his prison cell, Jacob reflected as he took his seat moments later. The upholstery on the seats was tattered and worn, there were candy wrappers strewn throughout the floor resting on week-old soft drink spills, and the smells emanating from the bathroom in the rear of the bus were offensive. Good thing it was just a quick four-hour trip to Washington, Jacob rationalized, shaking off the condition of his transport.

He pulled out his phone from his pocket and called Regan.

"Hey," she answered.

"You're a miracle worker," Jacob gushed.

"I take it you're out, then?"

"You got it. I'm heading to D.C. Do you want to meet?"

"Yeah. When do you get here?"

"I'm scheduled to get into the Union Station area in four hours."

"Sounds good. I have an appointment at three, but we can meet at five."

"Great."

"I know a nice little cafe around there. I'll send you the directions."

"Okay, see you then."

"Bye," she said and ended the call.

Jacob lowered the phone then brought his curled fingers up to his mouth and rested his head on his hand. He looked out the window to the blurred North Carolina countryside.

Forty-One

As Jacob Tanner stepped off the Greyhound bus in cloudy central Washington, D.C., he took a moment to look around. Regan had agreed to meet him for dinner at a nearby restaurant, but he had a few hours to kill in the meantime. He set out south toward Union Station and it took only a couple steps before his eyes were compelled skyward toward a menacing, dark gray storm cloud forming to the west.

He picked up his pace but before he reached Massachusetts Avenue, which ran into Union Station, drops of rain started pelting Jacob. He looked around for a coffee shop where he could spend a few hours, but saw nothing welcoming. Across the street, however, Jacob spotted a cell phone store and he checked the traffic before jogging over.

A small bell rang as Jacob pulled the retailer's door open. He wiped his damp feet on the doormat placed just inside the door and nodded at a rotund, mustachioed man behind the counter. A young Latino woman in the store browsed the cell phone accessories, batteries, and chargers that lined the walls of the store, but Jacob was interested in the phones themselves. A quick survey of the products revealed no Viper phones.

"Can I help you with somethin'?" the mustachioed man asked curtly.

Jacob turned to the man. "Yes, perhaps. I wonder if you have the new Viper phones here."

"We got everything," the man said as he eased off of his perch on a stool. He walked away from Jacob along the glass display counter that separated the man from his customers. With a clank, the man tapped a ring on his finger on the glass above the latest Viper phone and turned to Jacob who had followed him. "Want to take a look?"

"Yes, please," Jacob said eagerly.

Without a word or other acknowledgement, the man bent over, unlocked the display case from behind and pulled out a small, flat, black electronic device. He handed it to Jacob who recognized the design from the model he used to own.

"That's the bestselling phone on the market right now—selling like hotcakes. They got that zero-interference feature that makes every one of your conversations sound like you're in the room with the person you're talkin' to. And it's got the highest quality standard on the market."

"Oh?" Jacob faked surprise.

"Yeah, it's the only one of its kind."

"Really? Can you tell me about the safety? What kind of radiation does this thing put off?"

The mustachioed man shrugged his lips. "It's better than the others. But if you're worried about radiation . . . ," he said turning around and pulling a packaged Bluetooth headset from the wall behind him, "you should get you one of these too. We're having a sale on the Viper. If you sign up for a two-year plan, it's yours for just $19.99. I can throw in the Bluetooth for $49.99."

"Nineteen ninety-nine? That's cheap," Jacob noted.

"Yep, we want to move these puppies."

"Oh? Why's that?"

"They're really good sellers."

"But how can they be so inexpensive?" Jacob inquired.

"Well, since they're the only phones with them standards and features I just told you about, they give us a credit for each one we sell."

Jacob tilted his head toward the man behind the counter. "Who gives you a credit?"

"The FCC—that's the Federal Commission for . . . Cell Phones. They're the ones that license the phones."

"The Federal Communications Commission?" Jacob corrected the proprietor. Just then, Jacob's phone vibrated in his pants pocket. He pulled it out and pushed the talk button.

"Oh, I see you already gotchya a phone," the man behind the counter said and leaned in to pull the Viper out of Jacob's hand.

"Anne, hi" Jacob said into his phone. "I was going to call you."

"Yes, well. Do you remember what you said after the trial? You wanted to know why there were sales for the Viper phone despite the failed audit by Burnett?"

"Actually, I already know. The FDA was supposed to catch the faulty product but they gave it a pass."

"Well, there's more," Anne said.

"Right."

"It appears the high sales might stem from an amendment tacked on to an FCC bill by Congress last year that requires—"

"Requires retailers to carry the Viper phone?" Jacob preempted Anne.

"Yes, how'd you know?"

"I'm getting sold on one right now." Jacob looked at the mustachioed man who was trying to appear aloof.

"Right, so I looked up that amendment and it's all right there. It doesn't specify Viper per se, but it states that all retailers must carry at least one FIPS level two-compliant phone. And do you want to guess what the only phone of that kind is on the market?"

"The Viper?"

"Correct. And what's more," Anne continued, "the amendment mandates that retailers get a per unit tax credit if the price of the phone surpasses market average."

"Wait, what does that mean?"

"That means that retailers get money from the FCC for each Viper phone they sell in much the same way as the cash for clunkers provided federal money for automobile upgrades."

"You're kidding me."

"I don't kid," Anne replied dryly. "I thought I told you Mr. Tanner."

"That's right. Look, how did this amendment get signed into law? Who proposed it?"

"That I'm not sure of. I'm emailing you the PDF. Will you be able to view it on your phone?"

"Yes, I think so."

"Okay, I have to go," Anne said abruptly.

"Thanks, Anne."

Jacob pulled his phone away from his ear and navigated to his email program. He opened Anne's email and attachment and scanned the document, starting in the middle of the screen. It read, "On page 397, after line 9, insert the following: TITLE IX--MANDATORY AVAILABILITY REQUIREMENT . . . every licensed retail shall be required to provide a FIPS-II compliant phone for retail . . . ," It was exactly what he was looking for, Jacob thought. Martin Gall had connived some congressman to shill for his product. Instead of selling his product fairly on the open market, he had swindled somebody into *forcing* retailers to sell his product. This was what Gall was talking about when Jacob had first met him. He couldn't sell his defective product in Ur because of the intense audit by Burnett & Jones, but he could sell it in the rest of the country. Not only that, but Gall somehow got one of his cronies in Washington to practically make the sales for him.

Jacob stared at his phone wide-eyed and furious. But when he scanned to the top of the document to read the name of the senator who submitted the bill, Jacob's face turned white and he let out a stunned moan. "It can't be . . . ," Jacob whispered. It was.

Forty-Two

The flash flood warnings didn't stop the senator as he opened the door of his Lincoln in front of his three-story brownstone, situated on a cozy, drenched block of Georgetown in western Washington, D.C. The senator was in his early sixties and maintained a perfectly combed coiffure of silver and black hair. He displayed a charming smile that had been able to disarm any political adversary over the years as well as a few unwitting and witting females. He wore a perfectly fitted black suit naturally and comfortably and a pair of Italian leather shoes. The senator extended his umbrella outside of the door and let his guests—a lavishly dressed couple in their late fifties—exit the car. The driver had stepped out and, trying to avoid the downpour, offered another umbrella to the back seat door for his passengers.

"You deliver Margaret," the senator declared to his driver with a light-hearted chuckle, "then come back and get me!"

The driver escorted the woman out of the car and up the concrete steps to the door under one umbrella and her husband followed with the other.

The driver came back and held out the umbrella while the couple shook off the rain under the town home's small porch roof. The senator stepped out of the car and led his driver to refuge under the porch.

The chaos of the weather held so much of their attention that no one noticed a soaking woman standing next to them on the sidewalk. She had no umbrella and stood motionless as gallons of water poured over her head and body.

"Daddy," she called out. "Daddy, it's me."

The senator recognized the voice he had known well as a child but no longer. He slowly turned toward the sopping woman and dropped his jaw.

"Regan?" he asked, knowing the answer.

Senator Hank Masden handed his keys to his driver and told him to escort his guests inside, then walked back down the front steps to his daughter with his umbrella. The driver took the couple in the house as Senator Masden covered Regan. "What are you doing out here? You're soaking. Where's your umbrella?" He reached his arm around her and offered a hesitant embrace. "Are you okay?"

"I'm fine dad," Regan said, maintaining a stoic facade. "I need to talk to you."

"Well, come inside. Dry off. Of course you can talk to me."

* * *

Regan Masden sat on the arm of a chair in her father's townhome library drying her hair with a fluffy green towel. Hank Masden walked in with a steaming hot cup of water with a steeping green tea bag.

Regan put the towel down and accepted the teacup from her father. She smelled the tea and smiled. "My favorite," she said warmly.

"Now, what in blazes were you doing out there in the rain like that?" Hank asked with a strained face. He remained standing next to Regan and folded his arms.

"I have to talk to you about something."

"Well, couldn't it have waited? I mean I haven't seen you in God knows how many years; you don't return my calls; you just show up soaking wet like this? You worried me half to death."

"It couldn't wait daddy. It's about . . . ."

"Yes?" encouraged Hank, opening his arms as if to embrace.

"It's about Martin Gall."

A puzzled face on Hank Masden grew more contorted as he looked around the floor of the room in response to his daughter. "Martin Gall? What about?"

"I know everything, daddy. I know about the boat, I know about the home in Malibu, I know about the offshore account. And I know how you've paid for it all."

"How I paid for it all?"

"Legislation, daddy. You've paid for it all with legislation that helps Martin Gall."

"Honey, are you sure you know what you're—"

"Daddy, please, don't patronize me. I know everything. And I need you to listen to me. One of the amendments you wrote on behalf of Gall is killing people."

"Honey, is this about that environmental cause you're working for?"

"Daddy, I haven't been active in Sierra for years. It's about the FCC amendment last year."

Hank looked to the floor and lowered his arms slowly. "Regan, my staff introduces so many amendments . . . ."

"It was 'SA' 329. It was a deal you made with Martin Gall to push his product—the Viper phone." She waited for a response.

Hank looked to the door from which he had entered. Past the threshold he could hear his friends conversing and laughing. He turned back to his daughter. "Look Regan, what's this about?"

"Daddy, those phones are killing people. Your amendment is pushing a product that kills people." Her face was contorted in worry and strain.

"Regan, honey, I have no idea what you're talking about." He stepped toward her to perhaps offer her comfort. "You've had a rough day, why don't you—"

"Don't do this, daddy," Regan said with a fragile voice.

"Look, the Stevensons are here . . . maybe we can talk another time." Hank inched toward Regan and reached for her arm to raise her from the chair.

Regan slapped back her father's arm and tears began welling up as she looked at him. "I knew you would do this."

"Regan . . . ."

"You are . . . you are so far entrenched in this crony-capitalist system . . . that you can't listen to reason." She wiped tears from her eyes. "After all that you've done . . . after what you did to me . . . do you realize what you did to me, daddy? How much therapy I went through? So much work to get to where I am."

Hank huffed and looked disappointed at Regan.

"You can't even just listen. I knew you were hopeless, but someone talked me out of it. He said I should give you a chance. Well, what do you know? You *are* hopeless."

Hank Masden pursed his lips and eyed his daughter wearily. He stood up, turned away from her and slowly walked out of the room without a word.

Regan nodded. She called herself an idiot for coming and for thinking anything would be different between her and her father. He was a self-involved drunk and he was hopeless. After a minute, she heard the voices of her dad's guests and the front door close. Then she looked up to see her father return to the library with a concerned look on his face.

He pressed his hands to his face and breathed in, then released and sat down in a chair opposite Regan. "All right, you want to tell me about this?"

* * *

Jacob Tanner had been sitting at a table in the Bistro Americano for thirty minutes but there was still no sign or word of Regan Masden. He had perused the menu full of tasty Cuban dishes several times and was contemplating leaving when he saw her shuffle into the restaurant accompanying a gust of rainy wind. Her hair was disheveled, and as she neared Jacob, her blotchy skin and the remnants of running mascara revealed that she had been sobbing. She had a look of utter defeat.

Jacob stood up. "Wow, you look horrible," he said honestly.

Regan couldn't help but smile at his irreverence. "Thanks."

"But yet, still beautiful somehow," he said under his breath. He extended his right arm, which she accepted. They embraced and Jacob softly asked, "Is everything all right?"

Regan shook her head and breathed in deeply as she eased out of the embrace and plopped down in her chair. She looked up at Jacob who had sat down as well. "I've got a lot to tell you."

Jacob smiled. "You always do."

Regan didn't return the smile. "Do you remember me saying I knew someone on the HELP committee?"

Jacob smiled and nodded. "Your father."

Regan opened her mouth in astonishment. "How'd you know?"

"I didn't . . . until my attorney found an amendment to a Senate bill that requires cell phone retailers to carry the defective Viper phones. That amendment was added by one Hank Masden."

"Shit . . . so you know?"

"Well, I know that much."

Regan slouched back in her chair. "My father has been dealing with Gall for years, Jake. He's been the little Washington lackey for that pig ever since I've been out on my own."

Jacob shook his head as he listened.

"Every time Gall needed legislation that supported his products or muscled out his competition, good old Hank Masden was there for him and, in turn, Gall has made daddy a very rich man throughout the years. Of course, very little of that wealth is on the books."

"So, you had known about Gall for years—even before your whole Ur excursion?"

Regan nodded. "That was all part of the plan. I was going to infiltrate Gall's lair and expose the bastard for the sadist he is."

"And get back at your father for all those years?"

"You have no idea," she said solemnly and shook her head.

Jacob pursed his lips and observed as Regan sunk subtly in her chair.

"I had been gathering all this evidence of the shady dealings between daddy and Gall—it was going to be an unprecedented exposé on crony capitalism. That is until I met you and found out about the phones. That story is much more important than all the other backroom deals put together. I mean, people are dying! So, I went to talk to him today—to try and talk some sense in him."

"And?"

"Oh, he said he wants to do the right thing and he would let you talk about this at the hearing but I wouldn't put it past him to change his mind. For all I know, he's chatting it up with Gall right now, figuring out ways to screw the little guy all over again."

"Well, with his name on the amendment to require those phones I can't imagine he'd be too eager to commit . . . well, political suicide."

Regan nodded. "Well, it's not just his career he's worried about, Jake. Daddy said that most of his assets were invested in contracts with Gall. If he turned his back on Gall, he would lose everything." She shook her head and puckered her lips.

Jacob shook his head. "Is there anybody this guy doesn't own?" he asked, raising his voice in frustration. "Are there any senators on the committee that we can count on to be on our side? Gall can't be in the pockets of all of them, can he?"

Regan nodded as she formulated an idea. "Well, strictly politically speaking, any Democrat would love to stick it to daddy but there is one in particular. Senator Delano from Vermont. He's a big crusader and he would love to have something on my father and on Gall's empire."

Jacob nodded. "Great, so we'll focus on Delano." He smiled at Regan who looked worried.

"Jake, there's something I haven't told you about my father. I told you he was a drunk and he took my mom away from us. But there's more," Regan said, holding back some tears. "He also abused me when I was a little girl."

"Oh God," Jacob said. He contorted his face with anguish over Regan's words. "How?"

"In every way imaginable," she said, voice quivering.

"Oh, Regan."

"It's taken me all my adult life to come to grips with it and I thought I was okay, but it's clear that I have a long way to go still."

"Regan, I'm so sorry," Jacob said.

She breathed in and out. "I never thought I would do this but I'm prepared to go public with this if he doesn't come clean."

"Regan, no, you don't have to do that."

She shook her head. "No, I want to. I'm ready. If he doesn't come clean about this mess with Gall, I'm going public about him—the accident, the abuse, everything."

Jacob pressed his lips together. "Well for your sake, I hope you don't have to go through that."

Regan smiled and mouthed the words "thank you."

The house where the dead dwell in total darkness,
Where they drink dirt and eat stone,
Where they wear feathers like birds,
Where no light ever invades their everlasting darkness,
Where the door and the lock of Hell is coated with thick dust.

Forty-Three

Jacob Tanner scanned over the pictures of Gary Javert with various dignitaries that were hanging in his office as the FDA inspector chatted into his phone at his desk.

"Okay, right," Javert said then hung up the receiver at the base of the phone. He grabbed a bag of sugary, fruit-flavored candies and dumped some into his mouth as he turned to Jacob. "Mr. Tanner," he said through a chew of candy. "Thank you for coming."

Jacob turned toward Javert and looked at him expectantly. "Yes, as you know from the documents I sent you, it is extremely important that we address this as soon as possible. Our report shows that CE strikes quickly and will likely affect most of the ten million consumers who have bought the Viper phone in the past few months. It could be catastrophic!"

"Yes, well, about that," Javert said, swallowing a chunk of flavored sugar. "While it appears this is indeed important, we're simply not going to be able to address this issue at the HELP hearing. I've pulled you from the witness panel."

Jacob lowered his jaw and released some tension in his neck. "Gary, but why?"

Javert averted Jacob's stare. "I have my reasons. I don't have to tell you."

"What?" Jacob raised his voice. "Gary, do you understand? People are dying. We need to get this out there as soon as possible!"

"I'm sorry, but the HELP hearing is not the proper venue."

"Well, where can we address this, then? What's the correct venue?"

Javert shook his head as he looked down to the bag of candy in his hand. "I'm afraid that there may not be *any* proper venue for this discussion."

Jacob inched toward Javert with his head projected out. "What do you mean there may not be a proper venue for this? You've spent your entire career trying to take down evil corporations like this and you finally have evidence of blatant criminal behavior. Now you're just going to sit back and act like nothing is happening?"

"Mr. Tanner, you're young. I think eventually, you will learn that some things just aren't as black and white as some people make them out to be."

"Black and white?" Jacob stood erect with his hands on his hips looking down at Javert. "He got to you."

"I don't know about what you're talking."

"Gall. He got to you, too."

"I had to pull you, Mr. Tanner. They were going to stonewall you. There's nothing I could do about it."

"Stonewall me? Gary, just let me speak!"

"Look Mr. Tanner, you just got a "Get Out of Jail Free" card out of this, I suggest you let this pass."

"Gary, do you remember calling me the modern day Gilgamesh?"

Javert nodded. "Yes, yes, the slaver who wanted to become a god."

"Well, I read the epic while I was in jail and you had it all wrong. You see Gilgamesh represented the city—civilization and the gods sent this untamed natural beast—Enkidu—to destroy Gilgamesh. But instead of warring, Gilgamesh and Enkidu became great friends and together they went on to defeat the real villain, the monstrous Humbaba who the gods put out there to scare us mortals."

"Oh, how nice," Javert said sarcastically.

"You see, you are Gilgamesh, I am Enkidu, and Gall . . . Gall is Humbaba. Gary, we can take him down, but we need to work together."

Javert swished around saliva in his mouth as he fidgeted in his chair. "It's a nice fairy tale, Mr. Tanner, but this is the real world. Things happen for a reason and you just can't do anything about them sometimes."

"Look, whatever it is that got to you, it hasn't gotten to me. Just let me speak. You know we need to fight this. You know it's the right thing to do. Just let me at least try."

"I don't think it could be done, Mr. Tanner."

"Gary, I know we've had our differences in the past, but I truly believe you have the best interest of the people in mind. I think you honestly are trying to do the right thing." Jacob let a silent moment pass, then said, "This is the right thing."

At that moment, Nicholas Debbs knocked on the open door to Javert's office. Jacob turned back to see who it was.

"What is it Mr. Debbs?" Javert asked, relieved to momentarily avoid Jacob's plea.

"When you're done, Palmer would like to see you. He wants to congratulate the new Inspector General."

Javert made an uncomfortable face and shook his head. "Very well."

Jacob looked back at Javert with an accusatory stare. "So, that's it? That's your price? A fucking promotion?"

Javert averted Jacob's stare. He searched for something—anything—on his desk. "I'm not sure to what you're referring, sir. Now if you don't mind . . . ."

"I see," Jacob said with a shrug of his lips. He slowly turned toward the door and walked out, defeated.

Gary Javert shook it off. The man was a dreamer, a child. He had no place in the nuanced world of politics and bureaucracy. Javert leaned back and his eyes were drawn to the picture frame on his wall. The script inside the framed paper, which was big enough for Javert to read from his desk, read, "We are responsible for protecting the public health by assuring the safety, efficacy, and security of drugs, devices, and consumer products throughout the country and the world. We are the FDA." Suddenly, a

mild panic attacked Gary Javert. He put his left hand to his forehead and tried to calm his conscience.

Five minutes later, as Jacob was nearing his rental car in the parking lot of the office complex, his phone rang.

"This is Tanner," he answered.

"I'll do it." It was Gary Javert. "I'll get you on the witness stand."

* * *

"Oh, Martin's not going to like that one bit," the deep, haggard voice of Senator Arnold Huskin pronounced. The white-haired Huskin, ranking member of the Health, Education, Labor, and Pensions Committee stood next to his colleague Senator Masden in a closed office in the Dirksen Senate Building.

Senator Masden, who appeared downtrodden and lifeless, responded with, "Arnold, Tanner has a right to tell his story."

"The hell he does," Huskin retorted. "*We* control what's said in that chamber, not some two-bit witness."

Masden shook his head but said nothing.

Huskin continued, "If he so much as strays from his written testimony, there will be hell to pay from Gall."

"Fuck Gall," Masden replied tersely.

With a crash, the door to the office flew open and Martin Gall stomped in, accompanied by his bodyguard, Jermaine. The senators looked at Gall like deer in headlights.

"You were saying?" Gall asked quietly looking over the senators.

"Mr. Gall," Senator Huskin blurted. "How did you—well, we weren't expecting you, sir."

"I just wanted to ensure we were all on the same page regarding this hearing," Gall said looking at Senator Masden. "Tanner is not to speak."

"Oh, we're on the same page," Huskin blurted out. "We won't let Tanner stray from his written testimony."

Gall shook his head. "No, I don't want him speaking at all."

Huskin produced a strained, artificial smile. "Mr. Gall, it's too late to change the witnesses, but I assure you that there is nothing antagonistic in his testimony about you. If he veers from it, we will stop him."

Gall turned his eyes toward Masden. "Hank? What say you?"

Masden returned Gall's stare but said nothing.

Martin Gall coldly recited a quote, staring down the senators, "Confront them with annihilation, and they will then survive; plunge them into a deadly situation, and they will then live. When people fall into danger, they are then able to strive for victory."

He slowly walked behind the motionless senators without a word. Senator Masden looked into the air, unimpressed by Gall's Sun Tzu quote and presumed intimidation tactics. Senator Huskin, however, was nervous. A bead of sweat dripped from his brow and his eyes darted around the room as Gall paced.

Gall broke the silence, "Senator Huskin, you seem to have lost control of your ship."

Arnold Huskin flinched and looked to Gall behind him. "Uh, no. Not at all." He looked at Senator Masden then muttered, "Hank is on board."

"Is that right?" Gall asked doubting.

"You can quit the crap Martin," Hank Masden said defiantly. "I'm sick of this bullshit."

Senator Huskin put his hand on Masden's shoulder. "No, no, what Hank means to say is that he's ready to play ball now."

Gall stopped pacing in front of Masden and looked him straight in the eye. "Is that right, Hank? Are you going to play ball now?"

Hank eyed Gall. "Martin, why can't you just let the guy talk and move on?"

"Let the guy talk, Hank? Do you realize what kind of money is involved here? If you just 'let the guy talk,' it would mean recalls, bad PR, and losing a very lucrative drug company. We're talking upwards of $4 billion, Hank. That's nothing to sneeze at, now, is it?"

Hank Masden said nothing.

"Well, I know where I would get $120 million of it. I think that just about accounts for your share in my company. I could easily wipe you out to cover some of my expenses. But truly, I would need to consider a bolder plan of action. I might have to reconsider my political connections . . . bring Delano into the discussion."

"My PAC money?" Huskin said, panting.

"*My* PAC money," Gall corrected the senator.

"Jesus, Hank," Huskin said turning to his colleague. "Do you know what this could mean? Stop playing games with the man—the stakes are too high!"

"Now you wouldn't want to single-handedly lose the fundraising edge for your party, now would you, Hank?" Gall asked.

Hank Masden said nothing but Arnold Huskin flinched at the idea and blurted, "Now, Mr. Gall, no one wants you to lose any money. I assure you he won't get a word in edgewise."

Gall turned to Huskin. "He better not. Either you shut him up or I'm going to start dealing with Delano instead of you incompetents."

"You got it Mr. Gall," Huskin replied.

"You're forgetting that I am allowed the floor to ask whatever I want, Arnold," Hank Masden said defiantly.

"Well, you will yield your time, naturally," Huskin offered.

Hank shook his head. "I'm done with this bullshit, Arnold."

"Are you?" Gall asked, seemingly surprised. "Are you done with bottomless campaign contributions? Are you done with 30 percent return on investment in your stock over the last twelve years? Are you done with your house in Malibu?"

"Don't give me that shit," Masden shot back, "I've helped you just as much as you've helped me. You would be nothing if it weren't for me and the political favors I've provided."

Martin Gall smiled. "Why Hank, you act as if you're indispensable. There are 99 other senators in your position who I could purchase, and some for considerably less money. Why do you suppose you're special?"

Hank Masden turned his head toward Senator Huskin but kept his eyes on Martin Gall.

"Are you sure you don't want to play ball, Hank?" Gall asked.

Hank hesitantly nodded his confirmation. "People are dying Martin. If Tanner's willing to speak, I'm going to let the man speak."

"Is that your final answer, Hank?" Gall inquired.

Masden nodded again.

Gall released his stare with Hank and turned around. "Fine. But whatever may happen to that punk is your responsibility."

"What do you mean, Martin?" Hank demanded.

"Just know that whatever happens could have been avoided if you had done your duty." Gall abruptly walked out of the room and Jermaine followed then shut the door.

Huskin stood silent and looked sternly at Masden, then spoke slowly, "Do not fuck me on this, Hank. Don't even give him a chance."

Masden shook his head.

"If that witness talks, it won't be just Gall and you that go down. He'll bring down the entire party," Huskin warned. "You heard Gall, he's going to give the power back to the Dems."

Masden breathed in deeply. "It's time, Arnold. This needs to come to an end." He then walked past Senator Huskin toward the door.

* * *

The finely appointed Room 430 in the Dirksen Senate Building maintained a steady roar from the viewers and journalists awaiting the Senate hearing. The room was divided into two sections—the gallery, which corralled the crowd of press agents, visitors, and concerned citizens, and the committee area which consisted of an imposing, rounded wooden desk for the senators in front of a long witness table. The table was covered with a green felt-like fabric and aligned with four thin black microphones, one for each witness.

Jacob Tanner had sat patiently at the witness table for almost an hour watching the committee chamber come alive. At regular intervals he had turned around to scan the room in search of Regan Masden to no avail. She had told him she would come despite the futility, but she had not shown her face. *She's going to be late for her own funeral,* Jacob thought.

Gary Javert fidgeted uncomfortably in the seat next to Jacob Tanner. And on the other side of Javert sat a calm and collected FDA administrator. Jacob eyed an empty chair on the opposite side of the FDA administrator. He had spotted the nameplate in front of the empty seat, which read, "Martin Gall, CEO Gall Enterprises."

"You have a lot of fucking nerve, Tanner," a piercing voice declared from behind Jacob. "What the hell do you think you're doing here?"

Jacob turned in his chair to see Martin Gall opening a wooden gate leading into the committee area. Jacob stood up to confront the man.

"You're finished, Gall. I'm cutting you down."

Martin Gall looked away with a smile. "You're such an idiot, Tanner. You got nothing."

"One of these days, Gall, your big head is going to be too big to carry around any more and I'd like to be there to see when it's taken off." He gave Gall a fake smile. "So to speak."

"Out of all the heads around here, I think you should be most concerned with yours."

"Is that a threat?"

"No, no. It'd be a shame, though, if I had to ship your body back to Ur to feed my gator."

Jacob shook his head. "You can't touch me here, Gall. This is D.C., there are rules here."

Martin Gall threw his head back and let out an uncontrollable guffaw. "Oh, that's funny, Tanner. You're a real comedian." Jacob gave a sour response and with that, Gall walked to the end of the witness table and sat down in preparation of the hearings.

Forty-Four

"The Senate Committee on Health, Education, Labor, and Pensions will come to order," Senator Arnold Huskin grumbled over the speaker system of the committee chamber. The white-haired Huskin sat in the middle of a long, sturdy, semicircle desk with twenty-one comfortable leather seats to his left and right. The seats were intended for the other committee members, but just six of the seats were occupied for the hearing. To Huskin's immediate left was the ranking Democrat on the committee, Duane D. Delano of Vermont. He was a rotund, balding man of his late forties with glasses and an unnaturally even tan. To Huskin's right was the debonair Senator Hank Masden complete with his usual, finely tailored Italian suit and well-manicured looks. His aristocratic, confident appearance belied his reticent attitude as he looked down at his papers pertaining to the hearing. Behind the senators was a collection of various staffers from each senate office.

Senator Huskin continued, "I'd like to thank you all for joining us today for the first in a series of hearing focused on the extension of FDA authority to the charter city of Ur, Texas. As we all know, safety in our pharmaceutical and drug industries is paramount to the interest of average Americans and the Food and Drug Administration has done its part to ensure quality manufacturing processes and, in the end, consumer products throughout the country. Last year, we passed the Health Enterprises And Liabilities of America Act, the so-called HEAL America Act, which increased the scope and power of the FDA originally granted by the Food, Drug, and Cosmetic Act of 1938. The HEAL America Act allowed the FDA to investigate companies who were in violation of the Good Manufacturing Practices and to insure those practices by tempo-

rarily administering any corporations who continually failed to meet the GMP standards of excellence. Predictably, not an insignificant number of pharmaceutical companies have decided to flee the auspices of the federal government to the charter city of Ur, which, as you all know, is outside of the jurisdiction of any federal agency."

After fifteen minutes of long-winded pontification on the subject, Senator Huskin wrapped up. He looked to his left where Senator Duane D. Delano was seated for an indication of what was next, then addressed the crowd with the microphone again. "We're now going to hear from Dr. Peter Michelson, the Lead Deputy Commissioner of the Food and Drug Administration."

The middle-aged Michelson, seated next to Gary Javert at the witness table cleared his throat into his microphone to start his testimony. Jacob Tanner tried to pay attention to the dry monologue Michelson gave the committee, but failed. It was long-winded, self-congratulatory, and seemed antagonistic to corporate interests, the same corporate interests that Jacob understood had produced all of the life-saving pharmaceuticals on the market. Those companies weren't saving lives, they were gouging consumers. They weren't inventing cures; they were making it difficult for patients to get the medicine they needed. The senators took turns asking Michelson about the HEAL America program and he responded in an informative manner for another fifteen minutes.

The next witness was the newly promoted Inspector General, Gary Javert. Jacob listened intently to Javert as he produced an incessant glorification of himself and the HEAL America Act. Javert cited a number of cases in which his team of inspectors had used the HEAL America Act to seize manufacturing plants and prevent abuse of the FDA's Good Manufacturing Practices guidelines. "We have been taking back the medical industry for the American people, one corporation at a time," he proclaimed at one point with his index finger in the air as if he was running for political office. "Big pharma has been gouging medical sufferers for decades now and we're finally turning a corner on the fight to lower costs and truly help the public unlike any time in our history.

The Congress needs to extend the authority of the FDA to this special administrative zone or risk the consequences!" The committee members again followed up Javert's speech with questions and Javert answered in a consistently threatening tone.

"All right," Senator Huskin said after Javert finished answering his last question. The senator put his hand over his microphone and listened to a staffer, then returned to the microphone. "Right now, we'd like to get a little perspective from the business community. Today we have a CEO of a large multinational corporation, Mr. Martin Gall."

Gall, in his most eloquent tone thanked Senator Huskin and the other senators. Jacob listened intently as Gall gave his testimony, which surprisingly involved gushing praise of the FDA and their regulations over business. "It is with the assurance of the FDA that we can provide products that our customers can count on." He went on to welcome the FDA in his new home of Ur, Texas. "We've got to be honest. We need FDA regulation—even in Ur. It's just that simple. We cannot risk having some fly-by-night operation come in and produce a product that will make people sick or worse. All of the factories and plants under the Gall Enterprises umbrella have kept up with FDA standards for manufacturing and marketing and it is my wish to see that every organization be forced to do the same." Gall finished his testimony by praising the committee and answering a few questions with reiterations of his testimony.

After a moment's pause, Senator Huskin cleared his throat and spoke into his microphone, "Right now we welcome, uh, Jacob Tanner, uh, a business owner who operates a small pharmaceutical company in the region in question." The senator said it as a question as he eyed Jacob preparing his testimony at the witness table. Jacob sensed his palms beginning to perspire and he took in a deep breath to calm his nerves.

Gary Javert put his right hand on Jacob's shoulder and offered a terse, "Good luck."

Jacob smiled at the unexpected gesture.

"Thank you for joining us, Mr. Tanner," Huskin said. "Uh, I believe you are to give testimony on behalf of the business community regarding the HEAL America Act, is that correct?"

"That is correct," Jacob said leaning in to his microphone.

"All right. As you know, Mr. Tanner, we are running short on time, so if you could keep your statement brief so that we could proceed to the question and answer portion of your testimony as soon as possible, that would work to the committee's benefit."

Jacob nodded as he adjusted his microphone to the level of his mouth.

"At this time," Senator Huskin continued, "we'd like to go ahead and hear your testimony."

Jacob nodded again. "Thank you Mr. Chairman, Ranking Member Delano. On behalf of my employees and the business community as a whole, I thank this committee for allowing me to speak." He took a moment to review the script that had been composed by Javert's staff, then began reading it, "As a businessman, I find it difficult at times to balance my desire to compete in the open market and to provide a . . . ," Jacob hesitated while contemplating the next few words in the script then continued, ". . . provide a safe, inexpensive product intended for public consumption. Business, even the pharmaceutical business is riddled with bad apples that make fair competition impossible . . . ."

Jacob paused and looked at Gary Javert next to him who was looking at the senators. He saw Martin Gall who was staring into the air, carelessly.

Jacob returned to face the senators then continued his testimony, ". . . bad apples that make competition impossible—look this . . . this is no good," Jacob interrupted himself. He continued over a murmur from the gallery and despite questioning glares from the senators. "Look I didn't come here to read some script written by some FDA intern and condemn all businesspeople and beg you to extend the FDA authority. I came here to say one thing. The FDA does a fine job at what it does and all, but it has no ability to stop real travesties from occurring."

Next to Jacob, Gary Javert's eyes bulged and Dr. Michelson looked to the witness, confused. Martin Gall nodded to a staffer behind Senator Huskin, who stood up then leaned toward the committee chairman and whispered in his ear.

Jacob continued, "For instance, while my team was researching the disease that our drug treats—it's a horrifying disease called Chinese encephalitis—I discovered that it was actually caused by—"

"Uh, Mr. Tanner," Senator Huskin interrupted Jacob, who politely acquiesced. "Is this part of your written testimony?"

Jacob shook his head. "I have all the documentation with me—"

"Is what you're saying right now part of your written testimony?" Huskin repeated and held up a stack of stapled papers.

"No, sir," Jacob acquiesced."

"If you don't mind, Mr. Tanner. We are short on time so we're actually like to move on to the question/answer portion of your testimony."

"Excuse me but I was told I would have at least ten minutes to address the committee."

"Yes, well, extenuating circumstances. I'm sure you can understand. Now, if you would please comment on the particular case before us. Do you or do you not support extension of the HEAL America Act into the charter city of Ur?"

Jacob moved his head around, visibly grappling with the question. "Yeah, sure. And it would be great if the HEAL America Act actually healed the country. It'd be great if it actually prevented things like Chinese encephalitis, which we've discovered is actually—"

Again, Huskin interrupted Jacob. "Okay, thank you Mr. Tanner." Jacob tried to talk over the committee chairperson, but was unable. Huskin continued, "May I remind you Mr. Tanner," he repeated louder, "may I remind you . . . that you are here as a guest of this committee and I would ask that you respect the procedure by answering only the questions posed to you and not adding superfluous commentary."

"I don't think it's superfluous, Chairman. There is a very important issue that I'd like to bring up regarding the health of the nation."

"And I thank you, Mr. Tanner, for that." Senator Huskin turned to his left and nodded to Senator Delano. "I'd like to now recognize Senator Delano of Vermont."

Jacob let out a slight sigh of relief as he watched Senator Delano prepare to speak.

"Thank you, Chairman Huskin," Senator Delano said. He spoke with a speech impediment, part lisp, part phonetic disorder that prevented him from articulating clearly. The senator had usually made up for his obvious condition by speaking very loudly and using an erudite vocabulary. "I'm grateful for this opportunity to speak with you, Mr. Tanner. Presently, you mentioned your concern over the health of the nation, but you, in particular, have quite a questionable history concerning this regard. I cite a complaint by the FDA brought up three years ago concerning your company at the time. You were proliferating a nutraceutical that you promised would cure depression, joint pain, and complexion conditions. You marketed this pill as a wonder drug that would save the world from all of its ailments. Of course, it eventually came out that this . . . snake oil you were pushing was nothing more than an inert substance—a placebo—that did nothing to save people from their painful, often-times life threatening conditions. When the FDA stepped in to shut you down, you fought tooth and nail to preserve your precious nostrum racket and your unjust profits. Now, are we to believe that you have changed your tune about the FDA and have come to accept its true value?"

Jacob leaned into his microphone. "With all due respect, Senator Delano, the nutraceutical of which you speak was effective about 60 percent of the time—higher than similar active pharmaceuticals. The amazing thing about the placebo effect is that if someone genuinely believes that a pill will cure them, it actually does. Study after study shows this to be the case. With regard to depression, placebo has been seen to be just as effective as various powerful drugs."

"So," Delano interjected, "Am I to believe, Mr. Tanner, that you maintain your position on your nutraceutical—that you believe you were unfairly treated by the federal government?"

"Senator, with all due respect, I didn't come to discuss Amelior, I came to—"

"It matters not what you may have thought you came here to discuss. You are here, before the United States Senate Committee on Health, Education, Labor and Pensions, to represent corporate America and its ilk and you will answer the questions as they are presented to you or you will be held in contempt of Congress. Do I make myself clear?"

"Senator, if you would just let me finish—"

"Mr. Tanner, I think what you did with your snake oil was absolutely abhorrent. I knew people who counted on Amelior for their well being and when it broke that that drug was nothing more than a placebo, well, let me just say, it was not a pleasant enlightenment."

"This is just my point. The pill was working until—"

"Mr. Tanner, you are a disgrace to the world community. It is quite clear that you, in your Dionysian haze, have no concern for the well being of sufferers of these myriad conditions and that your only concern is maximizing the profits of your snake oil sales. It is people like you and companies like yours that the HEAL America Act was designed to constrain and as long as I have anything to say about it, I will be a steadfast supporter of this legislation. You come here with the nerve to tell *us* what we're going to discuss? You can save your preposterous ramblings for a criminal jury, which, Mr. Tanner, is who you deserve to be presented in front of, not a prestigious body such as ours." He let a deafening silence hang in the air after his rant, then said slowly, "I yield back."

A stunned Jacob Tanner sat slouched and stared at Senator Delano who was busy looking over the papers in front of him and not paying attention to Jacob. That was it, Jacob thought. He had lost. Out of the corner of his eye, Jacob saw Martin Gall lean forward at the witness table and stare at Jacob. He turned toward Gall, who mouthed the word "nothing" at Jacob, then eased back in his chair.

Forty-Five

"All right," Senator Huskin said chuckling and looking wryly at his colleague Senator Delano.

He's laughing? Jacob Tanner thought to himself as he shrank in his witness chair.

"Well, if there aren't any more questions for Mr. Tanner, we will ask to see our next witness." Huskin turned toward the few Democratic committee members to his left, then to his right at the fewer Republican committee members. Senator Hank Masden showed a contorted face looking down at his notes and averting Jacob's eyes. No one spoke up.

"If I could just say—" Jacob blurted into his microphone.

Huskin immediately dropped the gavel on his sound block and pointed at Jacob. "No you cannot just say. You will speak when you are asked a question, sir! One more peep out of you and you will be held in contempt of Congress."

At that instant, one of the main doors in the back of the room opened and Regan Masden, dressed in a black skirt suit strode into Dirksen Senate Building Room 430, a *Face the Facts* press pass dangling from her neck. She walked up to the front of the gallery and sat down in a vacant seat in plain sight of the committee desk.

Senator Hank Masden swallowed hard as he watched intently as his daughter took her spot in the press area. She was so beautiful and confident, he thought. And he had done nothing to help her ever since she was a child. His heart sank as he stared at her. I'm so sorry, he thought.

Jacob noticed the senator's reaction and turned to see what had gripped his attention. He gave Regan a regretful, defeated smile and she

responded with an empathetic nod. Regan then turned to her father and gave him a cold, hardened stare.

Senator Masden turned to his colleague, Senator Huskin, and hesitatingly said, "Mr. Chairman, I have a question for the witness."

Huskin soured at Masden's words. "Is that right?"

"Yes," Masden said.

Huskin had been prepared to move the proceedings along but turned to Masden. "Very well, the Chair will recognize Senator Masden."

Masden cleared his throat in preparation for the typical pontification that always came when a senator was recognized. Then he began, "I've been senator and been a part of these committee hearings a long time—almost thirty years—and I have never seen a witness treated the way you have been treated, Mr. Tanner. This has been a complete circus from the get-go and I apologize for that." A quiet murmur came over the gallery and the other senators lowered their heads. "Now this treatment could be for one of two reasons. Either you've been a surly sprite over there at the witness table or there is something you have to say that the distinguished gentlemen here to my left don't want to hear you say. Now, it's clear to me that you haven't been a surly sprite over there and I have a feeling that you have something very important to tell us. And right now, I'm going to allow that—"

"Will the senator yield?" Senator Huskin immediately interjected into his microphone.

"No," Masden replied curtly, "I will not. I'd like to hear what this witness has to say." He turned to Jacob. "Please . . . go ahead."

A surprised Jacob Tanner nodded at Senator Masden hesitatingly and leaned into his microphone. "Thank you Senator." He took a deep breath before beginning.

To Jacob's left, Gary Javert let an unsure smile creep over his face in response to Senator Masden's request. Martin Gall tilted his head back as if to assess Huskin's action then turned his eyes to Senator Huskin and slowly nodded. Huskin watched the nod, flinched, then turned to his left toward Senator Delano and whispered in his ear.

"Thank you Senator Masden. Last year," Jacob began, "it was discovered—"

At that, Senator Huskin slammed his gavel onto a sound block in front of him. "Okay, we're going to recess until tomorrow morning at nine-thirty. This hearing is adjourned until that time."

"You've got to be kidding me," Jacob muttered under his breath and sat back into his chair, throwing his hands in the air. "That's it?"

After a confused murmur from the gallery, Gary Javert hurriedly gathered his belongings together and muttered toward Jacob, "I was afraid of this. They're stonewalling you."

"They're what?" Jacob asked.

"They're not going to let you talk."

"So what do I do?"

Javert looked at Jacob and said sternly, "You wait for tomorrow to come and pray that they don't find some way to remove you from the panel."

Jacob squinted and sat back in his chair. He gripped his tense stomach.

A gentle hand came to rest on Jacob's shoulder accompanied by a sweet fragrance.

"Thanks for coming," Jacob said to Regan as he turned around.

"I had to," she said dryly.

"I should have known you would be fraternizing with the harlot," Martin Gall said leaving the witness stand.

"No," Jacob corrected, "that would be you. I'm fraternizing with a journalist."

Gall did not stay to hear the response. He walked into the gallery section and spoke to an associate who was waiting in the third row. Gall nodded toward Jacob and Regan, then left.

"You want to get out of here—get this hearing off your mind?" Regan asked turning back to Jacob.

Jacob nodded.

"I know just the place," Regan said.

Forty-Six

Regan Masden put her purse in a gray plastic container and moved it along the metal table toward the X-ray machine, then stepped in front of a walk-through metal detector. A bulky man stood on the opposite side of Regan and asked if she had anything metal on her person. The man wore a dark blue short-sleeve, collared shirt with a light blue badge sewn onto the left sleeve. The badge contained a ribbon reading "United States Capitol Police" and a two-color depiction of the Capitol above the date "1828."

The officer motioned Regan into the metal detector and she walked through, and then collected her purse on the other end of the X-ray machine. Jacob Tanner followed suit.

"They will be starting a tour at the top of the hour at the other end. You'll need a tour pass."

Regan nodded. "Thanks." And she and Jacob walked into the exhibit room of the Capitol Visitor Center. As they walked through the dimly lit room full of large display boards with historic texts and pictures, Jacob tried to soak it up. Regan kept her head down.

"Do you . . . ," Regan said then looked up at Jacob before continuing. "Did I screw things up between us—you and me?"

Jacob scrunched his face but did not answer.

"Jake, I know I'm broken, but I'm working things out. I'm . . . I'm sorry."

Jacob shook his head. "You don't have to be sorry."

Regan nodded silently and looked away from Jacob. "I think you're a good man, Jake. You're not like anyone I know. "

The right side of Jacob's mouth curled up in a half-smile but he said nothing.

Regan reached into her purse, which contained a ringing cell phone. She looked at the number and clicked ignore, then turned off her phone.

"Who is it?" Jacob asked.

Regan shook her head. "A friend. I don't want to be interrupted right now."

Jacob nodded.

"So, do you think daddy will let you speak tomorrow?"

"I don't know, but I'm going to try. I'm going to keep pushing this until I get somewhere. Javert may have chickened out, your father may chicken out, but I'm going to do this whether or not it kills me."

"Don't say that, okay?" Regan asked of Jacob with a worried tone.

"What? I'm not going to delude myself. You saw what lengths Gall is willing to go to protect himself with those goons in Ur."

Regan smiled. "Well, you don't have to worry any more. We're back in the real world where we have police and some semblance of protection."

Jacob nodded and smiled. "Right." After a moment's silence, he turned to Regan. "You know, I think I've figured it out."

"Oh? What did you figure out?"

"Well, it's a problem that I've been thinking about since my time in," he paused and chuckled at the thought, "the *big house*. In our current economic system, the special interests lobby the politicians and the politicians make their decree and the people pay for it. It's a paradox; theoretically the most powerful party in the equation—the people—are getting screwed, so how does it persist?"

Regan scrunched her face. "Interesting. Right, so how does it persist?"

"Well, it persists because, evidently, it's more beneficial for everyone in the system to keep behaving as they are. It's obviously better for the lobbyists to continue lobbying because they gain government favors of billions of dollars with relatively little investment. The politicians over there in the Capitol are better off because they get wined and dined by

the lobbyists and they look good to their constituency because they bring money back to their districts. And the taxpayer is also acting rationally by going along with the system because it would cost them so much more as an activist to try to defeat a government favor than to just go along with it. A government subsidy may cost a few pennies per person, but it would take a ridiculous amount of effort to actually stop that legislation, so the people just sit back and take it."

Regan raised her eyebrows. "That's a pretty cynical take."

Jacob nodded slowly as they reached the tour guide at the end of the exhibition hall. Jacob turned in front of Regan and faced her. "But I figured it out. It doesn't have to be that way," he said thoughtfully.

"Well? What's the solution?"

"Remember when we were sitting on the pier and you mentioned how the problem with corporations was that they removed responsibility from the people behind the corporations?"

"Ladies and gentleman," an early-twenties female dressed in a navy blue sweater and pants with a bright red jacket declared. "We're going to go ahead and get started with the Capitol tour."

Jacob smiled at Regan. "I'll tell you after the tour."

Regan nodded and turned to face the guide.

* * *

The guide walked backwards, leading the group of tourists into the open expanse of colorful marble, sandstone, and large historic oil paintings. There were sculptures spaced throughout. Jacob recognized the likenesses of Abraham Lincoln, Martin Luther King, Jr., Thomas Jefferson, Ronald Reagan, and George Washington. The tour guide then directed the group through a series of red velvet ropes linked with brass stands that made a path through the hall and explained, "This is the Capitol rotunda. Begun in 1818 and completed in 1824, this "heart of the Capitol" was designed in the neoclassical style, which was popular at the time."

Regan and Jacob both looked up as they walked into the center of the dramatic room.

"The rotunda is 96 feet wide and rises 180 feet three inches to the canopy above. "

Jacob raised his eyebrows in astonishment and looked at Regan who was slightly less impressed. "It's a great monument," he whispered to her. "A monument to what, I have no idea."

Regan playfully slapped Jacob. "Hater," she said with a smile.

Jacob looked down one of the numerous hallways leading into the rotunda and noticed a Capitol Police officer running toward them through one. The officer approached the group and whispered into the tour guide's ear, then he immediately ran toward another hallway.

"Something's up," Jacob said to Regan.

"What?"

The group of tourists produced a confused rumble.

"Folks," the tour guide said, raising her voice. "We're going to take a small detour. I'm going to need you to head back the way we came." The guide stuck her arms in the air and pointed behind the group, which made a collective about-face and started walking toward the hallway in which they entered the rotunda.

Jacob looked past the few tourists in front of him and spotted two Capitol Police officers in the hallway where they were headed. He froze in place and gripped Regan's arm. His face became instantly pale and his eyes popped.

"What is it?" she gasped.

"That bastard!"

"What?" Regan was becoming frantic as the tourists were jostling around her and Jacob. She looked in the direction Jacob was staring and spotted the same whitish pale gunman from Jacob's apartment in Ur. He was wearing a Capitol Police uniform.

"We're going to need you to keep moving folks," the guard called out from behind. "This is not optional."

"Don't go downstairs, I'm going to try to draw their fire." Jacob ran through the red velvet rope blocking off the rest of the rotunda and two brass stands collapsed with a crash.

"Sir!" the guide yelled.

The albino jumped in his place and took steps in Jacob's direction.

Jacob darted across the rotunda and into a hallway leading west.

Forty-Seven

Jacob Tanner exploded out of the doors of the Capitol building and flew down the steps toward the sloping west lawn. After maneuvering past some white sandstone railings, he heard the doors behind him open and close again. They must be right behind him, he thought. The albino from Ur and another man, both dressed in Capitol Police uniforms raced down the stairs after Jacob.

Jacob ran as fast as his legs would let him, then he pushed harder down the sloping grass of the lawn. There was a brick structure ahead of him hidden behind lush foliage.

Refuge.

He heard yelling behind him and finally a shot from a gun fired, which caused him to involuntarily yell. The round ricocheted off of the red brick wall of the Capitol Summerhouse, sending splinters of burnt clay into the air. Jacob Tanner felt the back of his head and wiped blood off as he darted behind the structure. He had sustained a superficial wound on his neck but was fine otherwise.

"Get out of here!" Jacob yelled at two tourists passing by thirty feet further north.

The brick walls of the Summerhouse separated him and his pursuers but a rage boiled up in Jacob's chest. He was sick of running. He was sick of hiding. He was sick of being a prisoner of his tormentor and was going to confront them once and for all. He looked up to locate a suitable place to launch an ambush. Nothing. He tried to pull open the wrought iron gates on the north side of the small building but it was locked.

Inside the gate, however, Jacob spotted a loose iron bar that must have come from one of the gates. He reached through the gate and pulled

out the bar. He tiptoed around to the west side of the building and hid behind a rounded brick pillar and some lush, flowering bushes. He was hidden from the south but vulnerable from the opposite direction.

On the other side of the building, the albino assailant had his gun pointed to the north where he had seen Jacob disappear around the Summerhouse. He eyed his partner and, with a point of his free hand, indicated for him to walk around the other way.

"Time to come out, sir. You will be safe in our hands," the albino called out.

The other man walked slowly to the west side of the Summerhouse with his firearm drawn as well. He kept his distance from the building but as he inched around a brick pillar, his eyes were drawn to a bystander running away from the scene.

With a swift upward blow of the iron bar, Jacob cracked the perpetrator's radius and ulna bones with an audible crunch. The man cursed violently and dropped his firearm to the ground, involuntarily. Jacob swiftly traded the iron for the gun and darted around the stunned perpetrator. He put the man in a headlock and pressed the gun into the man's back.

"Fuck man!" the assailant said. "You broke my arm."

"Shut up. Where's the other guy?" Jacob demanded.

Just then the albino slowly appeared from around the other side of the Summerhouse, his firearm drawn.

"I'm sorry to have interrupted your nice evening tour," the albino said in a polite tone. "But that doesn't mean you should be uncivilized."

Jacob held his whimpering hostage tightly and tried to crouch behind his torso.

"Don't move any closer. I'll shoot your friend!" Jacob warned.

"What makes you think we are friends?" the albino asked taking a step toward Jacob.

"Don't worry, Klaus," Jacob's hostage said to the albino. "He's still got the safety on."

Klaus, the albino, inched forward. He was still ten feet away but Jacob felt like he was right on top of him. Klaus aimed his gun at Jacob's head and Jacob scrunched his face and tried to hide behind the other guard. Klaus abruptly angled his gun down and shot twice through the other man's chest projecting a splatter of blood into the still surrounding air.

"Fuck!" Jacob yelled in shocked disgust, then dropped the victim and darted behind a nearby brick pillar.

Klaus watched, amused, as his victim fell to the ground, lifeless.

Jacob stumbled through shrubbery and sprinted around the Summerhouse and along a trail up to the north side of the Capitol. His mind was drowning in confused intensity.

The retreating sun still shone on the Statue of Freedom resting atop the Capitol dome, but the Capitol grounds were bathed in the shadows of dusk making visibility difficult. Jacob Tanner hid behind the trunk of a lush oak just off the pedestrian walkway and peaked around the tree to see the albino assailant, Klaus, strolling in his direction as if nothing had just transpired. He held his gun down and surveyed the now empty landscape with a dispassionate thoroughness.

Jacob threw himself against the trunk and closed his eyes, whispering, "Please tell me you heard the shots. Please tell me police are on the way."

He tried to reconcile the fact that a man had just died in his arms and that his killer was walking toward him. He turned around to see Klaus just fifty feet away moving behind another tree. Shit, Jacob thought to himself. Did he see him? He eased back behind the tree trunk but attempted to keep an eye on his pursuer.

Klaus stealthily led with his firearm from behind one tree to the next, moving ten feet closer to Jacob, though it was unclear whether the assailant knew where Jacob was hiding. He was only forty feet away. He had to have seen him, Jacob thought.

Jacob looked down to the gun in his shaking hand. Was he going to have to use it? Did it come to this? He looked back up to the shadowy clump of trees to the west but saw no signs of Klaus.

"Shit, shit, shit," Jacob whispered. He instinctively crouched down and lifted his gun in the direction he last saw Klaus. There was no movement. He squeezed the trigger. The gun vibrated and recoiled, stinging Jacob's hand and sending it in the air. The bullet hit a tree and sent splinters in a ten-foot semi-sphere.

After the shot, the thick dusk air was still and rustling leaves made the only sound.

Jacob thought he heard a branch crack and he shifted his aim to his right. No sign of his assailant.

"Put the gun down." A cold, steady voice demanded of Jacob. It came from ten feet behind him and was accompanied by a click of a gun's hammer.

I'm dead, he thought.

"This is the Capitol Police," the voice said flatly. "Put the gun down and raise your hands where I can see 'em."

Jacob was frozen, still looking away from the police officer. It wasn't the voice of the albino, thankfully. "Sir, there's a man—" Jacob blurted.

"I said drop your weapon!" the officer yelled. He maintained a sturdy stance with knees bent and his firearm extended toward Jacob.

Jacob slowly moved his arm down and placed his gun on the ground.

"Sir, there's another man in those trees—" Jacob tried again.

"All right, now, just take it easy," the officer said ignoring Jacob's warning. "I want you to raise your hands and back away from the tree."

"But officer—" Jacob blurted.

"Do it now!" the officer commanded.

Jacob pursed his lips and silently fumed but did as the officer said. He raised his arms, slowly stood up, and backed away from the tree, his cover.

"That's it . . . ." the officer said softly.

In a flash, the albino gunman flew from behind a nearby tree and shot the police officer twice in his chest, knocking him off his stance and drawing inaccurate return fire. Jacob ducked behind the tree, avoiding a third round from the assailant, which buzzed by Jacob's ear. The officer collapsed, headfirst into the dirt ground.

A blood-curdling yell directed at Klaus forced hesitation from him before he fired in the direction of Jacob a second time. It was Regan's voice. She had lunged at Klaus from behind another tree and clenched onto his gun-wielding arm. She dug in with her nails and clamped her mouth on the man's forearm like a rabid animal eliciting a scream from the man. He knew how to handle a gun, Regan thought, but he was physically weak.

"Regan!" Jacob yelled. He jumped up and flew at the fracas. He pulled Klaus's gun down with his left hand and slammed a blow from his right fist into the man's skull.

A shot was fired and the albino gunman wobbled to the ground, unconscious.

Jacob wrested the gun from the man's hand and turned it back on him. With a contorted face, he fought off the urge to shoot the man in his chest.

"What happened?" Regan asked, breathless.

"I knocked him out," Jacob surmised, looking at the man.

"My God," Regan said and pointed to Jacob's abdomen. It was inked with a dark red stain, growing larger by the second. "He shot you!"

"No, I'm not—" Jacob said, then looked down and put his hand to his stomach. Stunned, he pulled it away and stared at the red fluid on his hand. Jacob fell to the ground and looked up at Regan's contorted, worried face.

Three Capitol Police officers swarmed the area, guns drawn. "Put it down!" one yelled.

In shock, Jacob's swimming mind took in the activity around him as he kicked his legs out from under him. He watched as the officers secured Klaus and pulled Regan away. One officer directed Jacob to lie down and

put pressure on his bullet wound. Jacob blinked deliberately as his eyes began to cloud over. He stared up at the towering lighted Capitol dome contrasting the darkening sky.

Of the plant's fragrance a snake caught scent,
Came up in silence, and bore the plant off.
As it turned away it sloughed its skin.

Forty-Eight

"Dead?" Senator Arnold Huskin asked in an angry tone. He was speaking with Senator Masden in a closed-session meeting before the HELP Committee was set to resume. "They fucking had him killed?"

Senator Masden shook his head. "Well, I heard he was in critical condition."

"That is absolutely unacceptable. The man needs to be stopped," Huskin screeched.

"This is what I've been talking about Arnold. He's a lunatic," Masden said. "The man has absolutely no scruples. He will stop at nothing for a buck."

"Unbelievable."

"I mean we are U.S. senators—we have the authority of the United States federal government—and he has us scared shitless. It's not worth it, Arnold. I don't care what he's worth to the party, it's not worth it to me—my sanity."

"Dead?" Senator Huskin repeated. "I had no idea he was capable—"

"I guess we're all at fault," Masden said. "But I'm done. I'm wiping my hands clean of that bastard."

"So, what do we do?" Senator Huskin asked of Masden.

Masden shook his head. "I don't know. We wrap things up with this hearing and deal with Gall later? This hearing is about the FDA, not Martin Gall, right? It looks like he won this time."

Huskin turned away from Masden, stunned. "I just don't believe it. Dead?"

The two senators shared a conciliatory stare, then slowly paced out of the room.

* * *

"The Senate Committee on Health, Education, Labor, and Pensions will come to order," Senator Huskin said with a strike of the gavel in front of him. The room was full of the same people—senators and staffers behind the main desk and reporters and other viewers in the gallery. The witness table was lined with the same witnesses as well, Martin Gall, Peter Michelson, and Gary Javert—all but one Jacob Tanner.

"This is the continued hearing on the extension of the HEAL America Act into the charter city of Ur, Texas." Huskin turned to his right where Hank Masden sat, arms crossed in a defiant posture. "Senator Masden, I believe you have the floor."

Masden looked at the empty chair behind Jacob Tanner's nameplate and huffed before leaning into his microphone. "It appears, senator, that our witness is absent."

Martin Gall grew a grin as Senator Masden shook his head.

Huskin maintained his gaze on Masden but paused before asking, "Will you yield, then?"

A click from the back of the room was heard as the doors opened. A murmur accompanied the entrance of Jacob Tanner. He wore hospital scrubs and used a metal crutch under his left arm. The chamber fell silent as Regan Masden and Eli Tanner assisted Jacob down the aisle toward the witness table.

Martin Gall had turned around and dropped his jaw at the site. "Son of a bitch," he whispered. His body appeared to deflate as he turned back toward the committee desk and fumed.

Hank Masden smiled at Jacob as he sat down. Then the senator spoke into his microphone, "Chairman, I believe we have our witness after all."

"Very well," Senator Arnold Huskin replied into his microphone.

After Jacob situated himself in his seat with a grimace, he looked to Senator Masden expectantly. At the other end of the witness table, Martin Gall tried to appear aloof.

"Mr. Tanner, you were saying . . . ," Masden said.

After a pause to compose himself, Jacob Tanner began, "Thank you Senator Masden, Chairman Huskin, Ranking Member Delano," Jacob said then paused to collect his thoughts. He grinned. "Sorry I was late. Last night I was attacked and shot—"

"Senators, do we have to listen to this?" Gall asked into his microphone.

"Mr. Gall," Huskin declared, "you are out of order."

"This whole hearing is out of order!" Gall exclaimed.

"You've had your time to speak, Mr. Gall," Huskin said respectfully. "We have to allow others their chance."

"Please," Senator Masden said, "continue."

"The bullet pierced my side and ruptured my large intestine, causing a number of complications. Another man died last night at the hands of the same perpetrator."

A murmur stirred in the gallery.

"Both men were dressed in Capitol Police uniforms but both were under the employ of Keynes Aegis, the security firm run by one Martin Gall."

The room erupted in a confused roar as they digested the accusation.

Martin Gall fidgeted in his chair. He fumed and gave the senators long, cold stares, but when they didn't respond, Gall turned around to find his lobbyist, Leslie Benedict, watching helplessly. Gall mouthed, "Do something!" but Leslie shrugged his shoulders and gave Gall a look of helplessness.

Jacob tried to continue over the commotion from the gallery, "I have reason to believe that Mr. Gall wants me dead to prevent me from saying what I'm about to say."

"Oh, give me a break!" Martin Gall blurted into his microphone. "This man is clearly not fit to be giving testimony—"

"Mr. Gall," Senator Huskin shouted, "you are out of order!"

Gall pointed at Jacob. "He is out of order."

"One more word, sir and we will be forced to remove you," Huskin added.

"You weasely little . . . ," Gall shouted back.

Huskin slammed his gavel onto his sound block several times then turned to a Capitol Police office. "Officer, can we have this witness removed?"

"You're going to remove me?" Gall said jumping out of his seat. "I'll remove you, you piece of shit!"

The officer directed Gall away from the witness table and through the wooden gate to the gallery.

"You all are being conned!" Gall yelled. "He's conning you!"

"Thank you, Mr. Gall," Huskin said dryly over a rumble from the crowd.

A frenzy of activity from the press followed Gall as he exited Room 430 and the heavy doors crashed shut behind him. Senator Huskin slammed his gavel three more times then turned to Jacob as the noise from the gallery subsided. "Please, Mr. Tanner, go on."

Jacob cleared his throat then continued, "Yes, I have a hole in my side right now caused by a bullet from one of Gall's private security forces, but, quite frankly, I am one of the lucky ones. Gall has hurt many more people in much more insidious ways. One of them was my sister, who died because of that man out there. You see, two years ago, Martin Gall approved the production of an electronic chip that was to be used in the new Viper cell phones—yes the very phones that many people in this room have in their pockets right now. These chips were defective, however, and leaked radiation, which would eventually cause damage to the nervous system in the form of Chinese encephalitis.

"Gall knew about the danger his chip would cause yet he approved it anyway to save on costs—it's all in the addendum to my testimony that I've provided for the committee. In essence, to save money, Martin Gall was willing to risk the lives of hundreds of thousands—no millions—of people."

Jacob turned to his left side to see Regan and his father watching on intently from the gallery. With another grimace, he turned back to the senators. "You see, I've learned a great deal in the last few weeks about human nature. I've learned that quite a few businessmen are interested in only money. They aren't in business to help people and in fact don't mind hurting them as long as it meets their current budget requirements.

"But what allows these people to harm people and get away with it? As it turns out, the legal entity called the corporation is to blame. The corporation allows people to do their evil deeds behind the mask of a brand new shiny corporate logo. If and when the public finds out about the evil deeds, the people responsible are never indicted, the corporation is. The gulf oil spill wasn't blamed on the CEO or the engineer who cut corners on the oilrig—it wasn't *their* fault. It was BP's fault."

Regan, who was seated in the press section, smiled at Jacob's words, which sounded familiar to her.

"The blame for obesity doesn't fall on the food scientist who got paid to develop an impossible-to-resist French fry, the blame falls on McDonald's as a corporation. And the financial crisis wasn't the fault of the fund manager who bought risky loans in the name of Goldman Sachs; it was the fault of the corporation. So, those corporations take a hit, and in extreme cases, the corporations actually go bankrupt and fold. But the actual perpetrators—the CEOs and the food scientists and the hedge fund managers—all escape unscathed. The actual people doing the harm go unpunished and sometimes, as in the case of some corrupt banking corporations, those perpetrators are rewarded with extravagant severance packages and golden parachutes. They were just trying to do their jobs, after all, to make the corporation more money.

"I had all my faith in capitalism. It was the divine economic system. It was going to save humanity. It was the perfect system, and Ur, which was based on unfettered capitalism, was the perfect city. But my experience in Ur changed my mind. There, I saw the dark side of humanity and came to an unpleasant realization: there is such a thing as too much freedom. Some people will just take advantage of their freedom and use

it to harm others—it's just how it is. As a result, it can rightly be said that there is no perfect economic system."

"Uh," Senator Huskin interrupted, "that's all the time you have."

Senator Masden and Delano both looked at Huskin and spectators throughout the room turned to the committee chairman with a collective look of disbelief.

"Um, but you're welcome to continue, Mr. Tanner."

Senator Masden maintained his disapproving stare at Huskin.

"Please, take all the time you'd like," Huskin added for good measure.

Jacob nodded and gave a sarcastic, "Thank you." He looked down at his notes and continued, "In the most recent case, it was Martin Gall. Martin Gall of Gall Enterprises—entrepreneur and author and someone I used to consider a great man. He chose to hurt people in order to make a profit and he hid behind his numerous corporate disguises to make it happen.

"I told him his product was causing Chinese encephalitis and he wanted to shut me up! But that's not the worst of it. That man went further and sought to profit off of the suffering by buying into my company, which treated the disease that his product was causing! He wanted to create a self-sustaining balance by selling the product that made people sick and profiting off of the medicine to cure it."

The crowd in the gallery rumbled as they weighed Jacob's accusation.

"And if you haven't heard of this debacle on the nightly news it's not because we haven't tried to get it out through the mainstream media. It's because the major news outlets are controlled by the same criminal who's hurting people. It would have been a conflict of interest to report negatively on Martin Gall, a majority shareholder of basically every company this side of Timbuktu.

"That's what happens when personal responsibility is taken away from the equation. People forget about the welfare of fellow humans and concentrate solely on their own personal gain regardless of who's affected. Those people—those corporate scavengers—are no longer human, they have devolved into animals—into beasts."

Regan pressed her lips together and nodded regretfully.

"But aren't there checks and balances for this destructive animalistic behavior? Of course. Here in America, we have government agencies like the FCC and the FDA." Jacob put his hand on the shoulder of Gary Javert next to him at the witness table, who smiled. "They do their best to make sure that no one is harmed by corporate impropriety. We citizens give government the authority and power to protect us from scoundrels like Martin Gall and that's why we're all here. We're here to promote some regulation into a place that is devoid of any.

"But—and this is the kicker—when we grant the government unique powers to protect us, there is absolutely nothing stopping it from using those powers to hurt us."

Gary Javert stopped smiling and Senator Huskin raised his eyebrows at the comment.

"People are flawed and tend toward greed and self-interest, but we citizens think, for some reason, that those tendencies are eliminated when we put those flawed people into the role of government. It makes no sense! People will always err, whether they're in a corporation or in the government and when you give people extraordinary powers, they will err extraordinarily.

"You look at the examples of corporate wrongdoing I named earlier. Yes, BP screwed up during the Gulf oil spill, but that's not to say the government had no role in the debacle. The United States federal government owns the Outer Continental Shelf on which the rig was drilling. The Mineral Management Service controls the leasing of the land to oil companies and charges one sixth of the proceeds for the rights to drill on the shelf. And that's not to mention the tax cuts oil companies get to operate within the country making it a much more profitable industry than, say, pharmaceuticals. Various government agencies licensed and allowed the rig to operate and approved its safety. Still other agencies profit on the rigs. So it can be seen how at least part of the blame of that oil spill—maybe most—should actually fall on the federal government, not BP."

Regan raised her eyebrows, then looked to Eli Tanner who was seated next to her. They shared a look of confusion. Where was Jacob going with this? they wondered.

"Maybe we should stop him," Senator Huskin muttered in Masden's general direction.

"Let him speak, Arnold," Masden replied dryly. "We owe him that."

Jacob continued, "The same applies to our food. Yes, there are people in corporations who sell cheap, unhealthy food that is making the population fat. But why are they allowed to produce such unhealthy foods at such cheap prices? Well, the unhealthy ingredients cost less. And why do they cost less? Partly, at least, the unhealthy ingredients are so cheap because of government subsidies. Congress spends anywhere from $2-10 billion a year on farmers to produce corn. But there isn't that much demand for corn itself in the market, so the farmers grow corn for other purposes. The result is that corn ends up replacing other, more natural ingredients in the form of high fructose corn syrup and feed for cows, which in turn makes the carbonated beverages and burgers at McDonald's cheaper for its customers.

"And let's not forget about the banks. The banks are quite possibly the worst actors in this tragedy. They're the ones that made all the risky investments with mortgage packages based on unstable mortgages that they pushed on people who couldn't afford them. The Wall Street banks caused the entire economic crisis of 2008, but did they act alone in an unregulated market? Of course not. As a matter of fact, it was government policy that encouraged banks to make bad loans. Federal policy forced Fannie Mae and Freddie Mac, the government-sponsored enterprises to buy riskier loans to encourage home ownership. That policy, accompanied with cheap debt from the Fed fueled the housing bubble, which eventually crashed and started the collapse of the entire economic system. And the worst part of it all was that the federal government bailed out the companies that were gambling on those inflated mortgage-backed securities—they rewarded the criminals—with *our* money. And the moral hazard created by bailouts of this nature is even more damaging than all the other damage of the crisis put together.

"And that brings me to the case at hand—my case." Jacob coughed and gripped his side, which had sent sharp pains throughout his body. After a pause to recompose himself, Jacob continued, "Martin Gall produced a harmful product. But if it were up to the market, no one would have bought it. In fact in the charter city of Ur, where there is no government regulation, there hasn't been one single sale of a Viper phone because the device failed the audit by Burnett & Jones. There have, however, been hundreds of thousands of sales in the United States outside of Ur because it is the only phone with a FIPS level two-compliance rating—whatever that means. An amendment that was tacked onto a recent bill passed into law requires all cell phone retailers in the country to carry at least one of these phones and, in fact, subsidizes each retailer for each sale of the defective product."

Hank Masden lowered his head and rubbed his brow in shame.

"Yes, Gall was at fault for selling a defective product, but as in the corn subsidies and the banking regulation, the federal government was complicit in the unintended consequences of corporate wrongdoing."

Another murmur filled the committee chamber as Jacob's accusation hit home.

"And that's what I've realized in these last few days," Jacob continued. "Corporations aren't perfect. There are some serious problems with the concept of corporations. But everything that's wrong or problematic with corporations is wrong with government as well. People in government are just as greedy and self-serving as people in corporations and they're allowed the same anonymity and protection as they are in corporations. Government is, in all practicality, just one big corporation with the president as the CEO, Congress as the board, and the voting public as its stockholders.

"There is one clear distinction however. Government is just like a corporation except for the fact that it has the authority to force its bad policies on the people, corporations do not. BP couldn't have drilled and spilled, McDonald's wouldn't be able to offer cheap unhealthy food, the banks couldn't have offered their bad loans, and Martin Gall wouldn't have sold one defective phone if it weren't for government making all

that possible—even encouraging or forcing it. We give government the authority to protect us from harm, but it ends up using that authority to actually harm us.

"But you can't just have no government, you'll say. There will be anarchy without government. The world would be run over by the Martin Galls of the world without government. And I agree, we need the rule of law, but we don't need 100,000 pages of federal law plus all the state and local laws. That much law necessarily means that the government has gone past its charter to protect from harm and means that it is in fact causing harm.

"We really only need one law: *vulnero nemo*—harm no one. You see, the people who made Ur figured it out. When government goes beyond protecting people from harm and tries to work to benefit some class of people, they actually cause harm to others, in effect contradicting the one law it was created to defend. And it can't last. I love Bastiat. He said, 'The State is the great fiction through which everyone endeavours to live at the expense of everyone else.' Yet we're all enamored by that fiction. It's a truly backwards, jumbled system we have."

Jacob's father shrugged and nodded at Jacob's ideas.

"However, as an acquaintance has pointed out," Jacob said, briefly turning toward the gallery with a grimace, "that's the unjust system that we're left with and the paradox is that everyone appears to be content with it. The corporations are making money, the government officials keep their power, and the people don't have enough incentive to fight against the subsidies and government favors that lead to unintended corporate misconduct, so they just sit back and take it. And it makes sense.

"A corn farmer stands to make hundreds of thousands of dollars from a federal subsidy so he's going to fight tooth and nail for that, but you and I are only forced to pay about a dime, so there's no sense in fighting it. But those dimes add up of course. They add up so that over half of what we produce is confiscated by the government and redirected to a program that some bureaucrat at some point thought was worthy. It's a disturbing conundrum, for sure.

"But this modern feudalism isn't the way it has to be. Our system, in which the elite minority keep their power at the cost of the vast majority only happens when the vast majority accepts that government has the authority to harm people. You get rid of that assumption and there is no problem—there is no willing submission to the coercive authorities.

"And our current system isn't the only option. Viable alternatives do exist and one of those alternatives is a charter city like Ur, a society that is based solely on vulnero nemo.

"Like I said earlier, there is no perfect economic system and Ur is no exception. If you have a society full of imperfect people, you're going to get an imperfect society. That's just the way it is. However, I would rather live in a society that expressly forbids harm to others rather than one that expressly authorizes one class of people to harm another in order to benefit a third. And yes, if you take that authority away, you take all the good government does away too, but it's better to live with the threat of illegal harm than to submit to legal harm."

"Uh, Mr. Tanner," Senator Huskin interjected, "are you going to come down from your soap box anytime soon?" Laughs were heard throughout the chamber.

Jacob nodded and realized his place. "Yes, of course. But, please, if I may . . . ," He looked down to his notes to continue his statement but suddenly gripped his side in agony. He sensed wetness seeping through his scrubs but struggled to mutter, "We can overcome this . . . this corporatism that has come to dominate this country. But to do so, we must allow an alternative. We must allow Ur to remain free. Give people the option to live in a free society with none of the benefits or drawbacks of government if they so choose. You may just be surprised at how well freedom works."

Jacob leaned forward and involuntarily wavered before collapsing on the witness table.

Regan jumped up and gasped. Eli Tanner ran to the witness table and to his son's side. Others in the room erupted in a jumbled roar of questions and discussion.

Senator Huskin slammed his gavel onto the sound block and called order, and then yelled, "Doctor! Is there a doctor in the chamber?"

Jacob heard the clamor and gavel strikes fade away as he slowly faded into unconsciousness.

Forty-Nine

The emergency room doors flung open with a crash as a group of medical personnel hurriedly rolled a stretcher through the triage area toward Trauma One. The semiconscious patient—Jacob Tanner—reached out with his right hand but could not find what he was seeking.

"He's lost too much blood," a nurse called out.

"Keep pressure on it," the resident doctor replied. "How the hell did this man get okayed for release?"

The group rolled the bed into the emergency bay and the nurse immediately injected a needle into the patient's arm.

"I want a liter of RL hooked up stat!" the doctor shouted.

A nurse rolled over a stainless steel pole with a hook on top supporting a bag full of Ringer's Lactate solution. She inserted the RL tube into the IV and opened the drip chamber, allowing the solution to flow into Jacob's arm.

"Do we have labs? How about a blood screen?" the doctor demanded.

"We're on it. Thirty minutes out," a nurse responded.

Jacob trained his eyes on the chest of the emergency room doctor and he raised his arm toward it.

"You're going to be all right, big guy," the doctor patronized Jacob. "What? What do you want?"

A seemingly delirious Jacob produced an unintelligible sound and reached for the doctor's chest.

"What?" The doctor looked down and put his hand on his chest. He wore light blue scrubs and in his left breast pocket he noticed a folded piece of paper, a pen, and a pencil. He pointed to the piece of paper. "You want to write something?"

Jacob shook his head and pointed again in the same direction.

"Blood pressure is returning but slowly," a nurse called out.

The doctor pulled out his pen but again Jacob shook his head meekly. The doctor then took out the pencil and offered it to Jacob. With a faintly pleased look, Jacob took the pencil in his left hand and grasped tightly. The doctor scrunched his face and stared as Jacob let a smile creep across his face and drifted off into unconsciousness.

* * *

Colorful graphics swirled around the television screen and dispersed, leaving the perfectly symmetrical face of Michelle Torres.

"This is *Headlines Now*, I'm Michelle Torres. Shocking findings have linked the usage of one particular cell phone to the nation-wide epidemic of Chinese encephalitis today, federal authorities have announced."

A graphic of the Viper phone appeared over Michelle's right shoulder as she spoke. "The FDA has just reported that a chip inside the Viper smart phone emits dangerous levels of radiation, which causes the neurological condition called Chinese encephalitis. If you own one of these devices, it is strongly urged that you discontinue use immediately and contact the local Center for Disease Control office. A recall for each Viper phone will be conducted this week to ensure no further harm is done."

Contact information for the Viper Corporation appeared on the screen and after a brief pause, Michelle continued, "Criminal charges are being brought for a Billy 'Buck' Daniels, the president of Vizor Corporation, which issued the defective electronics used in the Viper phones. The attorney for Mr. Daniels refused a comment."

For whom have I labored? For whom have I journeyed?
For whom have I suffered?
I have gained absolutely nothing for myself,
I have only profited the snake, the lion of the ground!

Fifty

Something in Regan Masden's attire was wrong for the setting. Perhaps it was the shape of the dress or the awkwardness of high heels on muddy wet grass. Quite possibly, it was that black did not suit her. She required color to complement her persona.

She wasn't concerned with that, however, as she walked toward Eli Tanner who was seated on a bench next to the drive. He was staring into the cloudy skies, tears welling up in his eyes.

"I'm so sorry, Mr. Tanner," Regan said deliberately.

Eli didn't look at her but acknowledged her sentiment by pursing his lips and nodding.

"I can't imagine what you and your wife have gone through."

Eli threw up his left hand and smiled. "He always said it was something he would die for." After a pause, he added, "I just can't believe it happened." He bowed his head and let out a sigh as he wiped his eyes.

Regan sat down next to him and gently placed her hand on his back. "Well," she said, "it looks like he got what he wanted at least. The HELP committee rejected the extension of the HEAL America Act."

Eli looked up at Regan with a grin. "He was always very persuasive!" He chuckled.

Regan turned away and smiled. "Yes he was."

"And I hear big things about you as well," Eli said.

Regan shook her head. "Oh, well, it's nothing."

Eli leaned back in the bench. "No, I heard about your blog on the news. You're a celebrity!"

"I don't know about that."

"Fighting corporate corruption in style," Eli repeated what he had heard on the news. "You're bringing down the bad guys and looking good doing it!"

Regan smiled. "Well, I couldn't get the Gall story onto the major news outlets, so I had to figure something out myself."

"And I like the name, *The Whistle*."

"Thanks."

"Do you think they'll do anything about Mr. Gall?"

"Oh yes! There are charges being drawn up as we speak. He's going down."

"And all because of you."

"I couldn't have done it without Jacob."

Eli smiled and patted Regan on her knee. He surveyed Regan's friendly face and confided, "I think you two would have made a fine couple."

Regan nodded and pressed her lips together. "I do too," she agreed hesitantly. "I do too."

The two sat silently for a moment as black-clad groups got into their cars and slowly drove away.

"So," Regan asked, "what's in store for you?"

Eli stared off into the distance as a smile appeared. "I'm sure Jacob would have gotten a kick out of this . . . we're going to Ur!"

Regan turned to him, shocked. "Ur, really?"

Eli chuckled. "Well, we've looked into it, Regan. Did you ever hear about the region there called Amaurot?"

Regan opened his mouth. "Of course—the socialist sector?"

"That's the one, yes. I think they named it after Sir Thomas More's *Utopia* as a matter of fact. I know I was shocked myself when I heard about it, but, it's supposed to be a grand communal living experiment— they've designated an entire area for strictly socialist living. No property, no money. I've heard they're doing really well."

"Yes, I visited there once. I loved it."

Eli laughed. "And I heard they don't wear too much clothes either."

Regan laughed out loud. "Well, if that's your type of thing, I say go for it!"

"It just sounds exactly like what mom and I have been trying to do since after Berkeley. I've not heard of anything of its kind—I think it's actually going to work."

"Oh yeah?"

"Well, Jake and I always talked about this. You see at the other communities, they still made us pay taxes—property taxes, income tax, barter tax. But, of course, we had no money—we were socialists for God's sake—so we couldn't afford to sustain those places. I always thought that more government was the route to true communal living, but it turns out that no government is the only way to live the way we want."

Regan smiled. "I'm sure Jacob would have loved to hear you say that."

"Oh, I know. I know."

Regan turned and surveyed the serene cemetery, the lush green grass engulfing the weathered stone monuments. A small black bird with red stripes on its wings flew into her field of vision and landed in front of her. She watched it as it hopped around, every once in a while dipping its head to the ground. After a minute of searching, the bird found a suitable worm, which it tugged out of the ground with its beak and launched into the air flapping its wings.

Regan patted Eli on his knee and stood up. "Well, Mr. Tanner. The next time I'm in Ur, I'll have to come visit you and your wife."

Eli looked up to Regan. "I'd like that." He smiled and watched as Regan walked to her car.

End

Acknowledgments

When I became involved with this project, I found myself overwhelmed. I was writing a novel about a pharmaceutical entrepreneur with run-ins at the hospital. Besides an occasional doctor drama on television, I had had very little experience with these scenarios. Luckily I have friends who know what they're talking about. I owe much gratitude to Michael Kruse for his expertise in the pharmaceutical industry and his perspective on the benefits of the FDA and other government programs. I also want to thank Alyson Morse for her contribution in the medical arena and helping to make the introduction to this book realistic and entertaining as well as Kristine Finsaas for her perspective on character and plot. I'd also like to thank my very skilled editor Kristen Depken who saved me once again from countless egregious errors (in her free time this go around).

As always, I'd like to extend gracious thanks to my brother Eric Robert Morse for his invaluable insight into story. His excellent political economy book, *Juggernaut*, was a great inspiration for this book.

I'm also grateful for the economists of the Austrian, Chicago, and George Mason schools for trailblazing into the uncharted territories of economic science. I owe a debt of gratitude to Milton Friedman for bringing to light Leonard Read's article about the miracle of the pencil and demonstrating the price system (chapter nine) and his general brilliance on the subject of self-interest (chapter twenty-two). I credit Frédéric Bastiat for his analysis of the broken window fallacy (chapter thirteen). And I thank James M. Buchanan and Gordon Tullock for their perspective on public choice theory (chapter thirty-eight). My only hope is that I did all of their brilliance any justice.

Thanks to all my friends and family and thanks to you, the reader for your support, without which, this endeavor would have been impossible.

I am grateful.